The Dough Must Go On

Oxford Tearoom Mysteries
BOOK NINE

H.Y. HANNA

Note:

This book follows **British English** spelling and usage

There is a **Glossary of British Terms** at the end of the story.

CONTENTS

H.Y. HANNA

CHAPTER ONE

They say that showbiz is a cut-throat business and I got a front-row seat to what that means when I was invited onto Britain's hot new talent show.

Oh, not as a contestant, mind you—I was there simply to feed the many mouths backstage. Yup, I was Catering—or rather my business, the Little Stables Tearoom, was in charge of providing freshly baked scones, Chelsea buns, teacakes, and a host of other traditional English treats to the perpetually hungry members of the show crew and production team. It was a job that many a bakery or café would have killed for, and I still couldn't believe that I had picked up the lucrative contract. It had been the last thing I'd been expecting when a funny little man with shrewd brown eyes and an expensive suit turned up in my tearoom one morning.

"Cor... wossat fantastic smell?" he'd said, pausing just inside the door and sniffing in an exaggerated fashion.

I smiled as I approached him, holding the tearoom menu. "That's probably a new batch of scones coming out of the oven."

He rubbed his hands. "Ah! I've come ter talk ter yer about them... Yor scones," he said, at my blank look. "I 'ear they're the bloody best in Oxfordshire!"

I blushed slightly. "Thanks... they *are* our house special."

"You got some I can try?"

I was taken aback. I'd never had a customer march in and demand free food before. It was on the tip of my tongue to refuse, but something about his eager smile and bright-eyed anticipation made me feel petty about saying no. Besides, he was the first customer of the day; the tearoom was empty except for him and there was no one else to see, so it wasn't as if he was setting a bad example.

"Er... well, we don't usually offer samples but... um... sure, if you just hang on a moment..."

I popped into the kitchen and returned a moment later with a warm scone on a plate, then watched, bemused, as the man took his time breaking apart the golden crust to examine the light, fluffy centre. He took a big bite. He chewed thoughtfully. It was ridiculous, but I found myself watching him with bated breath and breathing a sigh of relief when his face split into a wide smile.

"Absolutely delicious!" He smacked his lips. "Would be perfect wiv some jam and clotted cream…"

Cheeky sod! Is he trying to scrounge more free food? Well, he can start paying for it, like all the other customers.

"Yes, that's how we normally serve them," I said, making an attempt to lead him to a table. "If you'd like to follow me, I can seat you at a table and you can order a proper serving of scones with all the trimmings. And you might also like to see the rest of the menu: we offer many other traditional British baking favourites, as well as finger sandwiches and—"

"Wot about delivery, then? Can yer do special orders ter be delivered?"

I relaxed as I suddenly realised where he was heading. "Oh, sure, I'd be more than happy to take a catering order. We've catered several events for various Oxford colleges, as well as private parties, wedding breakfasts, society meetings… we even did a funeral recently."

"Ah… and can yer do big orders?"

"Of course. We can bake as much or as little as required." I smiled at him. "How many scones do you need?"

"Seven hundred."

I blinked. "I… I'm sorry? *Seven hundred?*"

"Yeah—and I want them served wiv jam and clotted cream, innit? I like ter do things properly," he said, waggling his eyebrows. "Wot about sandwiches, then? Yer said sumfink about finger sandwiches. Properly cut, eh? In rectangles, wiv the crusts removed, and good ole-fashioned fillings, like fresh butter and cucumber... or egg mayonnaise... or that Coronation chicken stuff?"

"Well, yes, but—"

"Good, good..." He waved a hand. "Valerie, me PA, will contact yer and work out the details. Great ter meet yer—I like doin' business wiv pretty girls." He gave me a wink and a leer. "It's a bonus when they 'ave brains too." He shoved a card into my hand, then turned and trotted out of the tearoom, leaving me staring after him.

I was still standing there, staring into space with my mouth slightly open, when the tearoom door swung open a few minutes later and my best friend Cassie walked in.

"Morning..." She dropped her bag behind the counter, picked up one of the waitress aprons and tied it around her waist, then paused and eyed me curiously. "What are you standing there gawping like that for?"

"Oh! I... um... this weird little man came in a few minutes ago and..." I trailed off and shook my head. "It must have been some kind of prank. He told me he wanted to order seven hundred scones."

"*Huh?* Who was he?"

I shrugged. "I have no idea." Then I remembered the card he'd given me and glanced down.

"Someone called Monty Gibbs...?"

Cassie gasped and snatched the card out of my hands. "We got a catering order from Monty Gibbs?"

"Who's Monty Gibbs?"

"Gemma!" Cassie rolled her eyes. "Don't you ever watch TV? Monty Gibbs is the creator of *From Pleb to Celeb*, that new talent show everyone was talking about last year."

"Oh, a talent show..." I made a face. "You mean like *Britain's Got Talent* and *The X Factor*?"

"Yeah, except Gibbs says his version is much better, of course," Cassie chuckled. "Rumour has it that Monty Gibbs only wants two things in life: to get a knighthood and to be a judge on a talent show. Well, the former is out of his control but the latter... he's been trying to get invited for years, but he's never managed to wangle it. So, he decided to create his own show where he could play God."

"What? You're having me on."

"No, I'm serious."

"You can't just start your own talent show."

"You can if you're Monty Gibbs and you're one of the richest men in Britain. He's living proof that you can do anything, if you have enough money."

"Richest man? I've never heard of him."

"Well, he keeps to himself most of the time. He's not one of those 'loud' billionaires, you know, always turning up in the society pages or getting caught by paparazzi looking totally hammered coming out of some London nightclub. But he's rich, all right—and pretty eccentric too, from what I hear. He lives on this big estate out in the Cotswolds, where he's converted some old manor into a swanky modern villa and excavated a man-made lake because he wanted a home by the water and there aren't any natural big lakes in the Cotswolds, of course."

Cassie rolled her eyes. "So I'm not surprised that when no one would invite him to be a judge, he just decided to create his own show. And guess what? When none of the TV networks or digital channels would run his show, he went off and set up his own online streaming service to broadcast it. Then, when the show became a huge hit, everyone started subscribing to his channel—and he ended up making double the money! Now he's back for a second season, and apparently it's even more popular this time round. I'll bet the networks are all begging him to run it now and he's probably put his fee up, the clever sod."

"I'm beginning to see why he's one of the richest men in Britain," I said dryly.

"And he wants us to cater for him!" Cassie squealed. "Gemma, you could probably shut the tearoom and go on holiday for a month after this."

Despite having the benefit of Cassie's explanation, I was still unprepared for the eccentricity of Monty Gibbs's requests when his secretary rang me a few hours later.

"We'll be engaging the services of a professional

film and TV catering service, of course, to take care of the main meals and such, so you won't have to worry about lunch and dinner. We simply want you to provide morning and afternoon tea," said the efficient voice on the other end of the line. "You see, other talent shows have been criticised for the way they treat their contestants and crew—keeping people waiting for hours with no refreshment provided, for instance—and Mr Gibbs wants his show to be totally different. He wants to be known for his generosity in providing *more* than expected and for his attention to the finer details. So, for example, he would like all the tea to be brewed in porcelain teapots and served in proper china cups and saucers."

"Er… I don't think I have enough teacups here for all the crew," I said, doing a quick mental count.

"That will be no problem. You simply have to let me know which fine china brand you use and I will make sure that enough matching sets are purchased and delivered to the set."

Bloody hell. I was really beginning to understand the phrase "*money was no object*". By the time Gibbs's secretary ended the call, I was reeling—not just from the list of specific demands but from the sum she had mentioned as payment for this job. I was beginning to wonder if Cassie was right and I should shut the tearoom. I'd be pushed to capacity just keeping up with the huge orders and eccentric requests for the duration of the show. Could the tearoom kitchen support the catering order and provide normal service to customers as well?

Still, with what Monty Gibbs was paying, there would be more than enough when this was over to give everyone a raise *and* go on a very, very nice holiday! The thought of holidays made my mood darken for a moment as I remembered the one I had just cancelled because my workaholic boyfriend, Detective Inspector Devlin O'Connor, had been unable to leave his job commitments. Still, I had ended up having an impromptu adventure in Vienna, I thought with a smile, and had had a better time than I'd expected—despite dealing with a grisly death and four nosy old ladies who had insisted on meddling in the murder investigation...

The door to the tearoom opened and, as if conjured by my thoughts, the very four little old ladies I'd been thinking of tottered in. Affectionately known as the "Old Biddies", this little gang of octogenarians ruled the village of Meadowford-on-Smythe where my tearoom was situated, and—if rumours were to be believed—half of Oxfordshire too. They untied the headscarves covering their woolly white hair, wiped their sensible orthotic shoes on the doormat, and hurried towards me, their eyes gleaming.

"Oh Gemma, we are going to be on television!" cried Glenda Bailey, her cheeks so pink from excitement that they made the heavy rouge she applied look almost neon.

Florence Doyle nodded, a wide smile on her plump, kindly face. "That's right, dear, and we'll be performing before a real, live audience!"

"They said they might even feature my lace doily earrings," said Ethel Webb proudly.

"We are going to be the first of our kind!" declared Mabel Cooke.

"What kind? What are you talking about?" I asked.

"Our audition for *From Pleb to Celeb*, dear," said Glenda.

I stared at them. *The Old Biddies had auditioned for the talent show?* And why was it that up until that morning, I'd never even heard of *FPTC*—and now it was suddenly popping up everywhere?

"You went to an audition?"

Glenda nodded eagerly. "The Open Auditions were held a few weeks ago, at that lovely new concert hall in Oxford—you know, the one they've built near the business school and the train station. That's where all the judging for the show is going to take place, because Mr Gibbs wanted to keep the show near his home in the Cotswolds. He loathes London, you see, and didn't want to have to travel there every time for the shooting, which is what happened last year. Besides, he said that the other shows always feature big cities like London and Manchester and Glasgow, so it was time some of the other towns got a look-in, and as a resident of the Cotswolds, he likes to support local businesses and—"

"Yes, yes, never mind all that, Glenda—tell Gemma what the producers said!" Mabel cut in.

"Ooh... yes, they were ever so impressed with us and invited us back to perform before the judges. We have been keeping it a secret from you, dear, as we wanted to surprise you... Well, we went to the Judges' Auditions yesterday and they loved us! And we just heard this morning: it's official—we've been chosen as one of the twenty contestants to go into the contest!"

"But... I don't understand—what are you going to *do*?"

Mabel's chest swelled importantly. "We are going to be the first granny band in England."

I looked at her stupidly. "Granny—*what?*"

"Well, you see, there are girl bands and boy bands, dear," said Glenda, as if explaining something to a child. "So... why not a granny band?"

"We'll be singing and dancing to old favourite songs. Isn't it lucky that we have so much musical talent between us?" added Florence, beaming.

I winced slightly. The one time I'd heard the Old Biddies sing and dance, a man had come up to them and desperately offered them money to shut up. Still, I didn't want to rain on their parade.

"That... er... that sounds... great. Congratulations! So... um... you're going to perform as this granny band?"

"Ooh yes, we even have a special name for ourselves. We've given it a lot of thought, you see, and we've come up with the perfect name: The Pussy Puffs!"

"The *what?*" I blinked at them. "You're not serious. You can't call yourselves that!"

Ethel looked at me innocently. "Why not? It's a lovely name."

"Yes, but it's... um..." I groped around for a way to say it, then took the cowardly route. "Well, it's rather silly, isn't it?"

"It's not silly at all," said Florence indignantly. "We thought it was very apt. You see, people look at elderly ladies and think that we're just dull and frail, like a puff of air might blow us away—"

"—but in fact, we're clever and resourceful and full of surprises, just like pussycats!" finished Glenda with a proud smile.

I took a deep breath. "Look... just trust me—'The Pussy Puffs' is a really bad choice."

"Well, the producers didn't think that," said Mabel, bristling. "I told them it was a marvellous idea and they agreed." She folded her arms across her chest and nodded emphatically.

I wondered wryly if they'd had much choice. As the bossiest of the Old Biddies, with her booming voice and brisk, no-nonsense manner, Mabel Cooke was a force to be reckoned with. Even the head of Oxfordshire police had been no match for her. A couple of puny TV producers would have stood no chance.

"The band was really June's idea, Mabel—you have to give her the credit," Ethel chided in her gentle voice.

Mabel sniffed. "It may have been June's idea but *I* developed it."

"Who's June?"

"June Driscoll is an old friend of ours from bingo, dear," Glenda explained. "Her husband died last year and she's been finding it very hard—they were an extremely devoted couple, you see. She's been rather at a loss ever since. I don't think she quite knows what to do with herself—"

"Other than trying to save Bill's group, B.E.A.S.T.," Florence said.

"B.E.A.S.T.?"

"It stands for 'Bushy Eyebrows Activists Stand Together'. It's a support group set up to help people with thick eyebrows find sympathy and understanding. June's husband, Bill, had the most enormous eyebrows, you see—"

"They were almost like furry caterpillars," said Ethel. "I once mistook them for woolly bear caterpillars when he and June were visiting, and we were sitting out in the garden. I nearly sprayed some BugClear on his face before I realised."

"Bill was always very sensitive about his eyebrows," said Glenda in a hushed voice. "He felt that he was ridiculed and laughed at wherever he went, and it put him at a disadvantage in his career and community positions. So he decided to set up a support group to help others like him."

"A support group for people with bushy eyebrows," I said, not quite believing my ears.

Ethel nodded eagerly. "Oh, he had great ambitions for it. He hoped to promote awareness of the special needs of those with bushy eyebrows and even raise funds to provide scholarships for young men and women of certain eyebrow thickness." She screwed up her face in an effort to remember. "I think it had to be over half an inch thick to qualify."

I burst out laughing. "What? That's the most ludicrous thing I've ever..." I trailed off as the Old Biddies frowned at me.

"It may be a little silly, dear, but it's important to June," said Mabel, glowering at me.

Glenda sighed. "She misses Bill terribly and this is her last connection with him. If she can keep the support group going, then she feels like she's keeping him alive too, in some way. Isn't that romantic?"

"But the support group never quite took off, even when Bill was alive," said Florence sadly.

"I even made my Henry become an honorary member, though his eyebrows are really quite sparse," said Mabel. "But B.E.A.S.T. has been struggling over the years and now with Bill gone, it's in danger of fading away completely."

"But not if we win the grand prize in this talent show!" said Ethel. "June is sure there would be more members if only people knew about the group. She wants to print leaflets and make badges and do other... other promotions, you see, to raise awareness for B.E.A.S.T. But she needs money to do all that—that's why she came up with the idea of a granny band! She saw the advertisements about the Open Auditions—"

"—and asked us if we would join her band!" finished Glenda, beaming. She fluffed her white hair. "I've always rather fancied myself as a rock chicken."

Well, it seemed that the judges and the TV audience fancied the idea of ageing "rock chickens" too because—over the next two weeks—the Pussy Puffs sailed through the early rounds of the competition. Five contestants were eliminated in the live shows each week, so that the initial twenty were whittled down to ten semi-finalists, and to my utter astonishment, the Old Biddies and June were among them. Somehow the nation loved them, and there were even whispers that the "granny band" might be in with a chance to win the contest...

***

Which is how I found myself wandering backstage at the new Oxford Concert Hall three weeks later, looking for the contestants' Waiting Area. It seemed a bit crazy that I had been catering for the show for over three weeks now and I still didn't really know my way around, but so far, most of the time, I had simply dropped off the food at the Concert Hall kitchen and rushed back to the tearoom.

Against Cassie's advice, I'd decided to keep the Little Stables open while also catering for the show and now, three weeks later, I had to admit that it had been a mistake. Dora, Cassie, and I had been run off our feet, with crazily early mornings and exhausting late nights, trying to fulfil the orders and keep normal business running at the same time. Two days ago, after stern words from Cassie, I'd finally had to admit defeat and decided to close the tearoom for the remaining duration of the show. It had been so much more relaxed since then, that I wished I'd listened to her earlier!

So now, with no need to rush back to Meadowford, I decided to indulge my curiosity and see what it was like backstage. In particular, I was keen to see the Old Biddies and how they were getting on. I knew that all the semi-finalists would be here today, rehearsing for the big Semi-Finals show tomorrow. In contrast to other shows, which had been accused of setting up contestants to be stressed and humiliated in order to create artificial drama for TV, Monty Gibbs had wanted his image to be kindly and magnanimous. So, before each round of performances, he had been giving his contestants the opportunity to prep their acts *in situ* before the big day.

The reality, of course, was that the shrewd little businessman wasn't just being generous—he knew that with so many nervous and competitive contestants crammed together, all desperate for their turn to rehearse on stage, there would be more than enough drama and conflict to go around. Which is exactly what had happened. And since Monty Gibbs had cleverly arranged for a separate roving camera crew to shadow the contestants, all the petty squabbles and jealous tantrums had been captured for viewers to enjoy in the televised episodes each week. It was a formula that he had come up with for the show's first season and it had proved such a hit that he was repeating it for the second.

Oh yeah, the man is a master of milking drama for monetary gain, even while appearing to be virtuously above such manipulative practices, I thought. Then I paused as I rounded the corner and heard the sound of shrill voices raised in anger. *Hmm... it sounds like there's some drama going on now.*

The voices were coming from one of the rooms off the main corridor—a dressing room filled with a row of chairs before mirrors framed with lightbulbs. I caught sight of two women through the open doorway. I vaguely recognised them as two of the contestants: Lara, a voluptuous redhead in her late thirties with a sultry voice and improbably big breasts, and Nicole, a quiet, intense young woman who played the piano. Lara was standing with a hand on her hip, a cocky smile on her face as she addressed the younger woman.

"...nothing like the challenge of a married man," she purred. "Seducing him and watching him lie to his wife, just so he can meet you for a sweaty hour in a seedy motel..." She laughed, a deep, sensual sound. "And it's especially thrilling when they throw it all away—their wives, their kids, their safe home life—just to be with you. There's no feeling of power like it! I once had this chap leave his wife and son on Christmas Day—can you believe it? I waited until I knew they were about to eat Christmas lunch, then I rang him and told him he had to walk out on them and come away with me immediately— or never see me again." She gave a self-satisfied smile. "Guess what? He came. Didn't even say goodbye to his five-year-old son. And that's not even as bad as the guy who left his pregnant wife while she was in labour to sneak out of the hospital and meet me for lunch and a little bit... extra," she giggled. "Just think—it was their first baby and he should have been by her side; instead he was busy shagging me!"

"You're disgusting!" Nicole said, her face pale. "I can't believe you're just standing there, proud of saying those things. It's... it's despicable! There are loads of single men out there—why can't you leave the married ones alone? Don't you realise how much their families must suffer?"

Lara tossed her head. "It's not my problem if the wives can't hold on to their husbands. They should blame themselves. Who told them to turn into fat frumps with nothing to offer but constant nagging and boring sex?"

"How dare you!" cried Nicole. "They're... they're bringing up their children and cooking and cleaning... and they're tired and stressed... They can't be expected to look like... like sex kittens all the time just to keep their husbands happy—"

"Well, then they shouldn't whinge when their men run off to shag someone else."

"You cold-hearted witch!" Nicole's eyes smouldered as her hands clenched into fists. "It's women like you who ruin people's lives. You think you're so smug now but... but someday you'll live to regret it! Someday, someone will make you pay!"

"Ohhh, I feel so scared now," laughed Lara with a fake shiver.

Nicole flushed bright red and, with a shriek of fury, she launched herself at the other woman, her hands reaching for her neck.

"You... you... *AAAARRGGHHH!*"

CHAPTER TWO

The two women fell to the ground in a tangle of thrashing arms and legs. I stared in horror as they wrestled and fought, screeching like banshees. Nicole had her fingers around Lara's neck, squeezing hard, her eyes burning with hatred, while the redhead gasped and choked, trying to claw her hands away. Then, somehow, Lara managed to twist her body and tear free of Nicole's grasp; she grabbed the pianist's hair and yanked hard, twisting cruelly and causing the younger woman to shriek in pain.

"Stop!" I cried, rushing into the room. To my surprise, it was bigger than I'd thought, and a man and woman were tucked in the far corner: he had a video camera clamped on one eye and she hovered next to him, clutching a clipboard.

"Can you get them both in the frame?" she was asking.

"Yeah... but I think a close-up would be better..." he mumbled, approaching the fighting women.

I couldn't believe my ears. "Aren't you going to stop them?" I demanded. "They could hurt each other!"

"Ooh, that's an idea, Jeff," said the woman with the clipboard. "If either of them end up going to hospital, make sure you ride in the ambulance with them—"

"*What?*" I started to say something else, then thought better of it. Instead, I whirled and rushed over to Lara and Nicole. "Stop it! Stop it, the two of you!"

I pulled them apart and they faced each other like hissing, spitting cats, their chests heaving, their hair wild. I was relieved to see, though, that neither seemed to have serious injuries other than a few scratches and bruises.

"Keep rolling!" the woman with the clipboard hissed to the cameraman.

However, her voice seemed to bring Nicole to her senses. The pianist looked around and a mortified expression crossed her face as she saw the cameraman. She put a dazed hand up to her forehead, groping at her hair, which had come loose from its tight bun.

"I... I don't know what came over me..." she mumbled. "I... um... I need to go and get ready for my act..." Stumbling backwards, she turned and ran out of the room.

Lara was shaken as well, but she recovered quicker than Nicole and, when she noticed the camera on her, she brightened and leaned forwards surreptitiously, so that her open top displayed more of her cleavage.

"Are you all right?" I asked.

"Fine, fine," she said airily, tossing her hair. "Maybe that will teach that uptight little cow not to pick on me in the future." She blew a kiss at the camera, then sashayed out of the room.

"And... CUT!" said the woman with the clipboard. She frowned at me. "What did you think you were doing, barging in like that? That was some great footage there and you ruined it."

"They could have hurt each other! How could you just stand there and watch?"

She shrugged. "My instructions from the boss are clear: we don't intervene with anything the contestants are doing—we just film them." She wagged a finger at me. "What we had there was great TV! And you had to go and ruin it with your Little Miss Policewoman act."

"I—" I couldn't believe that she was making me feel defensive for what I'd done. "That's crazy! You can't let people hurt each other just for the sake of 'great TV'!"

"Welcome to the real world—or rather, the reality TV world," said the woman with a harsh laugh. She glanced at her watch, then said to the cameraman: "I need a quick ciggie break. Then we'd better go and cover that magician chap."

"Right-o," said the cameraman, lowering his machine and reaching in his own pockets for a packet of cigarettes.

Without another glance at me, they left the room and disappeared down the corridor. I stood fuming for a moment, then stomped off in the direction of the Waiting Area. There, I found the air thick with tension as the various contestants camped out in different parts of the room practised their acts feverishly. Slowly, I began to make my way through them, looking for a group of little old ladies. I dodged around a teenage boy practising hip hop dance moves and skirted a woman energetically manipulating a puppet, only to bump into a collie walking backwards, balanced on its hind legs.

"Oi—watch it!" his owner snarled. "He was almost at the end of that sequence! Now you've broken the flow. Do you realise how difficult it is to reverse chain the choreography?"

"Sorry!" I said, facing a thin woman with cold blue eyes. "I'm really sorry."

This must be Trish and Skip, the "dog dancing" duo, I realised. I remembered seeing this woman and her dog in one of the many show trailers being broadcast on TV and shared across social media. The producers had attempted to do one of those "warm, fuzzy" interviews of pup and owner, but

Trish Bingham had been dour and unresponsive. She had struck me then as an odd, hostile woman and I had to admit, meeting her in person didn't do much to change that impression.

She scowled at me. "It's taken me months to teach Skip the sequence—I don't need you messing it up for us at the last minute."

"I'm sorry—it was an accident. I just didn't see him," I said, starting to feel annoyed now. How many times did I have to apologise?

Then my heart softened as I looked down at the collie, who wagged his plumed tail and opened his mouth in a wide doggie grin. I crouched down to pat him, thinking that Trish was lucky: her handsome canine partner more than made up for her lack of charm.

Leaving the unfriendly woman calling her dog to Heel once more, I continued across the room, carefully skirting around a tense-looking woman with a pair of identical twin girls, and also a young man in a black cape, nervously trying to shuffle some playing cards. By the time I finally spotted the Old Biddies, I felt like I was walking on eggshells and I was relieved to find that they, at least, didn't seem to be unduly stressed. They were chatting to an elderly lady wearing large horn-rimmed glasses, whom I recognised as their friend, June Driscoll.

"Gemma, dear—how nice to see you!" said Glenda as I joined them. She smoothed down her outfit. "What do you think of our new costumes?

23

How do we look?"

"Er…" I stared at them, torn between honesty and politeness. "Um… you look… er… very eye-catching."

They looked hideous. For some reason, the Old Biddies had decided to take to the stage in replicas of Elvis Presley's white jumpsuit, complete with flared hems, huge upturned collars, and hundreds of fake precious stones stitched to the fabric.

"Do you think there are enough rhinestones?" asked Florence. "We wanted to make sure that we really sparkle on stage."

"Oh, don't worry—you'll definitely sparkle," I said, thinking that any more embellishments and the judges were likely to be blinded.

"I stitched on some extra stones myself," said June proudly.

"I still think some lace doily on the sleeves and collar would have looked nicer," muttered Ethel with a sulky look.

"No, no, we discussed this, remember? We're saving lace doily for our last costume for the Finals," said Mabel. "We need to have something that will really wow the audience."

"Er… do you think you'll make it through to the Finals?" I asked, surprised.

"We must!" said June. "I can't go home without the prize money—it's the only hope for keeping B.E.A.S.T. alive!"

"It *is* going to be very hard competing against the

twins though," said Glenda, with a doubtful look across the room at the two little girls. "They do dance beautifully and look so adorable. My great-nephew Mike told me that the bookmakers have Molly and Polly down as the favourites to win the competition. They always have the highest number of public votes, by a wide margin."

June looked indignant. "They might be cute but we have public appeal too! People love to see feisty old grannies. We might have slightly fewer votes but I'm sure we're not far behind. Surely, we must be in second place in the polls?"

"No, actually, that... er... lady, Lara, is in second place," said Glenda, stumbling slightly over the word "lady".

"Lara?" June screwed her face up. "That horrid woman? How on earth can people be voting for her?"

"Well, she *is* very sexy, dear, and she does have a wonderful voice. Her rendition of 'Feeling Good' in the last round got a standing ovation from the audience."

"She's an awful person! Did you hear her making fun of poor Mr Ziegler last week? She was jeering at him as he was warming up for his routine and saying the most nasty things."

"Who's Mr Ziegler?" I asked.

"He's the Yodelling Plumber, dear," Florence explained. She cocked her head. "Listen, he's on stage rehearsing now—can you hear him?"

I realised suddenly that the strange ululating sound I'd been hearing in the background was a man's voice warbling up and down, accompanied by the occasional *whoosh* of water that sounded like a toilet flushing.

"He's ever so clever." Ethel beamed. "He yodels while fixing leaks and blockages, and he's made a contraption of pipes and drains that he can take on stage with him, to provide water sound effects."

"Yes, although he does leave terrible puddles on the stage," said Mabel, sniffing disapprovingly. "The last time we had to rehearse after him, we nearly slipped in all the soapy water."

"Wow... he's doing pretty well to make it so far into the competition. I mean, yodelling is a bit of an acquired taste, isn't it? Once the novelty wears off, I wouldn't have thought most people would like it that much," I said, wincing slightly as the yo-yoing voice began to get a bit loud and repetitive.

"The judges like him," said June. "That's why he made it through the last round, even though he didn't have a lot of public votes." Her face turned serious. "Hmm... that's something to remember. The focus is always on the public votes but one must never underestimate the influence of the judges. Still, Ziegler isn't the competition we have to worry about. It's Lara and the twins..." she continued, pursing her lips and scanning the rest of the room. Then her gaze lit on Trish and Skip, and her eyes narrowed. "And that lady with the dog—

they're very popular with the audience... They could be a serious threat."

I looked at her in wonder. The words sounded so incongruous coming from her lips. With her soft, fluffy white hair, wrinkled face and petite frame, June Driscoll looked the stereotype of the sweet old lady. But there was a steely determination in her eyes and a shrewd calculation in her approach to the competition that reminded me of a ruthless military commander planning his battle strategy.

"What about that fellow, Gaz?" asked Mabel.

June frowned. "Oh yes, I'd forgotten about him."

I followed her gaze to the other side of the room where I saw Nicole—looking less dishevelled now—sitting in a chair, staring down at her hands. A young man was hovering beside her, trying to engage her in conversation. He had longish, almost shaggy blond hair and was dressed in a faded hoodie and ripped jeans, but somehow, the overall effect managed to be good-looking rather than unkempt. He radiated confidence and I could feel the strength of his charisma, even from this distance.

I saw Nicole say something to him sharply and turn her back to him. It couldn't have been a more blatant (and literal) cold shoulder, but he simply shrugged and laughed, then slouched away, his hands in his jeans pockets and an easy grin on his face.

"Gaz is the comedian who does impressions, isn't

he?" I asked. "I remember catching one of the previous episodes and seeing a bit of his act. He's very funny."

"Yes, but he does use the most dreadful language," said Ethel, putting her hands to her cheeks in a scandalised gesture. "Those... those horrible curse words—"

"Yes, someone ought to wash that boy's mouth out with soap," declared Mabel.

"Well, the audience don't seem to mind," said Florence.

"Yes," June agreed. "They seem to love him. Hmm... yes, Gaz is a strong contender. We'll have to watch him." She paused thoughtfully. "If the twins are in the lead to take the top spot, then that only leaves one other chance for us."

"I don't understand—are you saying only two semi-finalists get through?" I asked.

"Oh yes, dear. After we perform before the judges and audience again tomorrow night, only two acts will be selected to go through to the Finals," Glenda explained.

"And one of them has got to be us!" said June, shaking her fist.

I said nothing, but I didn't share her conviction. A granny band might have been able to beat Gaz's funny impressions and Trish's canine dancing routine, but somehow I didn't think they'd be any match for Lara. Sadly, "young and sexy" trumped "old and quirky" every time.

A young man with a walkie-talkie appeared suddenly next to us. "Pussy Puffs! You're on next!"

"Ooh!" squealed Glenda. "I haven't retouched my lipstick yet!"

I wished them luck and watched as they tottered off towards the wings. I was half tempted to go out and watch them from the auditorium but decided to save it for the real performance tomorrow night. As one of the perks of the job, I'd been given front-row tickets for the Semi-Finals and I was looking forward to a fun evening with Cassie and my other close friend, Seth Browning.

Carefully giving Trish and Skip a wide berth, I made my way across the large Waiting Area again. As I neared the back door, however, I stopped short as a grey tabby with white paws jumped down from a pile of props and trotted up to me. She looked exactly like my cat, Muesli, down to the black eyeliner around her wide green eyes and the little pink nose.

"*Miaow...?*" she said.

"Muesli! What are you doing here?" I demanded, shocked. I was sure I had left her safely locked up at home. I bent to scoop her up, but she darted away from me, pausing just out of reach to give me another cheeky: "*Miaow?*"

I hesitated. Was it Muesli? This cat sounded slightly different. But she looked so much like my little feline...

The grey tabby leapt onto a wooden trolley next

to us, which held a large, round container shaped a bit like a witch's cauldron. There was a lid on the container, so I couldn't see what was inside, but something was leaking from under the edge of the lid, almost like frothy liquid that was boiling over and flowing out. Except that it wasn't liquid—it looked more like a strange white mist or even smoke.

The cat approached the container and reached up to sniff the white smoke. I stretched a hand out too, curious. The smoke was unfurling in snowy, white plumes, surrounding the cauldron in a halo, and yet there was no heat emanating from the container and no smell of burning. What on earth was it?

I reached out to lift the lid, then froze as a voice behind me cried:

"Hey, be careful—don't touch that!"

CHAPTER THREE

I jerked my hand back and turned around to find myself facing a lanky young man in his early twenties, with sandy hair and a bad case of acne which had left pockmarks on his cheeks. He was dressed all in black, including a long black cape hanging from his thin shoulders, and I recognised him as the magician I'd seen earlier, practising his card tricks.

"Don't touch that container," he said urgently. "And get that cat away from it!"

Hurriedly, I reached out and grabbed the tabby, picking her up and holding her firmly in my arms as I stepped away from the container.

"What's in it?" I asked him.

"Liquid nitrogen," he said.

"Oh..." I relaxed slightly. "The way you were

acting, I thought it was · something really dangerous—like acid."

"Liquid nitrogen *is* dangerous," he said, frowning. "It's minus 195 degrees Celsius and can freeze your fingers off if you stick your hand in it. It's true," he insisted, seeing my sceptical look.

"If it's that dangerous, why do you have it here backstage?"

"I use it in my magic act. And, okay, it's not *that* dangerous, if you know how to handle it," he added grudgingly. "It's normally transported sealed in a dewar, but—"

"A what?"

"A dewar. It's a specially designed vacuum flask which keeps the liquid nitrogen below boiling point. At room temperature, it would evaporate and turn into this white mist, see? But I need an open container so the mist can flow out and cover the floor of the stage. It's fine as long as people aren't nosy and don't try to take off the lid before my act," he said, looking reproachfully at me. "The other contestants and the crew all know not to touch it."

"Sorry..." I said, thinking that I seemed to be spending the whole day apologising to various contestants. "Anyway, I know now and I'll be more careful."

Without another word to me, he grabbed the trolley handle and began wheeling the container towards the double doors that led to the wings and the stage.

"*Miaow!*" said the cat in my arms, squirming slightly.

I looked down. Now that I was holding her, I could tell immediately that she wasn't Muesli; I couldn't explain how, since she looked so alike that she could have been a doppelgänger, but somehow I knew that this wasn't my cat. She squirmed again, trying to wriggle free, and I was just wondering what I should do with her when I heard a voice behind me.

"Misty...? Misty! Oh, thank goodness you found her!"

A woman rushed up to join us and scooped the grey tabby out of my arms. It was the lady with the puppets. She hugged the cat close to her and looked apologetically at me.

"I'm sorry—she must have escaped from her carrier when I wasn't looking. She's terrible about wandering off—she disappears for days sometimes. I hope she hasn't been bothering you?"

"Oh no, no," I assured her. "She was just getting a bit too close to a container of liquid nitrogen and that magician guy—"

"Oh, that's Albert," she replied.

"Right... Albert... yes, well, he was worried, so I picked her up, just to keep her out of harm's way." I gave her a smile. "So this is your cat? She looks so much like mine, I nearly had a shock thinking that she'd somehow escaped and managed to come here."

She returned my smile. "Yes, I'm Cheryl and this is Misty. She's part of my act—or at least, she's supposed to be, although she's been so naughty today she's driving me crazy!"

I laughed. "That sounds familiar."

Cheryl gave me a rueful smile. "It's not even as if I'm asking her to do that much. All she has to do is walk on stage with me in a leash and harness—"

"Oh, if you're managing that, you're already doing well," I said, chuckling. "I've trained my cat, Muesli, to use the leash and harness too, but trying to get her to walk anywhere with me is a challenge!"

"Well, I didn't say Misty walks in a straight line," said Cheryl with a twinkle in her eye. "Half the time, she walks two steps then decides to sit down and wash herself."

"That's exactly what Muesli does!" I cried, laughing and feeling an instant camaraderie with the woman.

She seemed to share the feeling too, because she gave me a warm smile. "Still, I'm hoping that once I get Misty on stage, things will be okay. All she has to do is sit in a little basket next to me while I sing and do the puppet show. We've practised a dozen times at home and she's been pretty good." Cheryl leaned towards me and said in a conspiratorial voice: "I put a blanket sprayed with catnip in the basket, you see, and Misty *loves* catnip. She just nestles in and rolls around on the blanket."

"Oh, that's a good idea—why didn't I think of

that? Muesli loves catnip too and I've got a little bed for her at my tearoom, but I'm always having trouble trying to get her to stay in it. She's very friendly, you see, and she'd much rather be wandering around the tables and jumping up into customers' laps," I said, rolling my eyes. "I must try your catnip trick and see if I can convince her to stay on her bed more."

"Your cat sounds like the cheeky twin sister of mine," said Cheryl with a laugh. "I'd love to meet her."

"Well, if you're ever out in the Cotswolds, do pop in my tearoom. It's just on the outskirts of Oxford, in a little village called Meadowford-on-Smythe."

"A traditional English tearoom? That sounds lovely. Do you do scones and finger sandwiches and all those sorts of things?"

I nodded. "All the favourites. And all freshly baked on the premises."

"Oh, wait... are you the one who's been providing all the delicious treats for our morning and afternoon tea?" she asked, suddenly putting two and two together.

"Yes, hi... I'm Gemma. Gemma Rose."

"Oh my goodness, your baking is absolutely scrumptious! I don't think I've ever tasted such wonderful Chelsea buns. So soft and moist in the centre and with just the right mix of lemon zest and cinnamon sugar."

I flushed with pleasure. "Thank you. Yes, I was

very lucky to get this catering job."

We were interrupted by the sound of one of the producers calling the magician on stage.

"Oops... I'd better go and get ready," said Cheryl. "I'm on after Albert."

"Good luck," I said.

She looked down at the tabby in her arms and said with a sigh, "I think I'm going to need it. I just hope that after this rehearsal today, Misty will calm down enough to behave for the real show tomorrow night. She was so good at home, but I think she's too distracted here—all these new sights and smells—she keeps wanting to go off and explore."

"I'm sure everything will work out fine tomorrow night," I assured her. "Although maybe it wouldn't hurt to give that blanket a really whopping dose of catnip!"

She laughed and then, hugging the cat tighter to her, she walked away.

***

Several hours later that day, I picked up an identical-looking grey tabby cat and shoved her into a cat carrier, which I then placed in the front basket of my bicycle.

"*Meorrw?*" said Muesli, peering out through the bars of the carrier.

"We're late, Muesli, and it's all your fault," I muttered, climbing astride the bike. "If you hadn't jumped on the bloody bromeliad and knocked it over, I wouldn't have had to spend the last twenty minutes trying to get soil out of the carpet!"

"*Meorrw!*" said Muesli indignantly.

"Yes, you did! You did it on purpose!"

Then I stopped as I realised what I was doing and gave a self-deprecating laugh. I couldn't believe that I was arguing with my cat. I was barely thirty years old, and already I was turning into a crazy cat lady! I smiled to myself. And to think that I never even used to like cats. I had always thought I was more of a "dog person" and it wasn't until Muesli came into my life nearly a year ago that I'd realised how fun and fascinating felines could be. Yes, there had been many times since the day I'd adopted her when I could have happily wrung her little neck, but now I couldn't imagine my life without the naughty tabby.

With winter finally here and the days getting shorter, twilight had already fallen as I set off, and I was pleased that I had invested in new bicycle lights recently. The towpath along the river was not particularly well lit and I went slowly until it joined the larger road which led into central Oxford. My cottage was situated at the south end of the city whilst my parents lived in North Oxford, but traversing the city didn't take long, especially when you knew all the shortcuts and back streets like I did. My days as a student here—coupled with a childhood growing up in the outer suburbs—meant that I probably knew the university city even better than the back of my hand. I could probably cycle around it with my eyes closed!

Tonight, however, I kept them peeled, carefully scanning the road ahead. I was pedalling fast and cycling at this speed in the dark was asking for an accident, if I wasn't careful. Oh, I wasn't normally such a reckless speed demon, but in my mother's book, *"Thou shalt always be punctual"* was one of the Ten Commandments.

Fifteen minutes later, I arrived huffing and puffing outside an elegant Victorian townhouse in a quiet tree-lined street. I secured my bike to the front fence, then grabbed the cat carrier and hurried inside. Pausing only long enough to scoop Muesli out of her carrier, I rushed into the sitting room.

"Sorry I'm late!" I gasped as I burst into the room. "I was delayed at the tearoom and then Muesli knocked over the—"

I broke off in embarrassment as I realised belatedly that my parents had a guest. A tall man with a thin, clever face was sitting on the sofa with my father. He looked to be in his late fifties or early sixties, and he also looked vaguely familiar, but I couldn't figure out where I had seen him before. Perhaps he was a colleague or a foreign scholar who had come to visit the university? My father, Professor Philip Rose, was a semi-retired Oxford don, and over the years I had got used to various academics and scholars coming to visit or even stay at my parents' home.

Still—I eyed the guest thoughtfully—this man wasn't dressed like a typical academic. Unlike my father, who spent most of his days in brown tweed jackets (yes, the kind with elbow patches) and even the occasional bow tie when he was lecturing at the university, this man was wearing dark jeans that I'm sure had a designer label on them and a tight-fitting cashmere top in a trendy shade of teal. His hair was receding but long at the back and caught up in a grey ponytail, and he looked, for all the world, like an ageing pop star.

"Ah, Gemma, darling... how nice to see you. Your mother was just wondering where you were—she's gone upstairs to find her phone to ring you." My father gestured to the man next to him. "This is Stuart Hollande—but of course, you know him already, don't you?"

I racked my brains as I went forwards to shake hands with him, embarrassed that we might have met previously and I'd completely forgotten.

Stuart extended a hand and said with a smile: "You must be the young lady who's been providing us with all those delicious treats at morning and afternoon tea. Your father has just been telling me all about your tearoom."

Then it clicked, and I cried: "Oh! You're one of the judges!"

CHAPTER FOUR

Although we had never been formally introduced, I had glimpsed Stuart Hollande a few times backstage, especially when the crew had been filming the judges' segments for the show. I must have also seen him during some of the show trailers and previous episodes, but I had to admit, I'd never really paid much attention.

He inclined his head and said with a chuckle, "Yes, I'm one of the terrible trio. I hope you won't hold it against me." He turned back towards my father. "In fact, I'm honoured that you're still willing to speak to me, Philip, given that I've 'sold out' and gone into commercial television. I was almost embarrassed to contact you and let you know that I was in Oxford."

"Nonsense," said my father gallantly. "You know

I'm always delighted to see you, Stuart, and I'm sure you're bringing pleasure to many people, even if you've left the more classical arena."

"I used to work for the big theatre companies—places like the Royal Shakespeare Company," Stuart explained at my puzzled look. "Then I was headhunted by a studio in London for a music producer job, and it's been all downhill since then," he laughed. "Now I'm a judge on a TV talent show... Still, at least I have more legitimate claim to the role than the other two judges, I suppose. Monty Gibbs is only on the panel because he owns the show and Zoe Carlotti is only there because we needed a bit of totty and she was the only B-list actress available. Gibbs was pleased to get her because she was really hot for a while, following that 'Filler Pout' scandal—you didn't hear about that?" he asked as I looked blank.

"Sorry..." I gave him a sheepish smile. "I'm afraid I don't keep up with celebrity gossip."

"Ah... well, Zoe's always been famous for her pouty lips and she's always claimed that they're completely natural. But of course, they're not."

"They're not?"

He laughed. "Are you kidding? That pillowy pout is the result of gallons of fillers! Zoe Carlotti is a cosmetic surgery addict. There isn't one part of her face that hasn't been nipped and tucked and smoothed and plumped. But she'd never admit it. In fact, she claimed that the only thing she put on her lips was a home-made 'miracle salve' that she applied every night before going to bed. It was supposedly made from a secret recipe, passed down from her great-great-grandmother in Italy." He gave me an ironic smile. "And of course, she soon launched a cosmetics line, selling this salve to the public, as a 'natural way to create plump, beautiful lips'. She'd sold thousands of pots and made a tidy sum for herself, before it was leaked that the famous lips which were advertising the product were the result of injectable fillers and had nothing to do with any 'miracle salve'. There was a huge scandal on the news and social media—but all that happened was that she became even more famous and her sales shot up even more."

"What an extraordinary story," said my father. "You mean, people knew that she had lied and her product was misrepresented, but yet they bought it anyway?"

"I'm afraid that's the way of the world these days, Philip," said Stuart. "People worship celebrities and will do anything to emulate them. Just being famous—even if you're not famous for a 'good' thing—is still enough to give you power and influence." He gave us a cynical smile. "I shouldn't talk though—I'm part of the circus myself, taking part in this talent show. I mean, that title says it all, doesn't it? *'From Pleb to Celeb'*!"

"I can't believe he went with that name," I said, grimacing. "It's just so... well, so blatant."

Stuart laughed. "You have to hand it to Monty Gibbs: whatever else I don't like about him, I admire his *chutzpah* and blunt honesty. There's none of the mincing hypocrisy of the other shows, pretending to foster artistic talent and build dream careers... Nope, all Gibbs is offering is exactly what all these people want: their fifteen minutes of fame. As the show tagline says, we *'turn nobodies into somebodies'*. You know that slogan caused a furore when it was first released? There were cries of elitism, racism, celebrityism... you name it. But Gibbs was unrepentant. He refused to change it and he refused to apologise. That was what his show was really about and he wasn't afraid to be honest about it."

"Well, it doesn't seem to have hurt the popularity of his show," I observed dryly.

"Yes," Stuart agreed. "And all the controversy has just fuelled more interest in the show. You know the old saying: if you want to make a book a bestseller, ban it. This was a bit like that. Suddenly everybody wanted to watch this daring new show where contestants—and us judges—didn't have to worry about being politically correct all the time... It's been pretty liberating, I can tell you."

I started to answer, but at that moment a shrill ringing penetrated the quiet of my parents' elegantly furnished sitting room. I hastened to find my mobile phone and answer it, then paused in bemusement as my mother's voice rang out of the speaker, followed almost instantly by an echo drifting down from upstairs.

"Darling, where are you? We're all waiting for you to start dinner and it's really very bad manners to be tardy, you know."

"I'm sorry, Mother, I was a bit late—but I'm here now."

"Where?"

"Here."

"Here?"

"Here... downstairs."

"Oh, how lovely. Would you like a drink, darling, before dinner?"

Why are we having this conversation through the mobile phone when she could just come downstairs? "Um... no, I'm fine, thanks, Mother."

"Well, don't forget to wash your hands before we sit down at the table. And I hope you've put on something nice, Gemma, and not those dreadful jeans that you always wear. Really, a lady should wear a nice dress or perhaps a skirt and blouse—"

I flushed as I realised that Stuart Hollande could hear every word of this conversation and he was trying hard not to smile.

"As it so happens, Mother, I *am* wearing jeans," I said in exasperation. "But I'm already here—I can't go home to change now."

My mother made a *tsk-tsk* sound, then said, "Oh, well, I suppose if you're sitting at the table, no one can see your legs. And did you put on some make-up?"

"*Mother!*"

"Ooh! I just remembered, I bought a new Elizabeth Arden lipstick—it's a lovely, bright fuchsia shade—I can bring it down for you—"

Ugh. I wouldn't be seen dead in fuchsia lipstick. "No, thanks, Mother. I'm fine. I've got... uh... some tinted lip balm on already. Look, isn't it silly us talking on the phone when we're both here? Why don't you come downstairs and we can talk in person?"

"Oh yes, I'll be down in a jiffy... just noticed that the loo bowl needs a new toilet freshener..."

Several minutes later, we were finally all seated at the dining table and my mother brought out that old British classic, ham and split-pea soup, as the first course. I had to admit, while my mother's cooking was very "old school" and not the sort of things I'd usually make myself, I did enjoy eating at my parents' place. My mother was a fantastic cook and sometimes all the exotic fusion cuisine in the world didn't compare with a simple, home-made roast chicken.

Conversation over dinner was animated, with Stuart telling us more about the show and my parents listening with fascination. I had been shocked to discover that my mother actually watched *From Pleb to Celeb*. With my parents' tastes in TV usually running to highbrow programmes about the French art movement or roundtable discussions by leading sociologists on the conflict in the Middle East, a cheesy talent show was the last thing I'd imagined my mother enjoying. She seemed incredibly knowledgeable too. I was ashamed to realise that despite my backstage access, my mother knew more about the contestants than I did.

"Oh, I do like that teenage boy who does the hoppy dance," she said enthusiastically as she served the roast potatoes. "Although... he doesn't always look very coordinated, does he?"

"That's the type of dance, Mother. It's called hip hop."

"No, your mother's right," said Stuart, with a thoughtful look. "Tim tries very hard and he has the right technique, but as you say, Evelyn, there isn't a strong unity with the music... But of course, he's only sixteen and I imagine that would come with time and maturity."

"What do you think of the lady who plays the piano?" I asked, thinking of the fight I had witnessed earlier.

"Nicole Flatley? She's lovely... but she's very shy and quiet, isn't she?" said my mother. "It's almost as if she is apologising for being on stage."

"That's spot on, Evelyn!" said Stuart, looking at her admiringly. "Yes, Nicole is sweet, but she lacks stage presence."

"And the lady with the puppets?" I asked. "I met her today. She seems very nice."

"Oh, yes, Cheryl Sullivan—there was an interview with her in the last episode," said my mother. "She's a nursery school teacher, but her dream is to present a children's television programme and she's hoping to catch the interest of a network if she wins, so that she might host her own show."

"I don't think she's a strong contender to win," said Stuart regretfully. "I mean, her act is delightful—the puppet show combined with singing and telling stories—and I'm sure children would love it, but to win this competition, you have to wow the crowds. The adult crowds."

"What about the magician fellow?" my father spoke up.

I stared at him. "Dad? Have you been watching the show too?"

My father coughed sheepishly. "Well... I happened to see a few episodes... because your mother was watching," he hastened to add.

"Albert Hodge. Hmm... yes... he's an interesting young man," said Stuart. "He's not very confident and I would have thought that a career on the stage would be the last thing he wants. But I suppose the lure of the prize money is enough to make anyone overcome their fears, especially if it gives them the chance to get out of their current situation. I believe Albert lives with his mother in council estate housing, and from the little he's said, it sounds like he's had a tough childhood."

"Oh, the poor boy," said my mother. "You mustn't be too hard on him in the next round."

"Unfortunately, Evelyn, it doesn't work like that. We have to judge them based on their talents and performance, not on their background."

"But surely his challenging situation means that his performance is worth even more?"

Stuart shrugged. "You could argue that every contestant has his or her unique challenges. We can't favour one over the other, just because they come from more humble backgrounds. And in any case, much as I hate to say it, I don't think Albert has a real chance at winning the contest. I think he will be eliminated in the next round."

"Only two of them will go through to the Finals, won't they?" I asked, remembering what the Old Biddies had told me.

"Yes, that's right."

"And I heard that the twins, Molly and Polly, are the favourites to win the competition?"

Stuart smiled. "Well, you know I'm not officially supposed to comment... but yes, I think they've got a strong chance of winning the show. Of course, there are still a few weeks to go and anything can happen. Things are notoriously unpredictable when there's a public vote involved. So much depends on the popularity of the contestants and—as we've seen with politicians during election campaigns— that can change from week to week. The twins are certainly in the lead at the moment, but several of the other contestants are also very popular. Lara King, for example, is a huge favourite—there has been more coverage of her in the press and social media than of any other contestant..."

Probably because of the size of her fake breasts, I thought cynically.

"...then there's that chap, Gaz Hillman—the comedian who does the impressions—he's very good, very charismatic, and the crowds love him. And of course, there's the dog dancing duo."

"Oh, there've been so many dancing dogs now in so many shows..." said my mother, wrinkling her nose.

"Yes, you're right—they're not very original anymore," Stuart agreed. "But you know how much the British love their dogs. In fact, any contestant with an animal in their act probably has an advantage."

I thought of Cheryl with her naughty cat, Misty, and wondered if that still held true! Then I remembered the contestants who meant the most to me.

"Er... what about the Old Bid—I mean, the granny band with the old ladies?" I asked.

"You mean the Pussy Puffs?" said Stuart with a wicked gleam in his eye.

I winced. "Can't you get them to change their name?" I implored.

"Why? What's wrong with their name, darling?" my mother asked.

Oh God. Not her too. "Er... nothing, Mother. I just think they could have a better name."

"Oh, I think they're delightful as they are," said Stuart, chuckling. "It's just the sort of name you'd expect someone of that generation to choose, since they don't know the slang meanings of many perfectly innocent words. And Monty Gibbs likes to leave things as natural and genuine as possible, politically correct or not."

"But they're going to be the laughing stock of the country!" I said.

"They really shouldn't have joined the show then," said my mother with a disapproving sniff. "I was most astonished when Mabel Cooke told me that they were auditioning for the contest."

"I think they're doing it to help their friend, June. The prize money would mean a lot to her. And they're not bad," I added doggedly, out of a sense of loyalty to my geriatric friends. "I mean, I know they don't always sing in tune and... and... they forget the words sometimes... but it's pretty cool that they're willing to give it a go at their age."

"Yes, they're certainly inspirational, even if they're not aspirational," said Stuart, laughing. "And the public does love them. Who doesn't like a spunky grandma, eh?"

"So do you think they might have a chance to win?" I asked eagerly.

He rubbed his chin. "Well, first they'd have to get through to the next round and I'm afraid they've got some tough competition to beat, especially since there are only two places in the Finals. Several of the other contestants are going to put up a good fight." He gave a wry laugh. "In fact, some of them look ready to kill to win the contest!"

CHAPTER FIVE

At just five foot one, Monty Gibbs put the "micro" into micro-managing, but what he lacked in stature, he more than made up for in attention and fervour. Nothing escaped his eagle eyes and I watched nervously now as he hovered over the trays laden with freshly baked scones, teacakes, Chelsea buns, and miniature treacle tarts, all ready for the afternoon tea break.

"Mm... good... good..." he said, rubbing his hands. "And do we 'ave a cake as well?"

"Oh, yes..." I hurried to lift a large platter from the trolley and deposited it on the table, revealing a majestic Victoria sponge cake, resplendent with fresh strawberries and whipped cream.

"Ah...!" Monty Gibbs stepped back in admiration. "Fan-tastic!" He turned to the girl carrying the clipboard and said, pointing to the table, "Make sure yer cop close-ups of all the food and also footage o' the crew tuckin' in. And the contestants too—we want everyone ter see 'ow well we're feedin' them."

"Sir... I was thinking, maybe we could do, like, a food-poisoning scenario," she said eagerly. "You know, like one of the contestants had some cake with cream which wasn't fresh and they started getting sick just before their act. That could add some real drama to—"

"What? What are you saying? The cakes I provide are always fresh!" I said in indignation.

"Yeah, I know—but we could just, like, pretend," said the girl.

"No, you can't," I said, really starting to get annoyed now. "My tearoom is renowned for using the best and freshest ingredients, and I'm not having you spread lies and ruin my reputation, just to create fake drama for the show!"

"Well, it was just an idea," said the girl with a sulky look.

Monty Gibbs said: "Good suggestion, Natalie. I like the way yor mind works. But—" he held up an appeasing hand as I started spluttering angrily, "—I think we can get a right good story 'ere, wivout artificially raisin' the stakes. In fact, right, why don't yer play up the feel-good angle? That boy, Albert, tell 'im ter give yer some soundbites about 'ow 'e could never afford to 'ave cake as a child. 'e's the one who grew up on a council estate, right? And maybe a couple o' lines from that woman—the one wiv the puppets—she's a schoolteacher, ain't she?

"Nursery," Natalie supplied.

"Even better! Get 'er ter say 'er 'eart breaks ter see children gahn 'ungry. And then cut ter Albert stuffin' 'is face at the table, like a starvin' man who ain't seen food in days. There won't be a dry eye in the 'ouse!" said Gibbs with a satisfied smile.

"But... but you don't know if he couldn't afford cake as a child," I protested. "Maybe his mother baked lovely cakes at home. And you can't go putting words in Cheryl's mouth if she didn't think that herself. You should be telling people the truth—"

Monty Gibbs threw his head back and laughed. "The truth, isit? Darlin', this is TV! We're 'ere ter entertain people and what people want are stories: sob stories, luv stories, funny stories, scary stories... Nobody wants the borin' truth! Besides, we might bend the edges but we're still tellin' the truth, ain't we? Albert *did* 'ave a tough time growing up; whether he ate cake or not doesn't right matter. It's just a detail, innit? A... a—whatchamacallit—a symbolic thing, ter show everyone 'ow deprived 'is childhood were. And I'm sure Cheryl *would* be upset if she saw some poor kid gahn 'ungry."

Natalie nodded. "Yes, we're just helping her articulate it."

"Yes, but..."

Gibbs shot a glance at his watch. "Sorry, got ter

go! Need to do the judges' briefin'." His gaze went beyond us to the tall, ponytailed man on the other side of the room. "Eh, Stuart, mate! Where's Zoe?"

Stuart Hollande strolled over to join us. "Haven't seen her," he said, shrugging.

Monty Gibbs looked at his watch again and swore. "Always late! Somebody get that bloody cow on the phone and find out wot she's doin'—she's supposed ter be 'ere by now! We're on in a couple of 'ours."

Before he even finished speaking, a young man in oversized dark-rimmed glasses was rushing up to us. "Sir! Sir!" His face was a mask of consternation. "Oh sir—there's been a disaster!"

"Wot? Woss 'appened?"

"Ms Carlotti's agent has just contacted me and said that her client is unwell and unable to make it tonight."

"Whotcher mean, she can't make it?" Gibbs, demanded. "'ow can she be sick, then, eh? I seen 'er at the bloody breakfast meetin' this mornin' and she were fine."

The young man shot a glance at me, then gave a discreet cough and said: "Er... apparently, Ms Carlotti went for a Botox injection after that and something went wrong with the procedure... So... um... her face is frozen."

"Wot?" Gibbs gaped at him.

The young man shifted uncomfortably. "Yes, sir—she can't make any expressions at all. I don't think she can even shut her eyes properly."

"Maybe she can just pretend that she's astonished by every performance," suggested Stuart, grinning. "Then she can just keep re-using the same expression."

Monty Gibbs groaned. "This ain't funny, Hollande! Tonight's the bloomin' Semi-Finals. We 'ave ter 'ave three judges! W'am I gonna find a substitute for Zoe now?"

I stood aside, feeling a bit unnecessary as they huddled together to debate the best solution to the crisis. Deciding that they wouldn't miss me, I left and wandered through to the contestants' Waiting Area to look for the Old Biddies. As I entered the room, however, I nearly collided with a woman rushing out. It was Cheryl and she looked frantic.

"OH! Oh, it's you..." she said.

I caught her arms to steady her. "What's the matter?"

"I can't find Misty!" she wailed. "I put her down for one second, just to adjust my costume, and when I looked up, she'd disappeared!"

I looked around the large open-plan room. "She can't have disappeared—she must be in here somewhere."

Cheryl shook her head. "I've been searching every corner! She isn't here—she must have wandered out of the room. She often goes off by herself, you know, back home, and doesn't come back for days." Cheryl indicated the doorway I'd just come in. "This corridor leads to the rest of the backstage rooms—it's like a rabbit warren in there. I don't know how I'm ever going to find her!"

"Come on, I'll help you search," I said.

Half an hour later, however, I was beginning to share Cheryl's pessimism. We had scoured every room in the place but still, there was no sign of the little grey tabby cat.

"Are there any other exits from the Waiting Area?" I asked?

Cheryl shook her head. "No, the only other exit leads to the wings around the stage."

"What if she did go that way and went around the back of the stage... what's on the other side?"

"Nothing much... just some storerooms and... oh, there's a fire exit that's often left open because that's where people go out to have a smoke!" Cheryl gasped. "She could have gone out there and left the building altogether."

We rushed to the fire exit in question and, sure enough, found it standing wide open. It led onto a small car park at the back of the concert hall, obviously for production crew, cast, and suppliers. Beyond the car park was an area of wilderness, overgrown with weeds, grass, and shrubs, which sloped down to the canal in the distance. This was obviously what was left of the original land that the concert hall had been built on.

Cheryl's shoulders slumped as she saw the area of wilderness. "Oh God—I'll never find Misty if she has gone into that!"

I wanted to say something encouraging but I had to agree. The chances of finding the cat—especially if she didn't want to be found—were practically nil. Especially in the time we had left before the show began.

Cheryl was obviously sharing my thoughts because she wrung her hands and said: "What am I going to do? I'm on in a couple of hours."

"Can't you just do the act without her?" I asked.

"No, I planned the whole piece around the idea of me telling the story to my kitty friend. Even the songs have 'Misty' in them. I need to have her walk on stage with me and then sit in the basket, otherwise the whole thing is ruined!"

She looked on the verge of tears and I wished I could help her, but I didn't know what to suggest. Then she gripped my arm suddenly.

"Wait... I could use *your* cat!"

"I... I'm sorry?"

"Your cat! You said she's been trained to walk on a leash and harness, didn't you?"

"Well, yes, but—"

"Do you live far away?"

"No, I live in Oxford, about fifteen minutes' walk from here. But I don't think Muesli—"

"Oh, her name is Muesli? That's brilliant! That sounds so close to 'Misty'—I could easily swap her name in the songs and no one would even notice."

"Yes, but—"

"And she looks exactly like Misty too, doesn't she? You said so yesterday. So I wouldn't even have to tell the show people; they wouldn't know the difference. Not that I imagine they would have a problem with it, but you never know—"

"Wait, Cheryl—listen: Muesli has never done anything like this. I'm not sure she'd be okay on stage."

"You mean she'd be afraid of the noise and lights?"

"Well..." I thought of my confident little cat. "No, probably not. Nothing seems to faze her much. But she's very friendly and inquisitive, and I don't know if she'd stay obediently in the basket. She might decide she wants to say hello to the judges or the people in the audience and wander off instead."

"Oh, I'm sure she'll be fine. You said she loves catnip too, doesn't she? So I'm sure she'd stay happily on the blanket. And anyway, if she jumps out of the basket, I can always put her back in. My act is only two minutes. I doubt she can get up to much mischief in that time."

You haven't met my cat, I thought.

"Please, Gemma..." She looked at me pleadingly. "I'm going to keep looking now but if I can't find Misty before my act starts, then Muesli is my only hope."

I sighed. "All right. I'll go and get her—but be warned, you might be asking for even more trouble than you had with Misty!"

CHAPTER SIX

When I returned forty-five minutes later with Muesli in tow, the show had already begun and the area backstage was a hive of frantic activity. People rushed around, carrying props and unwinding cables, yelling for more lights, calling for sound adjustments... I dodged around them, careful to lift the cat carrier high and keep out of their way, as I searched for Cheryl. The nursery teacher wasn't in any of the other backstage rooms and I couldn't see her in the Waiting Area either. I paused by the double doors leading to the wings and the stage, and frowned, scanning the big room again.

Everybody else seemed to be here. Albert Hodge stood a few feet away from me. He was obviously due to go on next and he looked pale with nerves. He was dressed all in black, with a long cape and a pointy sorcerer's hat that was probably supposed to lend some mystique to his stage presence. Unfortunately, though, with his thin, gangly body and air of awkward nervousness, he looked more like a teenage geek about to attend Comic-Con or a *Dungeons and Dragons* convention than a masterful magician.

Beyond him, I could see the Yodelling Plumber, Franz Ziegler, busily polishing a length of metal pipe. He was dressed in a traditional costume of *lederhosen* and braces, and looked calm and confident. A few feet away from him, the Old Biddies were helping each other adjust their Elvis jumpsuits, and across from them was Tim the hip hop dancer. He was pulling faces at the twins, making them giggle, as their mother looked on indulgently. In the far corner of the room, I could see Skip the collie tied to his crate, although there was no sign of his owner.

And in the middle of the room, standing apart from everyone else, was Lara King. She looked stunning—her voluptuous body sheathed in a red sequinned gown which caught the light and shimmered with her every move. I could see why she was such a favourite with the public. Like Gaz, she had oodles of natural confidence and charm, and it radiated from her, giving her a powerful attraction. She wasn't wasting any of it, though, on the poor woman who was trying to put the finishing touches to her hair and make-up.

"Oh for God's sake, haven't you finished?" Lara snapped, twitching irritably.

"I'm sorry—I just need to make sure... *There!*" The woman gave her hair a final adjustment, then stepped back, satisfied. "I'll powder your nose again, just before you go on and—"

"Make sure you don't forget my drink," said Lara sharply. "I need it just before I step on stage."

"Er... is this that special gargle...?"

Lara gave an exaggerated sigh. "*Yes.* In the fridge, in the staff kitchen—didn't they tell you? And bring a bowl for me to spit into."

The make-up artist looked taken aback, and for a moment I thought she was going to refuse. But Monty Gibbs had obviously given strict instructions about indulging the contestants' whims, because after a moment she simply said: "Right. I'll see to it."

Lara didn't even acknowledge her with any thanks, too busy admiring her own face in a compact mirror. The make-up artist compressed her lips and walked away.

"*Meorrw?*"

I looked down at Muesli, who was peering out from between the bars of her carrier, and remembered my search.

"All right, Muesli," I said. "Give me a minute. We'll find her."

I scanned the room again, but Cheryl was still nowhere to be seen. *Where could she be?* Then I felt a flash of panic. What if I was too late and she had already gone on stage? I hurried over to the double doors that led towards the stage, nearly colliding with Gaz, who was just coming in from the wings. He looked at me curiously.

"You all right?" he asked. "You're not one of the crew, are you?"

"I'm looking for Cheryl," I said. "She hasn't gone on already, has she?"

"Nah, Nicole's on stage at the moment. I was just having a peek from the wings," he said, and as I cocked my head to listen, I realised that I could hear the faint sound of a piano being played, followed by dutiful applause as the piece came to an end. The notes had sounded timid, muted, and I thought back to my mother's words last night. She was right: Nicole's fingerwork was fantastic, but she lacked fire and passion in her performance.

The next moment, I froze, incredulous, as I heard my mother's voice, grossly magnified by a microphone, coming from the area beyond the stage.

"That was lovely, dear. And you sit so gracefully at the piano. I think it's dreadful how many women just don't sit in a ladylike manner anymore. I'm always telling my daughter, Gemma, that good posture is so important—she slouches terribly, you know—and people do judge you by first impressions, no matter what they say..."

Oh my God! What is my mother doing here?

63

I hurried to the edge of the wings and peeked through the curtains framing the side of the stage. My mouth fell open as I saw my mother sitting on the panel between Stuart Hollande and Monty Gibbs.

The former turned to her with a smile and said: "And speaking of first impressions, what did you think of Nicole's performance, Evelyn?"

"Well… it was very lovely, but…" My mother looked apologetic. "It did feel as if you were frightened to press the keys on the piano. It's important to have conviction, dear, when you do something—even if you don't feel it—you have to act it, so that people will believe you."

"Very true, Evelyn," said Stuart Hollande. "Fake it until you make it, as we say in the industry."

"Yes, yes," said Monty Gibbs, putting on a knowledgeable expression. "Yer didn't own that song, eh?"

"So… time for the judges' decisions," said Stuart. "Monty?"

The diminutive businessman swelled his chest and said grandly, "It's a no from me."

Stuart turned to my mother. "Evelyn? Is Nicole good enough to go through to the Finals?"

"Oh dear…" My mother looked distressed. "Can I tell you after I've seen everyone else?"

The audience burst out laughing and several people cheered. I stared. I couldn't believe my mother was a judge on the show… and it looked like the audience loved her.

"You have to give your decision now, Evelyn," said Stuart. "Although, of course, the public vote can still change things."

"*MEEEOOORRWW!*"

I jumped as Muesli's plaintive voice rang out suddenly, loud and clear in the waiting silence. *Oh bugger.* I'd forgotten that I was still holding the cat carrier. Muesli was obviously getting tired of being cooped up in the cage and wanted to be let out to explore. She put a white paw through the bars and rattled the door.

"*Meorrw? Meorrw?*"

The judges looked around in puzzlement whilst the audience burst into giggles. Hastily, I retreated from the edge of the curtains and backed away from the stage. In the distance, I could hear the crowd murmuring and Monty Gibbs saying:

"Is that a cat? Woot's a bloody cat doin' in 'ere?"

Oops. I hurried back through the wings, bumping into Albert, who was hovering just outside the double doors leading back to the Waiting Area.

"Is she finished yet?" he asked me.

"Almost. Listen, have you seen Cheryl anywhere?"

He shrugged, obviously not interested, and pushed past me, heading into the wings. I sighed and continued back to where I had seen Cheryl's things. The carrier was getting heavy now and my arm was starting to ache. I paused by the familiar chest with several puppets draped across the top and looked around indecisively. Where was she? Carrying the cat carrier over to a quiet corner, I set it down on top of a large trestle table and bent down to peek at Muesli through the bars.

"You be good. Wait here—I'll be right back."

"*Meorrw?*" Muesli pressed her nose against the door of the cage and pushed impatiently.

"Not yet, Muesli," I said. "Just wait here. I won't be long."

I hurried off, through the door on the other side of the Waiting Area and into the long corridor which connected the network of rooms backstage. Most of them were empty, but I diligently looked inside every one. Finally, I rounded a corner and found a door that I hadn't seen previously. To my surprise, it opened not into a room but a narrow corridor which snaked around the building. Curious, I followed it around and found myself suddenly in the crossover—the area behind the stage, concealed by screens and drapery, which provided a way to move from the wings on one side of the stage to the other, out of sight of the audience.

Onstage, I could hear the sound of mystical music and I noticed a strange white fog around my legs, billowing like white smoke and curling around me. *The magician Albert must be on*, I realised, *and this must be the liquid nitrogen that's part of his act.* It seemed like an awful lot of it, however. It swirled around me, rising as high as my knees, and was so dense that I couldn't even see my own feet. I waved my hand in front of my face to clear the air. At this rate, the audience wouldn't be able to see anything except clouds of white smoke!

Carefully keeping out of view, I skirted around the side of the stage, intending to head back into the Waiting Area through the double doors leading from the wings. As I walked past the rear screens, I saw the big cauldron-shaped container that held the evaporating liquid nitrogen, now with the lid off. It was tucked just out of sight, behind a fold of curtain, and there was a fan set up on one side to blow the white mist towards the stage.

However, the cauldron looked like it hardly needed any extra boost—it was already frothing and bubbling madly, like a pot of soup about to boil over. The billowing white mist rose like a cloud, obscuring the top of the container. Then the plumes of gas parted for a second and I caught my breath as I saw something slumped over the edge of the container.

No, not something. *Someone.*

I took a step closer, my eyes widening in horror as I took in the sparkling fabric clinging to the voluptuous body and recognised the red sequinned dress.

It was Lara.

Someone had shoved the sexy singer headfirst into the cauldron of frothing liquid nitrogen, straight into an icy death.

CHAPTER SEVEN

"Would you like to sit down, miss?" a young police constable asked, peering anxiously at me as he led me into the concert hall's administrative office. "The detective inspector is on his way, but he might be a few minutes yet."

"I'm fine... fine," I assured him.

"It's no shame to be freaked out by a dead body," he said earnestly. "Most people would be in a right state."

"Actually, it's not the first time I've come across a dead body," I said with a wan smile. "It was just the way she looked—her face..."

I shuddered as the memory came back to me: reaching out to grab Lara's body... yanking backwards... the way she fell back stiffly from the container... that icy lifeless mask of her face... then the awful moment when her body had slumped facedown to the floor and her frozen face had smashed, the nose splintering, the cheeks crumbling into a thousand pink fragments.

That was when I'd screamed.

And screamed and kept on screaming as people had come running from backstage, on stage, and even the audience, to see what the commotion was. I squirmed with embarrassment to think of it now. I'd always prided myself on having a cool head in a crisis and for not being squeamish about things like blood and dead bodies. Besides, as I'd told the officer, I had seen dead bodies before. Several, in fact. Not peaceful corpses either, but victims of brutal murders. And yet none of them had affected me like this one had. This had been like something out of a nightmare or a sci-fi horror movie. I had been practically having hysterics and not even my mother could calm me down. It was only when Mabel Cooke had said sternly in her booming voice: "That's quite enough, Gemma!" and dashed some cold water in my face that I had finally recovered my senses.

I wondered where Mabel and the other Old Biddies were now. They were probably outside in the Waiting Area, waiting to be questioned, together with the other contestants, the judges, and the rest of the crew. I wondered if the audience had been detained as well. I didn't envy the Oxfordshire CID the job of restraining the crowds and preventing them from leaving, although I had a feeling that a lot of people would probably have been more than happy to hang around out of ghoulish curiosity. After all, there was nothing as exciting as a real-life murder.

"How about a cup of tea then?" asked the young constable, obviously still worried about my emotional state.

I was about to decline when I realised that I would, in fact, appreciate the quintessential British panacea for every crisis. Several minutes later, as I sat alone in the room, sipping the hot, sweet tea, I felt the knot of tension slowly uncurl in my stomach and the shaky feeling leave my legs. Taking a deep breath, I found that I was able to think about what had happened much more calmly.

Murder. It was surreal to think that Lara had been murdered by liquid nitrogen, but that's exactly what had happened. Somebody had pushed her face into that lethal icy pool and she had literally frozen to death. The only comforting thought was that it had probably all happened so fast, she wouldn't have felt a thing.

But who could have done such a thing?

It had to have been someone close by, I decided. Someone backstage, probably, who could do the deed and then quickly return to their original position, before anyone missed them. And someone who knew enough about the competition to know that the container of deadly liquid nitrogen would be there, in the wings... which meant that it was likely to be one of the crew or the contestants. I thought of the various hopefuls that I'd seen nervously practising their act in the Waiting Area yesterday. It was ludicrous to think that any of them could be a murderer. But it was even more ridiculous to think that one of the crew might have murdered Lara. Why would they? Why would anyone want to kill the sultry singer?

The memory of the fight I'd witnessed yesterday between Nicole and Lara flashed through my mind. I just couldn't imagine the sweet, shy pianist as a murderer... but at the same time, I couldn't help recalling the expression of bitter hatred on Nicole's face as she'd flung herself at Lara. And she had certainly been livid at Lara's unapologetic attitude towards seducing married men and breaking up families. But surely you didn't kill someone just because you were disgusted by their morals?

The door to the office opened, and my heart gave a little jump when I saw the tall, dark-haired man standing in the doorway. With his piercing blue eyes and broodingly handsome profile, Detective Inspector Devlin O'Connor was the kind of man who made women's hearts jump everywhere. *But there's only one woman he has eyes for*, I thought with an inward smile. *Me.*

"Gemma." Devlin crossed the room and enveloped me in a fierce hug. "Are you all right? I heard that you had a bad reaction to finding the body."

"I didn't faint or anything," I said indignantly, pushing away from him. "It was just a shock... not so much finding her dead, you know, but rather seeing the way her frozen face smashed—" I choked and stumbled, "—um... well, it wasn't a pretty sight."

"I can imagine," said Devlin, wincing. He led me to the chair by the desk, then leaned against the latter himself and crossed his arms. "Can you bear to talk about it for a bit though? I'm afraid I can't avoid questioning you, since you're the one who found the body."

"Sure. I'm fine now—honestly," I said. "I've had a cup of tea and I've calmed down; put some distance between myself and the... the scene."

"Good." Devlin gave me an encouraging smile and switched on a portable tape recorder. "So tell me exactly how you found her."

I told him, trying to make sure that I described every detail, although I wasn't sure how helpful my rambling account was. Surely the Forensics team would be going over every inch of the crime scene? Still, I tried to give as full a description as I could. When I'd finished, I said:

"I've been thinking—the murderer must have been someone backstage. I mean, I saw Lara only ten, maybe fifteen minutes max, before I found her body. She was standing in the middle of the Waiting Area and she was perfectly fine. I don't think it was someone who came in from the outside—it had to be someone who was 'on the spot' already, so to speak. Someone who could sneak into the wings and shove Lara into the liquid nitrogen, then run back again to wherever they were before."

"Was Lara speaking to anyone when you saw her?"

"No. She was checking her appearance in the mirror. She didn't seem particularly friendly with any of the other contestants, in general."

Devlin raised his eyebrows. "Did you notice tensions?"

I gave a sarcastic laugh. "That's putting it mildly. Yesterday I walked in on her and one of the other contestants having a full-on hair-pulling, face-scratching match."

Devlin leaned forwards. "Really? Who was Lara fighting with?"

"Nicole Flatley. She's the girl who plays the piano. She and Lara were having an argument about 'homewreckers'—you know, women who purposefully have affairs with married men. I gathered that Lara was one and quite proud of it. She was boasting about her conquests and Nicole totally lost it. She attacked Lara and things got really ugly. And you know what the worst thing was?" I asked with remembered indignation. "Some of the TV crew were in there filming them and making no effort to stop them! They only cared about getting titillating footage for the show. I had to step in myself to pull the two women apart."

"I hope you didn't get hurt in the process."

"No, in fact, Nicole looked mortified. I think she got carried away in the heat of the moment and forgot herself."

"Did you see Lara getting into a fight with anyone else?"

"I didn't see that much of her, to tell you the truth—although I wouldn't be surprised if she'd got into a fight with the crazy dog lady at some stage," I added sourly. "That woman is waiting to pick a fight with anyone."

"Trish Bingham, you mean?"

I nodded. "The one with the collie. Her dog's lovely but she's a right grumpy cow. I bumped into Skip by mistake while they were practising and she practically bit my head off. She was completely unreasonable! None of the other contestants seem to like her much either."

"But you don't think there was any particular enmity between her and Lara?"

"No, except... well, there's something about Trish—she's very intense, you know. I wondered if..." I trailed off.

"Go on."

I gave an embarrassed laugh. "It's probably a stupid idea."

"No, go on... I trust your instincts, Gemma."

"Well... I did wonder if... you see, Lara was one of the favourites to go through to the Finals. Only two semi-finalists can make it through to the next round and the twins have pretty much bagged the top spot. And I think Lara was expected to take second place, based on popularity ratings. But if she was removed—"

"Then someone else would have a chance to step into that empty space and go through to compete for the prize," finished Devlin. He rubbed his chin. "Hmm... that's not a bad theory, Gemma. Certainly something worth following up. But couldn't the other contestants be equally guilty of this?"

"Only if they're high up in the polls. I don't think someone like Frank Ziegler, for instance, would have much chance. He's the Yodelling Plumber," I explained at Devlin's blank look.

"Oh... oh yes, of course. I should have known that," said Devlin, looking annoyed with himself. "I only arrived a short while ago and it's chaos out there. I haven't had a chance to familiarise myself properly with all the players yet." He shook his head and sighed. "But I can see that this is shaping up to be the longest list of suspects we have ever encountered. There are ten semi-finalists, including Lara, aren't there? So if your theory is correct, nine of those could be suspects—"

"Well, no, that's what I was trying to explain to you. I don't think they're all equally likely. We can probably rule the twins out, since they're not threatened by Lara, and anyway, they're just ten-year-old little girls. And we can rule out Albert since he was on stage at the time of the murder. That leaves seven other contestants: Frank Ziegler the Yodelling Plumber, Cheryl the puppeteer, Nicole the pianist, Gaz the comedian, Tim the hip hop dancer, and Trish with her dog. Oh, and the Pussy Puffs."

"The *what*?"

I grinned. "That's what the Old Biddies call themselves—they've formed a 'granny band' with their friend, June Driscoll."

Devlin groaned. "Nooo... Don't tell me those meddling old hens are mixed up in this too?"

"They do have a legitimate reason to be involved this time—they're one of the contestants." I shook my head, chuckling. "I never thought they'd make it through the initial auditions, but can you believe it? Not only did they sail through, but they've been storming up the polls. The public love them."

Devlin shook his head, looking bewildered. "But... why would they want to enter a talent show?"

"Oh, same as most people, really—they want the prize money. Or rather, June does and she's roped the Old Biddies into helping her."

"What does she want the money for?"

I laughed. "You really don't want to know."

Devlin sighed. "Okay. To get back to the case... So you're saying we can probably rule out those at the bottom of the ratings poll, since they have very little chance of going through anyway, even if they were to remove Lara."

"Yes. Right. There are too many other contestants who are better than them, who are likely to go through first."

"Okay... so who are the next strongest contestants after Lara? The ones with the best chance of filling her shoes?"

I frowned. "I guess that would be Trish and her dog, and the comedian, Gaz. They're the top favourites after Lara. Oh and..." I hesitated. "The Old Biddies."

"I think we can probably cross a bunch of geriatric pop-star wannabes off our list of suspects. And Trish you've already told me about. But what about this Gaz fellow?"

I thought of Gaz, with his warm friendly personality and endearing smile. I just couldn't imagine him being a murderer.

"I don't know," I said. "He seems like a genuinely nice guy, you know? And he's so confident and charismatic..."

"Just because someone is likable doesn't mean that they can't be a killer too," said Devlin. "Some of the most famous murderers were charming monsters."

"I suppose..." I chewed my lip. "We're really just randomly guessing here. Haven't you picked up any leads from the crime scene?"

"Have a heart, Gemma—the Forensics team only arrived a short while before I did. They've only had time for the most cursory examination. Oh, my constable did find this by the body though." Devlin reached into his pocket and pulled out a clear plastic wallet. Inside, I could see a crumpled piece of paper. As he handed it to me, I saw that there were a few words typed across it:

"If you want to win the competition, I could help you. Meet me by the cauldron during the magician's act."

I drew a sharp breath. "This is from the killer—this is how he enticed Lara there!"

"Or she," Devlin reminded me. "There is no evidence to suggest that the writer of that note was male or female. But yes, it looks like the whole thing was set up, which means that it wasn't accidental manslaughter but pre-meditated murder." He stood up and came around the table, pulling me gently up as well. "I'll get a police car to take you home. I *would* come by later and see you, but I don't know how late I'm going to be—I could be here most of the night—"

"It's okay," I said. "I'll be fine. Honestly. I don't need a police escort—I'd rather cycle. A bit of fresh air would do me good. And besides, my mother is still with the other judges—I can't leave without seeing her. And—*bugger!*" I gasped. "Muesli! I completely forgot about her!"

"Muesli?" Devlin looked puzzled.

"Yes, I left her in her cat carrier—I didn't want to

lug it around when I was looking for Cheryl. She's never going to forgive me!"

Without waiting for Devlin to reply, I rushed from the office and out into the Waiting Area. I was relieved to see Muesli's cage still standing on the trestle table where I'd left her and even more relieved to find my little cat safely inside, albeit in a very grumpy mood.

"*MEEEEEORRW!*" she said reproachfully as I bent to pick her up.

"Sorry, sweetie," I said, sticking a finger through the bars.

She rubbed her chin against the tip of my finger and, after a few moments, began purring. I smiled to myself. The nicest thing about animals was that they were so quick to forgive and forget. I sighed and looked up at the sombre faces around me, then repressed a shudder as a stretcher covered by a sheet was carried past me. Maybe if humans were better at "forgive and forget", the paramedics wouldn't have been carrying out the body of a woman who had been brutally murdered...

CHAPTER EIGHT

"Would you like a seat by the window? You get lovely views of the village High Street from there." I smiled at the two girls who had just entered my tearoom and gestured towards a table beside the large mullioned windows.

"Er... yeah, sure..." The girls exchanged looks, then one of them came forwards, her eyes gleaming. "By the way, are you the girl who found the body?"

Oh no, not another one of these.

In the two days since Lara had been found dead, frozen by liquid nitrogen, all activity on *FPTC* had been put on hold while the murder investigation got under way. And with no full-time catering job, I had decided to reopen the tearoom. Not that I had really needed to—Monty Gibbs had generously offered to continue paying my daily catering fee during the delay—but I found that I couldn't sit idly at home either. It wasn't as if it was a real holiday: we were all waiting on tenterhooks for the police to either make an arrest or, at the very least, allow us back into the concert hall. And so we woke up every morning, expecting the call to return, and went to bed every night thinking it had to come tomorrow... which meant that we were all jumpy and distracted.

Gibbs had been convinced that it would only be a short interruption and that we'd be back filming the rest of the show soon, but I had to admit, I hadn't shared his optimism. Having had some experience of how murder investigations work, I knew that they were long, drawn-out affairs and—unlike what was portrayed on TV—never wrapped up in under one hour, no matter how good the detective. So I decided that, rather than sitting at home trying to ignore the gruesome flashbacks, I'd be better off reopening the tearoom and trying to return to normal business.

It had seemed like a good idea initially. In fact, I'd been pleasantly surprised to find a long queue outside the tearoom on the first morning and a warm glow had filled me. *Everyone must have really missed the Little Stables while it was temporarily closed!* But when the doors opened and the customers began pouring in, I quickly realised that it was not the wonderful baking that had made my tearoom so popular. It was me. Or rather, my part in the exciting murder drama that was gripping the nation almost as much as the original show.

"So was she, like, really frozen?"

"What did you think when you saw the body?"

"Oh my God, were you terrified?"

"Who do you think murdered her?"

"Oh yes, some tea and scones, please... and by the way, you're not the girl who discovered the body, are you?"

I suppose I shouldn't really have minded. After all, they were usually ordering food and drink as well, and giving business to the tearoom. Still, I found myself clenching my teeth tighter and tighter each time someone asked:

"By the way, are you the girl who discovered the body?"

Now I took a deep breath and released it slowly as I faced the two girls giggling and whispering in front of me. They looked about sixteen and were only behaving like typical teenagers; I knew I shouldn't take my irritation out on them.

Keeping a pleasant expression on my face, I said: "Yes, that's right. I found Lara King."

"No way!" one of the girls shrieked. "Did she look like a human ice lolly?"

I felt my jaw tightening and hastily made an effort to unclench my teeth. "No, not really. Now, if you'll follow me to the table—"

"Oh... uh... actually, we've just remembered— we've got to get back home. Can't stay for tea after all. Sorry!"

Giggling, they turned and dashed out of the

tearoom. I resisted the urge to let out a frustrated howl, conscious that there were still other customers at the tables around me. Instead, I took another deep breath and returned to the counter.

"More snoopy free-loaders, huh?" said Cassie sympathetically, eyeing my face.

"I don't know what's wrong with people!" I said through clenched teeth. "They're treating it like some kind of circus freak show. For heaven's sake, a woman was murdered!"

"Well, I have to say, she doesn't sound like she was a very nice woman," said Cassie. "Have you read the things being said about her in the tabloids? They've been interviewing loads of people who knew Lara and no one has had a nice thing to say about her. They all said she was a selfish cow— didn't give a stuff about anyone else, didn't care whose feelings she hurt—as long as she got what she wanted."

"Yeah, I got that impression from the argument I overheard between her and Nicole."

"Ah, the man-eater thing? There was a lot of that in the press too. Loads of women coming forwards saying Lara made a move on their husbands and wrecked their marriage—"

"But I don't understand... How come all this is only coming out now?" I said, frowning. "I mean, Stuart Hollande told me that Lara had been in the papers more than any other contestant. There was a lot of media attention on her. Surely, they would have dug up all this before?"

Cassie shrugged. "You know what it's like. She was the nation's darling before this—one of the lead favourites to win the contest—and nobody wants to be the partypooper. It's like you being the only person to stand up and say something negative about a popular girl at school. People would probably accuse you of jealousy or trying to sabotage her out of spite. But now it's different. Now it's a murder investigation and the police are asking for any reason why somebody might have wanted to kill Lara. So now people feel justified in badmouthing her as much as they like."

Before I could reply, the air was split by a shrill scream. Cassie and I both whirled around. It had come from the kitchen. The only person in there was our baking chef, Dora. Exchanging a concerned look, we dashed into the kitchen together. There, we found Dora standing on a chair by the wooden table in the centre of the room, clutching her skirts in one hand and a rolling pin in the other.

"Where is it? Where is it? Can you see it?" she asked hysterically.

"See what?" chorused Cassie and I together.

"The mouse!"

"What? We don't have mice," I protested. "We just had an inspection last week and everything was clear. There were no traces of mice or any other pests."

"I don't care what the inspection said. I saw it! A

brown furry thing... It was there—scurrying under the table!" Dora said, waving the rolling pin around.

I bent to look under the table. "Well, I don't see anything now. Honestly, I think you might have imagined it, Dora—"

"No, no—I saw it!" she insisted. "I didn't imagine it!"

"Hey, you know what?" Cassie snapped her fingers. "The house next door is undergoing major renovations. It's stood empty for months and now the builders are knocking down walls and breaking up ceilings—I'll bet that the mouse came from there. There are always rats and mice living in derelict buildings and if the place gets disturbed, they all come scurrying out, looking for other places to live."

Ugh. I didn't like the sound of that. As an eating establishment, the last thing I could afford was a rodent infestation.

"Maybe it's not as bad as that," I said hopefully. "Maybe it was just one nest and... er... they decided to try this place and Dora scared them away." I looked back at the grey-haired, middle-aged woman standing on the chair. "Anyway, it's probably gone now. Here, I'll help you down—"

"Oh no!" said Dora, shaking her head vehemently. "I'm not coming down until you find that mouse!"

Suddenly Cassie, who had been looking behind some of the kitchen cabinets, gave a startled cry, and the next moment, a small furry creature shot out. It streaked across the floor and passed right by my legs, causing me to jump and yelp in surprise.

Dora shrieked again and pointed wildly. "There it is! There it is!"

The next moment, I saw a grey blur streak after the mouse and I gasped.

"*Muesli!*"

My naughty little feline was not officially allowed in the kitchen, since her presence at the tearoom was conditional on the fact that she didn't go near any food preparation areas. Still, she often tried to sneak in—partly because the kitchen was always warm, and she liked to snooze on one of the wooden chairs next to Dora, and partly because she knew she wasn't allowed in there. Like a typical cat, the more she wasn't allowed to do something, the more Muesli wanted to do it. This time, she must have followed me and Cassie when we had rushed in following Dora's scream.

Now she raced across the room, her green eyes dilated almost black with excitement, as she chased after the mouse. Cassie and I watched, bemused, as the animals zigzagged this way and that across the floor, with the mouse expertly evading Muesli at every turn.

"*Meorrrrrrrw!*" cried Muesli, pouncing and missing as the mouse shot behind another kitchen cabinet and disappeared. She gave a frustrated yowl and darted after the mouse, shoving herself into the narrow gap between cabinet and wall.

"Hey, Muesli—no!" I cried, hurrying after her as she too disappeared into the gap.

I had visions of my cat getting stuck behind the kitchen cabinets or, even worse, disappearing into the wall cavity and necessitating the fire brigade to come and knock holes in the wall to rescue her (yes, I'm speaking from experience). Crouching down, I squeezed a shoulder into the gap myself and caught hold of her back legs.

"*Meorrw!*" cried Muesli indignantly, thrashing her tail and trying to wriggle away from me.

"Oh no, you don't!" I said, reaching in deeper to get a better grip. The plaster on the wall here was old and crumbling, and as I wrestled with my cat, I was showered by specks of white.

"Argh!" I shook my head, letting go of Muesli as the dust went into my eyes.

"D'you need help, Gemma?" asked Cassie, bending down and eyeing me in concern.

"No... I'm all right... I just need to—"

"*He-llo!* Anybody there? Darling, where are you?"

I groaned as I heard the familiar voice. It was my mother! What was she doing here? At the same time, I realised suddenly that there was nobody in the dining room outside, looking after the customers. *Yikes.*

Standing up and brushing myself off as best as I could, I left Cassie groping around in the gap for Muesli while I hurried back outside.

CHAPTER NINE

I stepped out of the kitchen to find my mother and a strange woman standing by the counter. My mother was immaculately dressed, as always, in an elegant wool dress, with matching scarf and gloves, and not a hair out of place. I was suddenly conscious of my dishevelled appearance. My hair was covered in flecks of plaster, there was more white dust on my sweater and jeans, and I was flushed and sweating.

"Oh my goodness, darling—whatever have you been doing?" my mother gasped.

"Er... I just... I was doing a bit of tidying up," I mumbled.

I glanced at the strange woman, who was eyeing me up and down with heavy disapproval. She had fiercely plucked eyebrows and a very pointed nose in a thin, angular face. She was dressed, like my mother, in a ladylike outfit, with the kind of jewellery and coiffured hair that defined women of a certain class.

"Darling, this is Grace Lamont, the editor of *Society Madam*. You know, it's that lovely magazine for ladies I'm always telling you to read."

"Ladies of a certain refinement," put in the woman sharply. "We are not like those other women's publications cluttering up the racks in magazine shops, with their scandalous covers of barely dressed actresses and their revolting obsession with men and fornication. No, *Society Madam* is a publication of quality, with content that is appropriate for genteel members of the fair sex. We cover all aspects of home management and décor, gardening, cooking, fashion, and etiquette. We also publish several special editions a year which focus on important issues like the best methods for correct stain removal."

"Er... right. How nice," I said.

My mother beamed. "I was so delighted to get a call from Grace this morning. To think, after so many years of reading the magazine, I'm finally going to appear in it! What a great honour! Grace wants to do an interview with me about being a judge in a TV talent show—"

"Yes, a very brave venture, Evelyn. I commend you on your attempt to lift standards in our television broadcasting."

"Oh..." My mother gave a modest laugh. "I didn't have such grand designs, I assure you. I was simply asked by Stuart Hollande to step in temporarily, because one of the other judges was suddenly indisposed, and he said that he had been impressed by my observations during dinner the night before."

"But I believe that they have asked you to remain on the panel?"

I turned to my mother in disbelief. "Really?"

My mother gave another modest laugh. "I hadn't had a chance to tell you yet, darling. Stuart told me that they'd received so many messages from people who loved my commentary on the show—apparently, there is even something called a 'meme' on the Face Book about me!—that Mr Gibbs decided he'd like me to remain as a judge on the show."

"But... what about Zoe Carlotti?"

"I don't know, darling. I suppose they've asked her to step down."

Grace sniffed. "Good riddance! I can't imagine why they ever asked that shameless little trollop. Did you see the length of her fingernails in the last episode? And painted in two different colours!" She gave a shudder. "A lady should never have fingernails longer than a millimetre past her fingertips and always painted a classic, muted shade, although a French manicure is permissible."

I cast a surreptitious look at my own fingernails, with their ragged edges and chipped nail polish, and hastily shoved my hands behind my back.

My mother put a hand on my arm. "Now, darling—guess what? When I mentioned to Grace that you provided the catering for the show and owned a traditional English tearoom, she said she'd like to do a feature on you too! Isn't that marvellous?"

"Er... yeah... great," I said, trying to dredge up an enthusiastic smile. I could think of a million things I'd rather do than be interviewed by this scary woman for her archaic magazine. Still, I told myself that I shouldn't be ungrateful for the chance of extra PR for my tearoom.

Grace Lamont slowly and deliberately looked around the tearoom with a critical eye. I followed her gaze and thought with a secret smile that at least when it came to my tearoom, I had nothing to be ashamed of. Carefully renovated to preserve and highlight its period features, the fifteenth-century building, which had once been a Tudor inn, was the epitome of quaint English charm, from the exposed wooden beams to the wide mullioned windows and the genuine inglenook fireplace.

"Hmmm... yes... you've done a good job here," said Grace Lamont with a nod, like a schoolmistress during a class inspection. She reached out and ran a finger along a nearby shelf. "A little dusty, but overall the standards of hygiene seem remarkably good." She wagged a finger at me. "Tradition may be all very well but some of these old places seem to think that vintage charm includes a layer of vintage grease and dust. I was even invited to review a place once, and when I arrived, I discovered that they had mice!" Her nostrils flared in disgust. "Can you believe it? Mice! In their kitchens! Absolutely disgusting. I made sure to mention it in my article and I also personally wrote to Food & Safety, informing them of the gross breach of hygiene standards. I'm pleased to say that the place was shut down soon after."

As I stared at her in mute horror, Grace Lamont walked over to the pile of menus stacked neatly at the end of the counter and flipped one open.

"Now, I presume that you serve proper British baking here? None of those pretentious French patisseries or—God forbid—those silly Asian fusion things, like 'matcha cheesecake'?"

"Uh... no, we specialise in traditional British favourites, like scones with jam and clotted cream."

"Home-made clotted cream?" she said sharply.

"Yes, of course," I said. "And the jam is home-made too. In fact, almost all our food is made from scratch on the premises."

She nodded approvingly. "And I hope that the dough is kneaded by hand, as opposed to those dreadful machines people like to use nowadays?"

"Er... yeah, Dora, my baking chef, kneads all the dough by hand," I said, thinking that this was worse than when the food inspector had come to visit!

At that moment, the door to the kitchen swung open and Cassie burst out.

"Muesli got the mouse!"

Grace Lamont jerked around, her eyebrows

shooting up into her hairline. "*Mouse?*"

"Oh! Er... she means the computer mouse!" I shouted, giving my friend a frantic warning look. "My cat, Muesli, has been... er... pouncing on the mouse when we try to use it... It's... um... very annoying when you're trying to work at the computer."

"I never realised you had a computer in the kitchen?" said my mother, turning to Cassie.

My friend looked bewildered. "Oh... uh... yeah, that's right. New addition this week. To... um... help us keep track of orders."

"Do you mind if I pop in and use it for a moment?" asked my mother, making a move towards the kitchen. "Helen Green just sent me a text saying that she's received the new catalogue from John Lewis on email! She said it comes as an attachment and it opens up and looks just like a real catalogue, except it's on your screen! Fancy that! You can even turn the pages too, if you click on the little arrows at the bottom. I really must check my email and see—"

I jumped in front of my mother, blocking her way. "The... the computer in the kitchen isn't set up to check email, Mother." It was ridiculously lame and with anyone else, I would never have got away with it, but I was relying on my mother's ignorance of computer technology.

"Uh... yeah, right," said Cassie quickly. "The computer's really old and it's just for... um... taking catering orders."

Grace gave me a suspicious look but didn't comment. Instead, she pulled a slim, leather-bound diary out of her handbag and began flipping through the pages. "Now, Gemma, I have some time next Friday to do an interview—if that would be convenient for you?"

"Um... next week is ha—" I started to reply but was distracted as I saw the kitchen door swing open slightly and Muesli's little head appear. She wriggled out and trotted towards us, meowing excitedly. Her cries seemed strangely muffled, however, and my eyes widened in horror as I realised why. "...aagh—AAGGHH!" I yelped as Muesli stopped beside me and dropped the furry bundle she was carrying.

Cassie made a choked sound, her eyes bulging as she stared at the mouse. The little creature crouched, motionless, its eyes wide and its whiskers quivering. It was barely inches from Grace Lamont's high heels.

"I beg your pardon?" Grace said quizzically. "Haa-what?" She started to look around. "Is something the matter?"

"Uh... no! NO!" I said, shuffling my feet. "Um... I was just asking haa—haaw—how long it would take?"

"Half an hour should suffice. And I would be obliged if you could come to my office in Oxford. It's just on the High Street." Grace bent her head and began to write laboriously in her diary with a fountain pen.

"Right. High Street," I said, still groping around with my feet. If I could just nudge the mouse towards the tall potted palm next to us, hopefully it would climb into the pot before Grace noticed it. For the first time, I felt a rush of gratitude to my mother for insisting that I fill the tearoom with indoor plants to "freshen the air".

I felt my toes touch something soft and risked a glance down. The mouse had seemed paralysed by fright, but at the touch of my shoe it sprang suddenly to life. It turned towards the potted palm but, before it could move, Muesli reached out and clamped a paw on its tail. *Aghh!*

"Muesli!" I hissed, turning my foot towards her and giving her a shove.

"*Meorrw!*" she said indignantly, letting go of the mouse.

Grace looked up from her diary. "Is that a cat?"

Her gaze dropped to her feet. My heart stopped as I wondered if the mouse was still there—Grace was bound to see it!—but to my relief, I couldn't see it anywhere. There was only Muesli, sitting with her front paws daintily together, looking up at us with her big green eyes. I relaxed slightly. The mouse must have climbed into the potted plant, like I'd hoped. In fact, I saw Muesli turn suddenly towards the palm, her nose quivering, and trot up to it.

"*Meorrw?*" she said, sticking her head into the

clump at the base of the pot. It was a bushy palm, with fronds that splayed out in all directions, providing good hiding places for a small creature. Still, I didn't want to take the chance that Muesli might frighten the mouse and flush it out again.

"Oh... er, Muesli... come and give me a cuddle!" I said, hastily scooping her up.

"*Meorrw...!*" said Muesli sulkily, trying to wriggle out of my arms.

Grace gave a fastidious sniff. "I don't like cats. All those hairs everywhere." She took a step away from me, bumping into the palm tree, then clucked her tongue irritably as her handbag became snagged in one of the fronds. Pulling it free, she made a great show of brushing herself off. "I'm surprised that a cat is allowed on the premises," she said coldly.

"Oh, we've had approval from Food & Safety. The inspector reviewed everything and agreed that we could have Muesli at the tearoom, providing that she doesn't go near the food preparation areas—which means the kitchen—and that she stays off the tables. Which she does," I added hastily.

"Hmm..." Grace Lamont didn't look convinced. Then, to my relief, she shouldered her handbag and turned towards the door. "Well, I shall expect to see you next Friday then, Gemma. Ten o'clock sharp."

I smiled at her with false brightness. "Er... right! I'll be there!"

CHAPTER TEN

Whew! I sagged onto the chair behind the counter as the door closed behind Grace Lamont and my mother. Cassie, who had gone to serve one of the tables, returned and gave me a relieved look.

"Bloody hell, that was a close call. I thought she was going to see the mouse for sure!"

"Me too," I said with a groan. "I think I lost five years off my life just now." I glared at Muesli, who was sitting up on the counter, nonchalantly washing herself. "And you... you little minx! I'll bet you did that on purpose, bringing the mouse out like that and dumping it at my feet."

"They say it's supposed to be a sign of love, you know, when your cat brings you gifts," said Cassie with a grin. "Anyway, where did the little bugger go?"

"It went into the potted palm," I said, pointing.

Cassie bent to look but straightened again after a moment. "It's not here."

"What do you mean? I saw it go in there." I bent to look myself but after several minutes of rummaging through the base of the palm, nearly getting my eyes poked out by the spiky fronds, I had to concede defeat.

"It's not here!" I said in bewilderment, straightening to look at Cassie.

"Are you sure you saw it go in the pot?"

"Well... not exactly," I admitted. "It was there by my feet and then I looked up at Grace Lamont—and when I looked down again, it was gone. But it had to have gone into the pot—there's nowhere else it could have gone!" I gestured to the open area around us.

Cassie gave a shrug. "Maybe it crept out of the pot again when we weren't looking?"

I stared at her in dismay. "Oh God—don't tell me that! You mean it could be loose here in the tearoom?"

I turned to scan the room in trepidation. Everything seemed to be peaceful. Couples, groups, and families were sitting at the various tables, happily munching, drinking, talking, and laughing. There was no sign of even a mouse whisker anywhere.

"Surely, if it was loose out here, Muesli would smell it and be chasing after it?" I said, turning back to glance at my tabby cat, who was still sitting unconcernedly on the counter, washing her face.

"Yeah, you're probably right..." Cassie conceded. "Well, let's just hope we've seen the last of that mouse—wherever it's gone."

I started to reply but was interrupted by the shrill ringing of my phone. I fumbled in my pockets, pulling it out and hitting the button to answer.

"Hello!" I snapped.

"I suppose this is a bad time to ask you out for dinner," came an amused voice.

"Devlin! Sorry, I didn't mean to snap at you. I've just had a hell of a morning."

"That makes both of us," said Devlin with a sigh.

"No progress on the case?"

He gave another sigh. "So far, this investigation is going nowhere and Monty Gibbs is not happy about it. He's pressuring us to reopen the concert hall and let him get on with filming the show."

"Well, haven't your forensic team gone over the crime scene already?"

"Gemma, have you seen the size of that place? All those rooms full of props and equipment, the various stairwells and entrance ways... and that's just backstage. I'm loathe to reopen it and allow people to contaminate the area, when we haven't had a chance to go over all of it properly." He paused, then added, "On the other hand, we could scour it for weeks and still wouldn't be able to cover every corner. That place is like a rabbit warren."

"But it's not as if you need to find the murder weapon, is it? I mean, in this case, you know exactly what killed Lara."

"Yes, but if there's one thing I've learned, it's that crucial evidence can turn up in the most unlikely places. We don't know what's important—until we see it. There could be something incriminating hidden in one of those rooms or a trace left by the murderer in the Waiting Area..." Devlin made a frustrated noise. "I just wish I had a good lead! Right now, I've got a list of suspects as long as my arm and nothing to link any of them to the victim."

"What about Nicole Flatley? I thought she was the strongest suspect? Although I suppose her motive is a bit philosophical, isn't it? I mean, she'd be killing Lara just because she hates the woman's callous attitude and unethical behaviour."

"Actually, her motive might be based on more hard reality than you think," said Devlin. "We checked out her background and it turns out that Nicole split up from her husband recently. He'd had an affair with a neighbour, and when Nicole found out and confronted the woman, there was quite a nasty scene. It was witnessed by several of the other residents on the street, and according to them, the woman was completely unrepentant about breaking up their marriage. She just laughed at Nicole and said that it was her own fault for not being able to hang on to her husband."

"Oh my God, that's pretty much word-for-word

what Lara said!" I cried. "No wonder Nicole totally lost it and went for her. I saw the look on her face—she was absolutely furious."

"Yes, the question is whether that anger continued to fester—enough that Nicole decided to murder Lara the next day."

I thought again of the shy, quiet pianist. "I don't know, Devlin—I just can't see Nicole murdering anybody. I mean, I can see her getting emotional and losing her temper—in fact, I saw it first-hand—but based on that note you found by the liquid nitrogen, this murder was very calculated and I just can't believe that Nicole could plot to kill someone in cold blood."

"Well, appearances can be deceptive. On the face of it, none of the contestants are likely to be murderers."

"Actually, I can see that woman, Trish, plotting to murder someone quite easily," I said darkly.

"Gemma... you can't let your personal prejudices affect your judgement," said Devlin, sounding amused. "Just because you had a run-in with her and you don't like her doesn't immediately make her a villain."

"But have you checked up on Trish?"

"Well, we've only done preliminary background checks so far but yes, she seems to be kosher. She works as a dog walker and spends all her spare time with her dogs. She seems to be at some kind of dog sport or obedience competition every weekend.

Not how the average person spends their weekend, perhaps, but it's hardly a sign of homicidal tendencies."

"Yes, but it's a sign that she's competitive," I said.

"Being competitive isn't enough of a motive for murder," said Devlin impatiently. "I need more than that." He paused, then added thoughtfully, "You said the Old Biddies' friend, June Driscoll, wanted the prize money for a particular reason—what was it?"

"You don't think *she* could be the murderer?" I laughed.

"I have to consider every alternative."

"Aww, come on, Devlin! That's just ridiculous. You said yourself last night that we can probably cross a bunch of geriatric pop-star wannabes off our list of suspects."

"I can revise my opinion. Anyway, I'd just like to know."

"The money's to save her husband's support group."

"Support group?"

"Yeah, he passed away last year and his widow is desperate to keep his support group going, in his memory."

"You mean, a group to support him?"

"No, it's a group to support people like him— people with bushy eyebrows."

"*What?* You're taking the mickey."

"No, no, I'm serious. It's called B.E.A.S.T.—it stands for 'Bushy Eyebrows Activists Stand Together'."

Devlin was silent for a long moment, although I suspected I could hear the sound of muffled laughter coming from the other end of the line. Finally, he cleared his throat and said:

"The Pussy Puffs are one of the stronger acts. In fact, you could even argue that they're stronger than Trish or Gaz and would have been the most likely contestants to go through to the Finals, if Lara was no longer in the running."

"Yes, but... you're not seriously considering them as murder suspects?"

Devlin sighed. "Right now, I'm almost ready to consider anybody. Certainly those who don't have solid alibis. Most of the crew have checked out— other than a couple of the lighting technicians who were alone at the time of the murder. As for the contestants, the only ones in the clear are the twins, who are ten years old, and Albert, who was on stage at the time of the murder. But I think we can rule out Franz Ziegler and Tim the hip hop dancer. The former was talking to a member of the crew and the latter was playing with the twins, as confirmed by their mother. That leaves us with Nicole, Cheryl, Gaz, Trish, and the members of the 'granny band'. A few members of the cast say that they saw the Old Biddies, but they weren't able to identify each one individually. Nobody can confirm if they saw Nicole, Cheryl, Trish, or Gaz in the Waiting Area at the time of the murder."

"I saw Gaz," I said. "In fact, he spoke to me."

"But you said in your statement that there was a gap of several minutes between speaking to him and finding Lara's body."

"Yes, that's right," I admitted. "After speaking to him, I went out to take a peek at my mother on the judging panel, and then I went to search the other backstage rooms again for Cheryl. I found a shortcut into the area behind the stage, which leads to the wings, and then I stumbled across the body."

"So in fact, there would have been time for Gaz to sneak out into the wings and kill Lara after you saw him."

"I suppose so..." I said reluctantly.

"And you said you were searching for Cheryl?"

"Yes, she asked if she could use Muesli as a substitute for her cat, who'd gone off wandering, so I went home to fetch Muesli. But when I arrived back at the concert hall, I couldn't find Cheryl anywhere." I realised how that sounded and added quickly, "Although I'm sure I probably just missed her. As you say, that place is such a rabbit warren."

"But it's interesting that she was 'missing' around the time of the murder," mused Devlin. "When we questioned her, she was very vague and said she was moving around, looking for her cat."

"Well, that's true. She was worried about Misty. Besides, Devlin, Cheryl definitely isn't the murderer."

"How do you know?"

"I... I just do! I was chatting to her for quite a while yesterday. She's just not the type—"

"Gemma... you like her, don't you?"

Bugger. Devlin was always too sharp. "That's nothing to do with it," I said defensively.

"I think it is. And like I said with Trish—you can't let your personal feelings affect your judgement in a murder investigation. Just because you *don't* like someone doesn't make them a villain, and just because you *do* like someone doesn't make them innocent either."

"Oh, all right," I said. "But I tell you—I definitely didn't see Trish in the Waiting Area. I saw Skip, her dog, tied up to his crate but she wasn't with him. I know, I know, you're going to say I'm biased again... but the point is, she was 'missing' as much as Cheryl was. Did she say where she was when you questioned her?"

"She said she went out for some fresh air."

"I don't believe that," I said flatly. "That woman would have been practising to the last minute! And if she did go out for some fresh air, why didn't she take her dog with her? It would have been the logical thing to do."

"What about Nicole?" asked Devlin, abruptly changing the subject. "Did you see her?"

"No, I didn't see her either," I admitted. "What was *her* excuse?"

"She says she went to the Ladies. But, of course, no one happened to see her enter or leave the toilets."

"Bloody hell, this case really is a mess, isn't it?" I said sympathetically.

"Well, I've got the night off from it anyway," said Devlin. "Not a night off, exactly, but at least it'll be a change of scene and subject. Listen, this was actually why I called—I know it's a bit short notice but would you be free to go to a black-tie dinner tonight? It's for work, actually, but partners are welcome and since we haven't had much chance to see each other lately... It's not the same as a romantic dinner, I know, but it would be a chance to spend a bit of time together. And maybe we can go out for drinks afterwards."

"You're on!" I said, smiling. It would be nice to see Devlin, whatever the situation. "What is it— some police departmental function?"

"No, actually, it's the Oxford University Sherlock Holmes Society. They've got their annual Speaker's Dinner at Montague College and the Superintendent was invited as a guest speaker but he can't make it, so I've been roped in at the last moment. I'm giving a talk on 'The Psychology of Murder'."

"I can't believe people want to listen to that over dinner."

"Ah, well... this is Oxford..." said Devlin with a laugh. "'The Psychology of Murder' is probably pretty light fare—it could have been 'The Multiple

Identities of Dark Matter' or 'Classical Latin and How It Has Influenced Modern Oratory'."

"True," I agreed, laughing as well. "Okay, what time?"

"Pre-dinner drinks are at seven-thirty, with dinner at eight. Shall I come and pick you up around seven?"

"I'll be ready," I said, my mind already starting to drift as I wondered what to wear. I felt a pleasant sense of anticipation. It would be nice to have an evening out and forget about the talent show for a while. *And it's always a treat to see Devlin in black-tie*, I thought with a smile to myself. With his piercing blue eyes, lean, dark good looks, and tall, muscular physique, Devlin O'Connor could give James Bond a run for his money any day.

I hung up in a much better mood and was still happily contemplating the evening ahead when the Old Biddies walked into the tearoom a few minutes later. They were accompanied by June Driscoll, who looked tired and strained.

"...Gemma will know," Mabel was saying as she led her friend up to the counter. "Her young man is the detective in charge of the investigation, you know." She turned to me and said: "Have you had any updates on the case? Are the police planning to arrest anyone?"

"You know Devlin can't discuss the details of active investigations with me," I lied.

"Nonsense," said Mabel. "It's not as if you're a

normal member of the public—you've been involved in murder investigations before. In fact, you've helped the police solve many a past case. With help from us, of course," she added smugly. She crossed her arms and regarded me complacently. "So... what did your young man tell you when he called you just now?"

"How did you kno—?" I stared, then sighed and gave up. "Nothing much. The police are stumped at the moment. There are so many suspects in this case but no strong leads to tie any of them to the murder."

"Who are the suspects?" asked June in an anxious voice.

"All of you, really," I said. "Anyone backstage could have done it, although the contestants certainly had more motive than the crew for killing Lara."

"What do you mean?" asked Glenda.

"Well, with her gone, there's more chance for the other contestants to go through to the Finals."

"But surely Devlin doesn't think anyone would commit murder just to win the contest!" cried Ethel.

"That would be despicable!" said Florence, her usually kindly face contorted in an expression of disgust.

I couldn't help noticing that while Mabel, Glenda, Florence, and Ethel all looked flushed and indignant, June had gone very quiet. Devlin's words came back to me and, for a moment, a crazy thought flashed in my mind. Looking at the pale woman in front of me, I couldn't help recalling the way she had seemed so determined to win, and the military precision with which she had assessed the other contestants. Just how far was June Driscoll willing to go to keep her husband's memory alive?

Then I pushed the thought away with an inward laugh. Surely I didn't think that a little old lady would murder someone just to save her husband's ludicrous support group for bushy eyebrows?

CHAPTER ELEVEN

Montague College was not one of the bigger Oxford colleges, but its beautiful quadrangles and ivy-covered neo-classical buildings were still majestic by any standards. I followed Devlin through the main gate, past the Porter's Lodge and across the main quad into a second quad which was enclosed by cloisters. Darkness had fallen and the college was lit only by vintage lamps, which emitted a feeble yellow glow and threw sinister shadows along the cloister walls. By the time we arrived at the large, arched doorway at the other end of the arcade and climbed the creaking wooden stairs up to a private antechamber, I felt like I was walking in a Gothic horror movie.

The feeling was quickly dispelled, however, as soon as I stepped into the brightly lit antechamber, with medieval tapestries lining the walls and an antique wrought-iron chandelier dominating the ceiling. We were slightly late, as Devlin had been delayed at the station, and the room was already filled with people milling about with drinks in their hands, the men looking suave in their black tuxedo jackets and bow ties, and the women elegant in their cocktail dresses and evening gowns.

Devlin gave me an apologetic look as he was hailed by a member of the society committee and quickly became embroiled in a discussion on police ethics. I didn't mind—I was quite happy to mingle by myself and chat to strangers. As it happened, however, I had barely accepted a glass of champagne from the roving waiter when someone tapped me on the shoulder.

"Gemma! Fancy seeing you here!"

I turned around to find myself facing a young man with thick dark-rimmed spectacles. I broke into a wide grin as I recognised Seth Browning. After Cassie, Seth was one of my closest friends, and the three of us had been inseparable during our time at college together. And while Cassie and I had both been keen to leave student life at Oxford— me for a fast-track graduate position in Sydney, and Cassie for a chance to pursue her artistic dream— Seth had opted to remain in the bosom of the university. The life of an academic suited his shy, quiet personality and he was now one of the youngest Senior Research Fellows in Chemistry at

Gloucester College.

"Seth! This is a nice surprise," I said warmly, giving him a peck on the cheek. "What are you doing here? Don't tell me you're a member of the OU Sherlock Holmes society!"

"Well, as a matter of fact, I'm considering it," said Seth with a laugh. "I've heard that they have very thought-provoking debates. One of my colleagues is a member and he suggested that I come along and see what the society events are like." He glanced across the room at Devlin. "I hadn't realised that Devlin was speaking tonight."

"He wasn't supposed to originally—they'd invited his boss but the Superintendent couldn't make it, so he asked Devlin to step in."

We were interrupted by the sound of someone striking an old-fashioned gong and, a moment later, a pair of double doors leading into the dining hall were opened and people began to file in. I was pleased to discover that there was no seating plan, and with Devlin still occupied by the society committee members, I decided to sit with Seth. As the white-uniformed staff began serving the four-course meal and I gazed down at the formal place setting in front of me, with the dozens of different forks, spoons, and knives laid out in concentric layers around the plate, it felt for a moment almost as if I was back in college again. Life as a student at Oxford involved many unique quirks, one of which was the number of black-tie and formal events you were expected to attend. In fact, in my first term at college, I probably spent as much time trying to remember the correct fork to use as the correct answers for my tutorials. *Start from the outside and work your way in*, I reminded myself, picking up the outermost set of knife and fork as the starter was placed in front of me.

"It's a shame Cassie isn't here," said Seth. "We could almost have had the night out that we missed."

"Yes, I'd been so looking forward to catching up with you both on the night of the Semi-Finals," I said ruefully. "And then it all went crazy and I never even saw you guys."

"Imagine how *we* felt! We were sitting in the audience, wondering where you were... and then the next thing we knew, all hell had broken loose. All we could see were people running backstage and all we could hear was this terrible screaming—"

"That screaming was me," I said, embarrassed.

"Yes, Cassie told me that you'd had quite a nasty shock," Seth said with a sympathetic look. "Hardly surprising... finding a dead body like that."

"It wasn't so much discovering a dead body as seeing the way her face smashed to bits when it hit the ground..." I shuddered at the memory. "It was horrible, Seth! I just can't get the image out of my mind. I mean—how can flesh just shatter like that?"

"Ah, well, you see, liquid nitrogen is a cryogenic fluid—its boiling point is minus 195.79 degrees

Celsius or minus 320 Fahrenheit; that's only 77 kelvins above absolute zero, which is when all thermal motion ceases. And at that temperature, you encounter the Ductile-to-Brittle Transition. Even materials which are ductile at normal room temperature can become highly brittle when super-cooled, due to the change in the directionality of the chemical bonds, and with the high percentage of water in organic matter, it's hardly surprising that brittle fracture occurs—"

"Seth!" I said in exasperation. "In English, please."

"Oh. Right." He gave me a sheepish grin. "Basically, living tissue such as our flesh is made up primarily of water, so when it comes into contact with something as cold as liquid nitrogen, it freezes completely, and we turn into something a bit like an ice sculpture. And ice is very brittle, as you know. Of course, a very dense object wouldn't break unless an extreme force was applied—that's why her entire head didn't shatter—but thinner objects, such as her nose or the other features on her face, would crack and crumble easily if put under stress, such as when her face hit the ground."

"But what about the murderer?" I asked. "Wouldn't he or she have been affected too? I mean, they must have had to shove Lara's head into the cauldron and hold it immersed in the liquid nitrogen for a few seconds, until she... er... froze solid. Wouldn't their hand be affected too?"

"Well, they could have worn insulating gloves... but even if they hadn't, they would probably have been protected by the Leidenfrost effect."

"The what?"

"It's a physical phenomenon which occurs when a liquid comes into contact with something that's much hotter than its boiling point. Part of the liquid evaporates and forms an insulating vapour layer around itself," Seth explained. "You see it sometimes when you drop water on the hotplate on an electric stovetop: you'd expect the water to evaporate immediately, wouldn't you? But instead, the drops just move around on top of the hotplate for a few moments."

"Oh yes, I've seen that!" I cried. "I always thought that was weird, the way they skitter around."

"Well, the drops are being protected by an invisible layer of vapour between themselves and the hotplate. The same thing happens if you plunge your hand into liquid nitrogen for a short while—the nitrogen immediately in contact with your skin vaporises, forming a cloud of vapour which coats your hand and protects your skin from the freezing effect of the rest of the liquid nitrogen. But the vapour doesn't last forever—so if you kept your hand in there, after a few minutes, it would freeze solid."

"You know, I'm wondering if most people know all this stuff. I mean, it might help to narrow the suspect list," I said excitedly. "Surely someone would only use liquid nitrogen as a murder weapon if they were familiar with its properties? Which means that the murderer is probably someone who is used to handling liquid nitrogen on a regular basis."

"That doesn't narrow the field hugely, I'm afraid," said Seth. "Liquid nitrogen is used in all sorts of places these days—really, you don't have to be much of a specialist to encounter it. It's used as a coolant in superconductor systems, for example, and to shrink-weld machinery parts together. It's even used in some fancy bars to create those smoking, bubbling drinks for novelty effect."

"Oh." I sat back, disappointed.

Seeing my expression, Seth said, "But it certainly wouldn't hurt to check and see which of the suspects might have experience using liquid nitrogen." He glanced down the table to where Devlin was sitting, then turned back to me and said, "Is the show going to be on hold much longer?"

"I don't know. I think the police are getting a lot of pressure from Monty Gibbs to reopen the concert hall and let them continue filming... and with the lack of new developments, Devlin may have no choice."

"Oh good," said Seth, looking pleased. "Then we can watch the rest of the Semi-Finals performances."

I stared at him. "Seth! Don't tell me you follow

From Pleb to Celeb too?"

"Well…" Seth looked down and fiddled with his fork, a line of colour on his cheeks. "I know it's not very highbrow… but it *is* very good telly."

"Yes, I suppose… Do you vote as well?"

"I haven't yet. But Cassie and I were planning to vote in the Semi-Finals." He gave me a grateful look. "Thanks for the tickets, by the way. It was fantastic getting to see the acts live, even if things got cut short. I hope they let that magician chap repeat his act—I was really enjoying it when it was interrupted. Did I tell you I used to be really into magic as a boy?"

"Really? You mean you wanted to become a magician?"

"Well… I did have an amateur magic set, but what really interested me was the evolution of magic as a performing art. You know it's one of the oldest performing arts in the world? During the eighteenth and nineteenth centuries, large magic shows in big theatre venues were really popular, and illusionists were treated like great stars. I used to spend hours reading up on the different magicians and their individual styles, and learning all the different categories of magic tricks."

I rolled my eyes and laughed. "Seth! Trust you to turn a fun hobby into a geeky obsession."

"It wasn't an obsession," said Seth indignantly. "I just liked to find out how the tricks are done. From an academic point of view. It gives great insight into the human capacity for misdirection and self-delusion, you know. Like the 'Zig-Zag Girl' trick, for example, when the magician divides his assistant into thirds—and she's still smiling and waving at you from each section—and then he 'rejoins' the pieces and she emerges from the box completely unharmed."

"Yeah, I've seen that—I just don't understand how they do that!"

Seth laughed. "It's all about having the right props. It's actually fairly easy—the assistant just has to contort her body in a particular way, inside the specially constructed box. It's the same with the chair trick that Albert does at the end of his act— you know, when he covers himself in a sheet and sits in a chair... but then he suddenly reappears on the other side of the stage... I'll bet that chair has a seat with a false bottom which opens—"

The sound of a fork being struck against a glass made everyone stop talking and look up. The president of the society stood facing the room with a welcoming smile. He made a little speech, then introduced Devlin and invited him to the podium. The room fell silent, everyone's attention rapt as Devlin gave a fascinating talk on why people were driven to murder, the different types of motivations, and the range of reactions to the aftermath of the deed, from those who immediately confessed in a fit of guilt and remorse, to those who would happily murder more people to cover up their crime.

As I listened, I couldn't help thinking of Lara's death and the potential suspects in the case. What was the reason for this murder? Was it greed and gain? Bitterness and revenge? Fear and self-defence? Or just plain insanity?

CHAPTER TWELVE

Although we didn't leave Montague College until well after ten o'clock, Devlin followed up on his promise and took me to the Quod Restaurant & Bar for late-night drinks. The bar was part of the Old Bank Hotel, located in prime position on the High Street, sandwiched between some of Oxford's oldest colleges, and facing St Mary's Church and the iconic buildings of the Bodleian Library. The hotel also had special meaning for me because it used to be my father's bank—in fact, it had been the main Oxford branch of Barclay's Bank for over two hundred years, before the building had been bought by a millionaire art collector and turned into a boutique hotel. I could remember my father taking me with him when he'd gone in to do his banking there. Now, the beautiful fourteenth-century building—with its Georgian alcoves, wood-panelled walls, and large sash windows—played host to tourists, businessmen, and other visitors to Oxford, and revelled in its status as the only hotel right in the heart of the university city.

Despite the late hour, the restaurant was still humming and we were lucky to find two empty stools at the white onyx-topped bar that dominated the room. Devlin glanced at the bar menu, then handed it to me and said with a grin:

"I bet I know what you're having—the Rose & Rhubarb Bellini."

"Oooh, that does sound nice..." I perused the menu myself, then gave him a teasing look. "And I suppose you're having the Basil Daiquiri?"

Devlin pulled a face. "Not unless someone gives me a lobotomy! No, it's a pint of beer for me. I'm having the Cotswold Premium Lager. What about snacks—do you want something to nibble with the drinks?"

"Good grief, no..." I said, clutching my stomach. "That sticky toffee pudding they served at Montague College for dessert just about finished me off." I looked down at the menu again and added wistfully, "Shame, as some of these sound very interesting... hmm... 'Cornish brown crab on toast'... and what on earth is 'black radishes with celery salt'?" I gave him a bright smile. "I know! We can come here to have a celebratory dinner when the case is closed."

Devlin raised his eyebrows. "You're very

optimistic. You do know that a large percentage of murder investigations never get solved?"

"Yes, but I have complete faith in your abilities," I said with a smile.

He chuckled and leaned close for a kiss, but at that moment I happened to glance up and my eyes met the gaze of a man rising from a table near us. His face brightened as he recognised me and he hurried over, followed by his dinner companion.

"Gemma, how nice to see you!"

Devlin straightened, a look of chagrin on his face, but he turned and gave the newcomers a perfunctory smile. I looked warmly at the tall, good-looking man with the humorous brown eyes and open, pleasant smile. I had known Lincoln Green most of my life: his mother, Helen Green, was my mother's closest friend, and in fact, the two mothers had always (and not so secretly) hoped that Lincoln and I would end up together. With his upper-middle-class background, Cambridge education, and impeccable "English gentleman" manners—not to mention being a doctor to boot—Lincoln was considered the perfect match.

He was also a genuinely nice guy and I found his company very enjoyable. In fact, if I was honest with myself, I had to admit that if I hadn't met Devlin again after all these years, things might have been very different between Lincoln and me. As it was, we were good friends, although sometimes I couldn't help feeling that Lincoln still harboured a hope that we might become more than that. Devlin certainly seemed to think so and had always remained tense in Lincoln's presence. It hadn't helped that my mother had struggled to accept Devlin, with his working-class roots and unconventional upbringing, and—for a long time, I'm ashamed to admit—I had let her disapproval affect my own attitude too.

Still, that's all in the past now, I thought with an inward smile of relief. Since Devlin had demonstrated his technological sleuthing prowess (that is, he'd found her beloved missing iPad), my mother had suddenly decided that my old college flame was the best thing since organic sourdough bread and had welcomed him into the family with open arms... while *I* had finally realised that I didn't need my mother's approval to be happy.

"What a marvellous coincidence," said Lincoln, beaming and leaning down to give me an affectionate peck on the cheek.

Devlin stiffened slightly, but took Lincoln's proffered hand equably enough. "Good to see you, Lincoln," he said.

"Yes, we haven't seen you in quite a while," I said.

"It's been ages!" said Lincoln. "In fact, I think the last time we saw each other was during that morning tea your mother hosted, when *your* mother—" he glanced at Devlin, "—came to visit."

Devlin winced slightly at the memory of that day and looked even more uncomfortable when Lincoln added enthusiastically, "Your mum is brilliant, Devlin! I hadn't realised how young she is. She's a very attractive woma—" Lincoln broke off and flushed as he seemed to recollect himself. Clearing his throat, he finished lamely, "Er... I hope she comes down to Oxford more often."

Devlin looked like he was struggling to unclench his jaw to say something polite and I stepped in hastily.

"Um... so how's work, Lincoln?"

"Oh, it's going well. In fact, it's Research Week at the hospital and I'm chairing the panel of guest speakers." Belatedly, he remembered his companion and turned apologetically towards her. "Forgive me—this is Dr Elsa Kruger. She's come all the way from Melbourne. We're collaborating together on a research project about septic shock."

The pretty blonde woman stepped forwards to shake hands, her eyes lingering on Devlin with interest.

"You're not a doctor, are you?" she asked him.

Devlin smiled. "No, my oath involves arresting people, not curing them."

"Oh—you're a policeman?"

He inclined his head. "Detective. CID."

"Wow, I've never met a real-life detective," she said, fluttering her eyelashes and looking up at him admiringly.

I resisted the urge to roll my eyes.

Devlin chuckled. "I wouldn't get too excited—it's

not as glamorous as they make us look on screen."

"Oh, I don't know about that," Elsa purred. "You could give any of those sexy TV cops a run for their money."

Oh, for heaven's sake... I didn't know whether to be irritated or amused by her blatant flirting. And judging from his wicked grin, Devlin was enjoying my discomfiture. Pointedly turning my back to them, I said to Lincoln:

"How's Jo? I haven't seen her in ages either."

"Jo? She's great," said Lincoln, smiling as he mentioned his pretty forensic pathologist colleague. "She's gone on holiday with a friend. They're visiting Finland and hoping to see the *aurora borealis*."

"Oh, I'm so jealous! I've always wanted to see the Northern Lights. Although... it's a cold time of the year to go, isn't it?"

"Well, you have to go between September and March for the best chance to see the lights, but I agree with you—it's mid-winter now and a really brutal time of year. I can't imagine how cold it must be up in the Arctic. Jo and her friend are probably freezing to death!" He realised what he'd just said and winced. "Sorry! That was a bit tasteless, given your experiences with the recent murder—"

"It's okay," I said. "It's been a few days and I'm getting used to it now. I think part of it was that it was so bizarre... almost unreal, in a way. I don't know why but I think I would have coped with it better if it had been a stabbing or something."

"That's understandable," said Lincoln. "We deal better with things that we can make sense of. It's probably why early man developed so many myths and superstitions—it helped us cope with natural phenomena which puzzle us. You know, many people believe that the legend of the werewolf originated from medical conditions such as porphyria, which causes reddish teeth and psychosis, or hypertrichosis, which causes excessive hair growth all over the body. Some even think it came from people's fear of rabies. Of course, now we know the scientific bases behind all those conditions, but in medieval times it was probably comforting to blame the symptoms on a 'werewolf' curse." Lincoln gave a self-deprecating laugh. "Sorry... this is probably boring you."

"No, no, it's really interesting. I can see what you're saying. It makes me feel better, actually, for getting so freaked out." I paused, then added thoughtfully, "You know, I thought having such an unusual murder weapon would make it easier to catch the killer, but Seth told me that liquid nitrogen is used in lots of industries and it's actually pretty accessible. Apparently, they even use it to make fancy cocktail drinks!" I glanced across the counter at the bartender, wondering if they used it here.

"Yes, you do encounter liquid nitrogen in a lot of places. We use it a fair bit in medicine—to preserve tissue samples and biological cells, and also in cryosurgery to burn off warts."

"But you'd have to be a scientist or medical personnel to get hold of it, right?"

"No, I believe you can order it easily on the internet." At my incredulous look, Lincoln added, "The thing is, in the overall scheme of things, liquid nitrogen isn't considered *that* dangerous. If it's handled correctly and with respect, it's a very useful element to have. There are far more dangerous, reactive substances that are found in every household, such as products made from chlorine."

The barman came over for our orders, interrupting the conversation, and Lincoln gave Devlin an apologetic look.

"We'd better head off and leave Devlin and Gemma to their drink," he said, putting a hand under Elsa's elbow.

The blonde woman pouted. "Oh, we don't have to go yet, surely? I'm sure they wouldn't mind if we joined them for a bit."

I do mind very much, especially if you're going to keep leaning into my boyfriend like that, I thought sourly, watching her. *Any closer and you might as well climb into his lap!*

To my great relief, Lincoln said: "Don't forget, Elsa, you're speaking at the breakfast symposium tomorrow morning and that starts at seven-thirty. So we'd better get an early night." He turned to me, saying with a smile, "I hope we'll catch up again soon, Gemma," and held a hand out to Devlin.

"Good to see you too, mate," said Devlin, clasping Lincoln's hand. Then he offered his hand to Elsa, but she ignored it, leaning close instead for a lingering kiss on his cheek.

"It was sooo nice to meet you, Devlin," she purred. "If you're ever in Melbourne, you must look me up..."

A few minutes later, we were alone again and I settled back on my stool with a sigh of relief. "Bloody hell, I thought that woman was going to invite herself into bed with us next. She was practically climbing into your lap! Not that you seemed to mind," I added tartly.

Devlin burst out laughing. "Well, I have to say, it makes a nice change from watching Lincoln drool over you."

"Lincoln does not drool over me! He's... he's just being friendly."

Devlin mimicked Lincoln's posh accent: "*Oh Gemma—how marvellous to see you!*" Then he swooped close to give me a long, wet kiss on the cheek.

I squealed and squirmed away from him, giggling. "Yuck! Stop, Devlin... stop...!"

The barman delivering our drinks finally put an end to the horseplay and I sat back on my stool, flushed and happy. I couldn't remember the last time Devlin and I had clowned around like that. He worked so hard these days, and was often so intense and serious, it was nice to see a lighter side of him. It reminded me of our college days together. Since returning to England and meeting Devlin again as the shrewd, indefatigable "Inspector O'Connor", it was hard, sometimes, to remember him as the boy I had fallen in love with all those years ago.

Devlin picked up his pint and looked at me thoughtfully. "Penny for your thoughts, Miss Rose?"

"I was thinking of a boy I once knew... a long, long time ago, in a life far, far away..."

"Ah..." Devlin smiled. He reached out and drew me close. "Well, in this life... he's here to stay."

***

I didn't end up getting home until well after midnight, but despite the late hour I found myself awaking early the next morning. It was probably because I was anxious about what was happening with the show. There was still no news from the *FPTC* production team, but based on what Devlin had told me yesterday, the show was likely to resume any time. Knowing from experience that the producers could call me at short notice, I decided not to risk opening the tearoom and I called Dora to let her know.

"Oh, it's a good thing you caught me—I was just about to start baking a fresh batch of scones," said Dora. "As it is, I can refrigerate the dough to use tomorrow."

"Are you at the tearoom already?"

"Of course! I get here at five every morning. How else do you think we manage to have all the baking done in time for the doors to open at ten-thirty?" asked Dora tartly.

"Yes, of course," I said, thinking again how lucky I was to have found her. Not only did she bake like a dream, but she also lived just around the corner from the tearoom and was happy to come in early. This meant that I didn't have to be up at the crack of dawn every day and could even do a few chores in the few hours before the tearoom officially opened.

"Why don't you take the day off, Dora? You can put your feet up and lie on the sofa and enjoy a good book or something."

"Put my feet up? Lie on the sofa?" Dora gave a bark of laughter. "I don't know about you, missy, but some of us have chores to do and washing to get done. Hmm... actually, the weather looks fine today, even if it's chilly—I might take the chance to get on with my gardening."

"Gardening? Now? But it's November. What could you be doing in the depths of winter?"

"We're not in the depths of winter yet," said Dora. "And there are plenty of things to do. Leaves to rake up, pots to bring in, seeds to sow... By the way, speaking of seeds, did you or Cassie ever find that mouse?"

"No, I don't know where it got to but we never

found it. Why—have you seen any signs in the kitchen?" I asked anxiously.

"No, thank goodness. I've been checking the pantry daily, but so far it doesn't look like there have been any teeth nibbling on anything. But perhaps we ought to put down a mousetrap—"

"Oh no, those are so cruel," I protested. "I always feel awful thinking of the poor mouse."

"Gemma, this is vermin we're talking about, not a pet."

"But mice look so cute, the way they hold things in their little paws and—"

"Cute? You've got to be joking! Filthy, sneaky little creatures... ugh!"

"Well, anyway, I don't think we have to worry about it," I said. "I think it was just the one stray mouse and it's gone. If it was still around, we would surely have seen some traces, especially with all the food lying about."

"Hmm..."

Dora didn't sound convinced but she said nothing more and I soon said goodbye, to let her get on with her raking and potting and sowing. I wandered around my cottage for a bit, half-heartedly answering some email and trying to catch up on admin, but I was too restless to concentrate. Finally, I remembered that I'd spilled some Béarnaise sauce on my dress at the dinner last night and I decided to take advantage of the clear morning to take it to the drycleaners. Otherwise, with my usual hectic schedule, who knew when I'd next have a chance to go into town... probably not for weeks, by which time the stain might have set permanently!

The drycleaners was situated in a lane just off Cornmarket Street, the wide pedestrianised boulevard running through central Oxford, and after I'd dropped my dress off, I wheeled my bike slowly through the centre of town, enjoying the displays in the different shop windows. Pausing in front of a café on a street corner, I admired the little terracotta pots placed around their front door; they were filled with pansies and violas which were flowering valiantly despite the cold wintry weather. The colourful blooms gave a cheerful, welcoming vibe and invited passers-by to step in.

Hmm... I should do something similar outside my tearoom, I thought. I slid my phone out of my pocket to take a photo for reference, but as I was lining up the shot, I noticed the window next to the café. It looked into some kind of shoe store, but what caught my eye was the woman talking to a customer in the shop: it was Nicole Flatley, the pianist.

On an impulse, I went in. The shelves were filled with comfortable walking shoes and other support footwear for the elderly, and several old ladies were browsing the store. I hovered next to the counter until Nicole was free, then feigned surprise at seeing her.

"Hello! It's Nicole, isn't it? I didn't realise that you worked in Oxford," I said, giving her a friendly smile. "I'm Gemma—I provide the catering for the show."

"Oh, of course. I thought you looked familiar." She gave me a guarded smile in return. "Yes, I work primarily in Oxford, although I do a day a week at our branch in Reading. I'm a podiatrist," she explained. "It's one of the services offered by the store. Aside from fitting customers with the correct shoes, we also help treat a range of foot issues..." She indicated a poster on the wall next to us.

I glanced at the poster, then did a double take as I read the words:

Let us provide complete care for your feet!
Podiatry services to treat common foot problems such as bunions, cracked heels, ingrowing toenails, verrucae, and warts...

It was the last word that caught my eye. Suddenly I remembered what Lincoln had said last night. Turning back to Nicole, I asked casually:

"So you remove warts as well? Is it a complicated procedure?"

"Oh no, it's very simple, really. I'm trained in the use of cryotherapy for wart and verruca removal, which involves freezing the warts off in a controlled manner. This will usually cause the skin to blister and the tissue to die off, and then the wart is removed."

"Wow... but how do you freeze the wart?"

"Well, I normally use liquid nitrogen—" She broke off suddenly and stared at me, her eyes suspicious. "Why are you asking all this?"

"Oh... um, I have an elderly aunt who has warts on her toes and... er... she was wondering how to remove them," I said. "So... um... is this liquid nitrogen the same as the stuff that Albert uses in his act?"

Nicole went pale. "You think I killed her, don't you?" she whispered.

"No, I—"

"Is that what everyone thinks?" she asked, her voice rising. "Is that what they're saying about me behind my back? Just because I had a fight with Lara doesn't mean that I would murder her!" She paused and narrowed her eyes at me. "Wait... I remember... you were there that day, when Lara and I were having the argument. Was it you who told the police? Is that why they've been hounding me?" she demanded.

I glanced over my shoulder. The customers and other shop assistant had all stopped what they were doing and were staring at us. I flushed slightly and turned back to the hysterical woman in front of me.

"No one's talking about you, Nicole," I said soothingly. "We're not ganging up against you. But you have to admit, it's logical for the police to consider you a suspect, since you'd had a terrible row with the victim the day before the murder."

"She started it," said Nicole. "Lara was the one who was saying those awful things and laughing at me... just like that woman Steve was—" She broke off and I saw tears shimmering in her eyes. I felt a surge of pity for her.

"I'm sorry, Nicole. I didn't mean to upset you," I said, putting a gentle hand on her arm.

She shook her head, taking a tissue out of her pocket and blowing her nose. "No, it's all right. I'm just a bit sensitive about it still..." She sniffed for a few moments, then composed herself and looked up at me. In a calmer voice, she said:

"Don't you think that it would have been stupid of me to have a very public fight with Lara and then murder her the next day? I'd just be making myself the obvious suspect."

She had a point. It would be the silliest thing to do. Of course, it was possible that she had been so bitter after the fight that she had acted on impulse. But this murder didn't feel like a crime of passion. And besides, if Nicole *had* still been furious at Lara and lashed out in revenge, she was much more likely to have simply hit the other woman on the head with a heavy object or stabbed her with a knife. Why bother with the elaborate plan of using liquid nitrogen as a murder weapon?

"But you did hate Lara, didn't you?" I said doggedly.

"I can't pretend that I'm sorry Lara is dead," said

Nicole quietly. "She was a horrible woman and I'm sure I'm not the only one that she hurt terribly. Yes, I hated her." She lifted her chin and looked me square in the eye. "But I'm not the one who murdered her."

CHAPTER THIRTEEN

I was still mulling over my encounter with Nicole when I arrived back at the tearoom later that day, and I was so deep in thought that I didn't notice the Old Biddies ensconced in their usual corner by the window. They had obviously been waiting for me, however, because they got up and hurried over as soon as I walked in, and surrounded me, all talking at once.

"Wait... sorry... I can't hear properly..." I protested, trying to understand what each of them was saying. "You're changing your name?"

Glenda nodded earnestly. "Yes, we've decided that our granny band needs to have more edging."

"More edging?" I looked at her in confusion.

"To compete with the younger contestants," explained Florence. "We were chatting to one of the other tearoom customers and they said that nowadays, it's all about your *image.*"

Ethel piped up, "And your name is a very important part of your image."

"Yes, the 'Pussy Puffs' doesn't have the right connotations," declared Mabel.

Bloody hell, you can say that again, I thought.

"We want a name that sounds younger and has more edging!" said Glenda, beaming. "The Semi-Finals are our last chance to impress the audience—"

"And don't forget all the people watching us on telly across the country," Florence said. "They'll be voting for us too."

"—yes, so we've decided to change our band name to something else," Glenda finished.

"Oh, thank God—I mean, that's great! Wonderful," I said fervently. "So what are you changing it to?"

"Well... we've been busy thinking about it all morning," said Mabel. "Ethel called one of her old librarian colleagues, who happens to collect magazines, and she told us about a very famous English girl band. It's a group called the Spice Girls."

"Oh yeah, I remember them: Ginger Spice, Scary Spice, Posh Spice, Baby Spice, and Sporty Spice," I said, smiling. "I liked a lot of their songs."

"Well, we're going to call ourselves the Herb Girls!" Mabel announced. "I shall be Tarragon."

"I'll be Chives," said Florence.

"I'll be Dill," said Glenda.

"And I'm going to be Parsley!" said Ethel, beaming.

"We haven't decided a name for June yet—maybe Chervil or Borage," said Mabel thoughtfully.

"Um... don't you think it'll be better to pick nicer-sounding herbs? Like Rosemary? Or Thyme?" I asked.

"*Bah.* Rosemary is so common. We want something different and memorable."

You'll certainly get that if you start calling yourself "Borage", I thought. I started to protest again, then shut my mouth. On second thoughts, considering that the alternative was calling themselves the "Pussy Puffs", going by "Chives" and "Parsley" was probably the lesser of two evils.

"Ooh, we must tell June," said Glenda. "Maybe if we all meet at the concert hall later, we can have a rehearsal with our new names."

"Has the concert hall been reopened?" I asked in surprise.

"Hadn't you heard, Gemma? The police have released the crime scene and they're resuming filming for the show! We'll be continuing with the Semi-Finals performances tomorrow night."

"Oh... I wonder why they haven't contacted me..." I dug in my pocket and pulled out my phone, then realised that there were several missed calls and text messages waiting for me. I had put my phone on silent before bed the night before and I'd forgotten to switch the sound back on.

"I'd better tell Dora—we'll have to start baking things for tomorrow's morning tea," I said, heading for the kitchen. I hadn't gone three steps, however, when I remembered something.

"Oh, bugger!" I muttered. Our large serving platters were still at the concert hall. I'd used them on the day of the murder and in the mayhem that had followed, I'd forgotten to collect them afterwards. And with the place shut for the last three days, I hadn't had a chance to retrieve them yet. I was going to need them tomorrow when I took in the fresh baking for morning tea.

I sighed and said to the Old Biddies, "I think I'll be seeing you at the concert hall. I need to go and collect—" I was interrupted by the ringing of my phone. It was a number I didn't recognise.

"Hello?"

"Oh, hello, Gemma—I hope you don't mind me calling you. I got your number from one of the show producers. This is Cheryl—Cheryl Sullivan from the show."

"Oh, hi! How are you? Have you found Misty yet?"

"Yes, she turned up the next day—one of the police officers found her. Goodness knows where she had wandered off to. Anyway, she's home safe and sound now, although she's a bit sniffly. The vet thinks that she might be having a bout of cat flu—

she's had it before, usually when she's been a bit stressed. She's a recue cat, you see, and many of them get infected by the virus when they're at the shelter."

"Is it serious?"

"Oh no, the vet thinks she'll be fine. She just needs to remain indoors and stay warm..." She hesitated. "Actually, that was the reason I was ringing. I hate to have to ask you again, but I was wondering—would you mind letting Muesli take Misty's place again?"

"Well, of course I don't mind—but are you sure that's a good idea? I really don't know how Muesli will behave. I don't want you to mess up your act because of her."

"I'm sure she'll be fine," said Cheryl warmly. "Especially if we have a chance to rehearse it a few times. That's why I was calling, actually. I know this is a lot to ask but... is there any chance I could 'borrow' Muesli this afternoon? They're reopening the concert hall and I thought it would be a wonderful opportunity to rehearse my act with Muesli on stage. I can come and pick her up from you—and drop her back later," she added.

"No, that's okay. As a matter of fact, I was just on my way to the concert hall myself. I need to pick up a few things I'd left there. I can swing by my cottage and grab Muesli on my way, and meet you there."

"Oh, thank you so much! I really appreciate it—

thank you!"

***

It was strange walking into the backstage area and seeing members of the crew hurrying around, carrying equipment, adjusting cables... just like a few days ago. It was almost as if a murder had never happened. And in fact, as I passed Monty Gibbs in earnest discussion with some of his show producers, it seemed that the head of *FPTC* had decided to behave as if it never had.

"...just cut straight ter Gaz—'e was supposed ter go on after Lara, right?—and give 'im a couple o' extra minutes longer in the programme," said Gibbs, flipping through the pages of the call sheet. "The audience always luv 'im anyway so they won't mind—"

"But sir..." One of the producers frowned slightly. "Don't you think we should mark Lara's death in some way? Maybe we can observe a minute's silence in her slot?"

"Wot? I'm not some bloody memorial service!" said Monty Gibbs. "I don't want one minute o' the programmin' wasted. We need to cash in on the 'ype around the murder, right? Everyone in the bleedin' country will be tunin' in tonight. This, 'ere, is a ratings dream." He rubbed his hands together, a satisfied expression on his face.

I turned away in disgust. I hadn't particularly

liked Lara but this sort of cold-blooded exploitation of her death seemed utterly despicable. Then I stopped in my tracks as a new thought struck me: how far would Monty Gibbs go to ensure a "ratings dream"? Would he go as far as murder? No, surely not. Besides, Monty had an alibi—he couldn't have been sitting on the judging panel outside and also shoving Lara into a cauldron of liquid nitrogen. I laughed and shook my head. The last thing I needed was to add another person to the suspects list!

I found Cheryl waiting for me beside her chest of puppets. Her eyes lit up when she saw Muesli in her carrier and she said:

"My goodness, she really does look like Misty!"

"Oh... I thought you'd met Muesli but I just remembered, I never saw you on the day of the murder," I said. "When I came back to the concert hall with Muesli, you weren't here in the Waiting Area."

Cheryl gave a nervous laugh. "Really? I was around; we must have just missed each other. It's so easy to in this place—so many rooms and corridors."

"I did search through all the backstage rooms—in fact, that was why I stumbled across Lara's body—but I didn't see you anywhere."

"Er... oh, I remember now—I must have been outside. I went out into that little car park again to see if there was any sign of Misty." Quickly, Cheryl reached out and opened Muesli's carrier, lifting my cat out of the cage. "Hello! Aren't you gorgeous?"

"*Meorrw?*" said my little cat, her green eyes wide as she checked out her surroundings.

"Here's her harness," I said, handing over the halter and leash. "Do you need me to put it on her?"

"No, I can manage. It will be a good bonding exercise," said Cheryl, smiling.

Leaving her cooing to Muesli, I went in search of my platters. They weren't where I'd left them, on the long trestle table at one end of the Waiting Area, and they weren't in the staff kitchen either. I sighed in frustration. Where could they be?

I set off through the warren of corridors, poking my head into each room and casting a swift look around. Most of them were empty—in fact, there were very few people in the corridors. Most of the crew seemed to be busy in the Waiting Area and on stage. It was almost eerily quiet and I couldn't help thinking of the last time I'd been wandering around these empty rooms. It had been just a few minutes before I'd found my way into the wings and seen Lara's body. I shuddered at the memory and pushed the thought away.

Hastily, I turned and began to retrace my steps. Then I paused as I recognised the doorway in front of me. This was where I'd been standing the day I heard Nicole and Lara fighting. Almost without conscious thought, my feet moved and carried me towards the doorway. I hesitated, then peeked in.

The dressing room looked exactly as I'd remembered, with a row of chairs standing before tables and mirrors framed by lightbulbs. There was someone huddled over the last dressing table, in the corner. The person jumped and whirled around when she heard my step in the doorway—and I saw that it was Trish Bingham.

"Oh! Hi..." I said awkwardly.

"What do you want?" she snapped.

"N-nothing," I said, taken aback by her aggressive manner. "I was just searching for my platters and I thought I'd check in every room, just to be on the safe side..." I trailed off, annoyed with myself for feeling the need to explain. Why did Trish always put me on the defensive?

"Well, they're not here," she said rudely. She pushed past me and hurried out of the room, leaving me staring after her.

What on earth was wrong with that woman? I turned back to scan the room. There was nothing unusual that I could see, other than the fact that some of the bottles and jars on the dressing table in the corner were moved from their usual neat rows and there was some powder spilled on the table surface.

Shrugging, I gave up on the mystery and continued the search for my platters. I found them eventually, in the last place I'd expected. They'd been emptied and neatly stacked in a pile beneath the long trestle table, and covered by a plastic sheet—which was why I hadn't seen them at first. I collected them, then went back to find Cheryl and Muesli. They were just about to go on stage and I watched nervously as Cheryl led my little cat into the wings on her leash and harness. To my surprise, Muesli trotted obediently along, only pausing to sniff the curtains by the wings for a few moments.

"Oh, she walks so much better than Misty!" said Cheryl in delight.

"She isn't normally that good," I said. "Usually she keeps stopping and sitting down, or wanting to go in the opposite direction... but she must be excited in this new environment and keen to explore."

I decided to go out into the auditorium to watch Cheryl's act properly and settled myself in the front row, where I had a good view of the whole stage. Cheryl was just placing Muesli in her basket, which was perched atop a stand, next to a large, old-fashioned brass-bound chest. I watched anxiously, half expecting my cat to jump back out, but to my surprise, she nuzzled the blanket, then lay down and began rolling around on her back, purring so loudly that even I could hear her from the front row.

Blimey. Cheryl's catnip trick really works! I thought. I really had to try it with Muesli's bed at the tearoom. It would be great if I had some way of getting her to stay put in one place.

Cheryl made cheerful pretend conversation with

Muesli, asking if the little cat wanted to hear a story, and I smiled as Muesli let out a loud "*Meorrw!*" in reply, sounding exactly as if she was answering the woman. It was incredibly cute, and I could see that it would be a great crowd pleaser. Then Cheryl picked up a pair of puppets and began manoeuvring them with expert skill. Muesli watched with interest as the puppets jerked on their strings in front of her, and again I expected her to jump out of the basket and pounce on them, but she seemed happy to remain in the basket, nestling against the fleece blanket. My doubts began to fade away; maybe Cheryl was right and this could work after all...

The nursery teacher began singing and even though she didn't have the advantage of backing music during this rehearsal, her melodic, sweet voice carried the notes beautifully. The combination of her song and lyrics, matched to the puppets' movements, was delightful, and Muesli's occasional "*Meorrw*" only added to the charm of the whole performance. I had never had much interest in puppets before and hadn't expected to be very interested in this act, but now I was pleasantly surprised. I could just imagine that with some proper backing music and maybe some lights and special effects, Cheryl's piece could be fantastic entertainment—especially for children. When she finished the song, I stood up and clapped enthusiastically.

"That was brilliant!" I said. "Really—I enjoyed it so much."

"Thanks," said Cheryl, beaming. "And Muesli did her part beautifully! I just hope we can repeat this tomorrow."

"If you do, I think you'll stand a good chance of going through to the Finals," I said excitedly. "I think your act could easily rival Trish and Skip for the 'aww' factor."

"Yes, it'll be cats versus dogs..." said Cheryl with a laugh. She lifted Muesli out of the basket and cuddled her close. "We're going to beat them, eh, Muesli?"

CHAPTER FOURTEEN

"You don't really think Trish was in the dressing room for no reason, do you?" Cassie gave me a sceptical look.

I shrugged and leaned back in my chair, enjoying the warmth of the open fire on my back. We were sitting in one of Oxford's historic pubs, and the cosy interior made me feel soporific. The place was packed, the air humming with conversation and laughter, as people queued at the bar to order drinks, sat with their friends at the various booths, or stood in small groups between the tables. A popular student hangout, this pub attracted a younger crowd—especially now in the middle of the Michaelmas term—and it wasn't normally the place I would have chosen to have a drink after a tiring day. But funnily enough, despite the noise and the crowds, I found that I enjoyed the lively atmosphere.

I cradled my mug of mulled wine, leaning in to inhale the wonderful cinnamon aroma rising from the steaming red liquid. I'm usually a bit of a lightweight and don't drink much alcohol, but I love the warm, spicy sweetness of mulled wine on a cold winter's day. I yawned, then belatedly covered my mouth, sending Cassie an apologetic look.

"Sorry... I feel knackered. All that cycling back and forth today, from Oxford to the tearoom and then to the concert hall and back again..." I smiled at my friend. "But I'm glad you suggested this drink. I didn't think I'd be up for it, but now that I'm here, I'm really pleased I came."

"Seth said he might try and join us later, if he could make it. He wanted to hear the latest on the murder investigation." Cassie sipped her own mulled wine and added, "Speaking of which, you never answered me about Trish."

"She's always like that," I said, shrugging again. "I've never met a woman who's such a stroppy cow all the time."

"Maybe she was filching some of the make-up and felt embarrassed when she was caught out," said Cassie. "I'll bet she was up to no good. Why else would she have been so defensive?"

I sighed. "Maybe Devlin is right—maybe we're just biased against Trish because she's so unpleasant. But that doesn't mean that she's a murderer."

"Okay, what about Cheryl then?"

"Cheryl? No, no, I'm sure she wouldn't murder anyone. She's a nursery teacher, for heaven's sake!"

"So?"

I thought back to the performance I had watched earlier that day, the sweet way Cheryl had sung and the obvious delight she had taken in entertaining with the puppets. I knew appearances could be deceptive, but it was really stretching the bounds of imagination to think that woman could be a murderer...

"She just doesn't seem like the type," I protested. "Besides, what motive would she have? Unlike Trish, she's not one of the front runners to go through to the Finals, so even if she *had* got rid of Lara, it wouldn't have made much difference to her chances."

Cassie shrugged. "Maybe she wanted to kill Lara for other reasons. I mean, you suspected Nicole and that wasn't because of the contest. You just thought she hated Lara and killed her out of rage."

"I've changed my mind now," I said. "I know it's just her word but after speaking to Nicole this morning, I... I believe her when she says she didn't murder Lara."

Cassie rolled her eyes. "Okay. So if it's not her... and it's not Cheryl... *and* it's not Trish... who's left? Gaz? He's the other person who would have really benefited from Lara being eliminated from the competition."

As if conjured by Cassie's words, a handsome young man in a leather jacket stepped into the pub. It was Gaz Hillman. He pushed his way through the crowd towards the bar, offering everyone his trademark friendly grin and getting a few flirtatious smiles from several young women in return.

"Hey, talk of the devil!" said Cassie. "I didn't realise Gaz lived in Oxford too."

"I don't think he does," I said. "I seem to remember the Old Biddies saying he's from Cheltenham. But he must have come for the Semi-Finals and he's obviously hanging around while the show's still on hold." I watched him greet the barman with easy familiarity and make a joking remark to a group of men next to him, causing them to roar with laughter. "Looks like he's going to be best mates with everyone by the time he leaves."

"Yeah, but—" Cassie broke off and did a double take. "What are *they* doing here?"

I followed her gaze to see four little old ladies trotting into the pub: the Old Biddies. They were wrapped up warmly in their ankle-length woollen coats, with old-fashioned plastic rain bonnets covering their heads, and they looked completely incongruous in the pub filled with students in hoodies and ripped jeans. Casting a furtive look around, they sidled after Gaz and took up a position near him at the bar. When he leaned over the counter and gave the barman his order, they leaned over as well, clearly trying to eavesdrop on what he was saying.

"What are they doing?" said Cassie in exasperation, watching them.

I groaned. "Doing some 'investigating' of their own, no doubt. You know how much they love snooping around, and now this murder has given them the perfect opportunity. They've probably decided that Gaz is the murderer and are following him around town, hoping he'll drop some incriminating clue."

Cassie shook her head, laughing. "Why can't they be like other little old ladies and spend their time knitting and gardening?"

As we watched, Gaz turned from the bar with a pint of beer in his hand and the Old Biddies darted out of his way with amazing speed for ladies of their age. Keeping a few feet behind him, they followed him across the room as he searched for an empty table. A couple at a table next to us were just rising and Gaz hurried to take their place, with the Old Biddies shuffling a few paces behind him. I wondered what they were going to do when he sat down—hover around him like avenging angels?

As it happened, the Old Biddies spotted me and Cassie, and their wrinkled faces creased into delighted smiles. They rushed over to join us.

"Gemma! Cassie! How nice to see you, my dears," said Mabel. She leaned forwards and added: "We're tailing a suspect!" She made an exaggerated head motion, indicating Gaz at the next table.

"Yes, we think Gaz is the murderer!" said Glenda in a melodramatic whisper.

I glanced at him, embarrassed that he might have overheard, but to my relief, he had his head down, busily texting on his phone, and he wasn't paying us any attention. In any case, the loud hubbub in the pub managed to drown out most conversation between tables.

"Why are you picking on Gaz?" asked Cassie. "He hasn't got any motive—other than wanting Lara out of the competition. But that's the same as several other people and they're far more likely than him to be the murderer."

"Ah... but you don't know what we know," said Mabel with a smug smile.

"What's that?" I asked.

Glenda leaned forwards and said in a dramatic whisper: "Lara and Gaz had a one-night sleep!"

"You mean 'one-night stand'," I said.

"Oh no, dear, it's an expression which means they were in bed together—so they couldn't have been standing."

"No, I mean... Oh, never mind. Anyway, how do you know this?"

"Well, when we were at the concert hall rehearsing last night, we had a chat with one of the girls in the crew," said Mabel. "Lovely girl, engaged to be married next summer, although I thought her chap sounded like a bit of a layabout and I told her so. Probably needs more fibre in his diet; constipation is known to cause lethargy, you know, and—"

"Yes, but what does all this have to do with Gaz and Lara's affair?" I asked, exasperated.

"I was coming to that." Mabel gave me an irritable look. "Anne—that's the girl's name—told us that she came into the concert hall one morning and overheard Lara talking on the phone. Apparently, Lara was boasting about the night she had just spent with Gaz."

"So Lara and Gaz knew each other much better than they let on!" said Glenda triumphantly.

"And they always say that most murderers are familiar to their victims," said Florence.

"We think Gaz murdered Lara out of jealousy!" squeaked Ethel.

I gave them a sceptical look. "That's a bit of a leap, don't you think? I mean, just because they spent one night together doesn't mean that Gaz developed a jealous obsession with Lara."

"Yeah, Lara sounds like the kind of woman who had 'one-night sleeps' with lots of people—especially if you believe half the things written about her in the papers," said Cassie, grinning. "By that token, half of the nation could be her murderer."

"Ah... but half the nation weren't backstage with her on the night she was killed," Mabel pointed out.

I frowned at her. "Are you sure about this information? Devlin never mentioned anything about Gaz and Lara when I spoke to him last, and I would have expected the police to have known."

"Bah! The police!" Mabel waved a dismissive hand. "Much as I like your young man, Gemma, I must say, the police are about as effective as a chocolate teapot. And the fact that they didn't know about Gaz and Lara's affair just proves my point."

"To be fair, this is the kind of thing that's hard for the police to dig up, unless people are willing to volunteer the information," I said, feeling the need to defend Devlin.

"They volunteered the information to *us*," said Mabel loftily. "It's simply a matter of technique, dear. For example," she glanced across at Gaz, still busily texting on his phone at the table nearby, "you could easily get that young fellow to confess just by lulling him into a false sense of security and then asking him suddenly about the murder. That'd catch him off guard."

Cassie snorted. "What? Where did you hear that stupid idea?"

"It's done all the time in books and films."

"Exactly!" said Cassie, rolling her eyes. "In fiction. Not in real life."

"The principles are the same," insisted Mabel.

"Bollocks! People don't behave like characters in books! They don't just conveniently blurt out the truth or confess guilty secrets, just because you smile nicely and get chatty with them. That whole Miss Marple thing is a complete myth!"

Mabel gave her a challenging look. "How can you be sure unless you've tried it?"

"All right—you're on!" said Cassie. "I'll go over and chat to him—get all friendly and flirty—and then ask him outright if he's the murderer. We'll see if he reveals anything!"

Cassie stood up and fluffed out her hair. Then she smoothed a hand down her top, pulling the clingy fabric over her hips, and sauntered over to Gaz's table. The Old Biddies quickly shifted their seats so that they were closer to the next table and could eavesdrop more easily, and I followed suit. Luckily, a large group had also just left the pub so it was suddenly a lot quieter and easier to hear the neighbouring conversation.

Gaz looked up and his eyes widened as he saw Cassie.

She gave him a dazzling smile and asked in a throaty voice, "Is this seat taken?"

"Uh, no... I mean, sure... sit down!" He jumped to pull out a chair for her. "Er... can I get you a drink?"

"I've got one, thanks," said Cassie, holding up her mulled wine. She leaned back in her chair so that he had a good view of her, with her deep-red sweater setting off her tumbling dark hair, and her tight-fitting jeans showing off her voluptuous figure and long legs to perfection.

Gaz swallowed and tried hard not to ogle her. I had to fight the urge not to laugh. Although I'd known about Cassie's femme fatale tendencies ever since our days in school together (when she'd left a trail of broken hearts in her wake!), I'd rarely seen her exploit her looks. Cassie's first love was her painting, and she spent more time cooing endearments to the canvas than to any lucky male. Not that it had stopped men flocking to her anyway, and she was never short of hopefuls wanting to fill the spot as her boyfriend. But for the most part, she treated romance with a casual indifference and never made much effort to attract a man's attention. Now, though, she was giving it her all and I was impressed. I also felt a stab of pity for Gaz. The poor man didn't stand a chance.

Cassie fluttered her eyelashes at him. "I hope you don't mind me just coming over like this but I noticed you from across the room..." She gave him a smile heavy with meaning. "I thought you looked like the kind of man I'd like to get to know."

"Uh... um..." Gaz's usual aplomb failed him and he stammered like a schoolboy. "I... I'm glad you did. You... you look like the kinda girl I'd like to get to know too."

Cassie laughed. Then she leaned forwards suddenly, feigning surprise. "Wait a minute—you look kind of familiar... You're not that chap who's on *From Pleb to Celeb*, are you?"

"Yeah, I am," said Gaz, grinning and puffing his chest out.

"Ooh, I love your impressions," said Cassie,

opening her eyes very wide. "You're so hilarious!"

Gaz's chest swelled even more and he looked like his head was rapidly expanding too.

"So, tell me..." Cassie gave him a coy smile. "What's it *really* like being on a talent show?"

Gaz grinned. "It's good fun. I mean, there's a lot of hanging around an' waiting for things to happen but they feed you really well an' it's pretty comfy backstage."

"It must be amazing to be treated like a star!"

"Yeah, it's kinda cool to have people fussing over you—although I don't like summa the things they make me do—"

"Like what?"

"Oh... like put on make-up. Blimey. Never realised that men had to put make-up on telly as well. The make-up woman's always fussing about 'shine' or something, an' dabbing bloody powder on my face before I go on stage." He wrinkled his nose. "She even wanted to put some lipstick on me once, but I told her: No way—I'd end up looking like a right plonker!"

Cassie laughed dutifully. Then she lowered her voice and said: "It's so awful about Lara's murder, isn't it? I couldn't believe it when I heard the news!'

Gaz's face sobered. "Yeah. Pretty shocking, it was."

"Did you... see her?"

He winced. "You mean her body? Well, I rushed over, just like everyone else, but I didn't get too close."

Cassie gave a delicious shiver. "Yeah, it's such a gruesome murder, isn't it? I mean, frozen by liquid nitrogen—what a creepy way to kill someone! I feel really sorry for Lara... although I must say, I never liked her much based on her TV appearances—did *you* like her?"

Gaz looked uncomfortable. "She... she was all right."

"Did you know her well?"

"Um... not particularly. She was just another contestant, really."

"Funny... I heard differently," said Cassie with a smirk. She leaned across the table and said in a suggestive tone. "I heard that you and Lara got very friendly... friendly enough to share a bed."

Gaz went pale. "Where did you hear that? It's rubbish! I didn't... we never..." he blustered. "That's a loada bollocks!"

"Well, it wouldn't have been a big deal if you had," said Cassie with a shrug. "She was an attractive woman—loads of men probably wouldn't have minded sharing a bed with her."

"Well, I weren't one of them," Gaz snapped. "Look, can we talk about something else?"

"Oh, sure... sorry..." Cassie's voice dripped with fake sympathy. "It must be really tough for you."

Gaz relaxed slightly. "It's not *too* awful since she didn't mean anything to me. I mean... of course, I'm sorry she's dead, but it wasn't personal, you know?

But, yeah, murder is always pretty nasty—"

"Yes, and especially when it happens so close to you!" said Cassie smoothly. She gave him a conspiratorial smile. "You must have a hunch about who it might be?"

"I... I dunno... It could've been anybody backstage—"

"But surely there must have been some people who might have had more reason to want Lara dead? You knew them all—who do you think might have had a grudge against Lara?"

"I... I said I dunno, okay? Jesus, why're you so interested in the murder?" He looked at Cassie with sudden suspicion. "Hey, are you a copper in disguise?"

"Would it be a problem if I was?" Cassie shot back. "Have you got something to hide?"

"No!" cried Gaz. "Bloody hell, you don't think that *I* killed Lara?"

Cassie leaned forwards suddenly, all traces of flirtatiousness wiped from her face. "Did you?" she asked bluntly.

"NO!" Gaz sprang up from his seat, his face outraged. "No, I bloody well didn't! Is this some kinda set-up? Fine! You want to know who might have wanted to kill Lara? I'll tell you who: that woman with the puppets. Cheryl Sullivan."

"Cheryl!" I cried, not caring that Gaz would realise I had been listening. "That's ridiculous! How can you say that? Cheryl is the sweetest, nicest—"

He turned to me, his face sneering. "Oh, you fell for that act, did you? Well, lemme tell you, Cheryl didn't always have this sweet, wholesome image. Oh no, our goody-goody nursery teacher used to spend her working days in a very different way."

"How do you know?" I demanded.

He smirked. "Well... let's just say, I enjoy a bit of solo time with some quality men's literature— y'know what I mean?" He made a lewd motion with one hand. "Summa the shops have vintage editions on their back shelves. I like to look through those sometimes... an' guess who I saw staring back at me from the centrefold one day?"

"You're saying that Cheryl..." I stared at him incredulously.

He nodded. "Don't believe me? Go to *For Your Eyes Only* on Cowley Road an' have a look. Check out a couple of editions from the '80s—you'll see."

"But I don't understand—how could Lara have known about this?"

"Because I told her! We were having a natter about the other contestants an' she said she thought Cheryl was too good to be true—an' I said she was right. I told her what I'd seen. I probably shouldn't have," he added with slight regret. "But y'know what happens with pillow talk—"

He broke off suddenly as he realised what he'd said.

"I assume this was during that one-night stand you insisted you didn't have, right?" said Cassie sarcastically.

Gaz flushed. "Okay, so I lied. Who'd want to admit having a connection with a murder victim, unless they really had to? But it was just one night—that's all. We never hooked up again after that and I didn't murder Lara!"

A few minutes later, after Gaz had stormed out of the pub, Cassie joined us back at our table and gave the Old Biddies a grudging smile.

"Okay—I have to admit, you were sort of right. Gaz did spill a lot of stuff."

"That's because you were brilliant, Cass!" I said, looking at her with admiration. "Seriously, if you ever want to give up painting, you could get a job as a spy for MI6 or even as a police interrogator! That was like watching a professional in action, the way you hooked him and reeled him in, then pinned him down just at the right moment."

"Yes, your technique was very good, dear," said Mabel, nodding like a proud teacher.

"He didn't confess to the murder though," Cassie said, looking disappointed.

"That's because he didn't kill Lara," said Mabel.

"You believe him?"

"I think he sounded very sincere," said Glenda. "Such a nice young man—and so handsome too. If I was fifty years younger..." She sighed wistfully.

"Yes, but Gaz does impressions, you know," I protested. "That's a type of acting, isn't it? He could simply have been acting his outrage and all that.

You really only have his word."

"Ah, but the whole point of this technique is that the suspect is not on their guard—like they would be in a police interview—and so their reactions are much more honest. I think Glenda is right: Gaz isn't the murderer," said Mabel.

"What did he mean about Cheryl?" asked Ethel, looking confused. "I don't understand what men's literature he's talking about. When I used to work at the village library, there were certain books that appealed more to men—like novels by John le Carré and Tom Clancy—but they don't have any photos in them?"

"He wasn't talking about that kind of men's literature," I said awkwardly.

"Well, what other kind is there?" asked Ethel, looking even more bewildered.

I looked helplessly at Cassie, hoping that my best friend would step in, but she grinned and held up her hands, as if saying: *It's all yours.*

"Um... you know what?" I said brightly. "I think I'm going to get another glass of mulled wine. Anyone else want a drink?"

CHAPTER FIFTEEN

"Well, this isn't really my idea of a romantic date, but I suppose at least we're spending a bit of time together," said Devlin with a smile as he leaned back in one of the plush velvet seats of the auditorium.

I sat down next to him and laid my head on his shoulder for a moment. Devlin slipped an arm around me and pulled me close.

"I can't remember the last time we went on a proper date," I said. "And that drink at Quod doesn't count."

He sighed. "I know... it's just been really crazy at work—"

"When is it *not* crazy at work? You told me things would get better after that last case was over—the one you cancelled our holiday for," I reminded him with a dark look. "But as soon as that case was closed, you dived straight into a new one."

"I'm sorry, sweetheart—I know how disappointed you were about cancelling the trip to Malta." Devlin looked at me with genuine contrition. "I really *was* going to take leave as soon as that investigation was completed. But that double murder in Wolvercote was just too big for me to ignore. The whole department was run ragged over that one—I couldn't, in all conscience, ask for leave in the middle of that. And, of course, then *this* happened..." He indicated the stage in front of us. "Lara's murder is a high-profile case and the Superintendent is putting pressure on me to have it wrapped up..."

"Which is the only reason I get to spend a bit of time with my boyfriend tonight," I said wryly. "You're only here so you can observe the suspects—"

"Well, no... I could have sent my sergeant or even one of the junior detective constables to sit through the show. It's not really high priority." Devlin tightened his arm, pulling me closer against him and turning his head so that his lips brushed my cheek. "But I wouldn't want anyone else cuddling my favourite tearoom sleuth," he added teasingly.

I laughed in spite of myself. It was hard to stay mad at Devlin when he was like this.

"Hey, you two lovebirds... mind if we join you?"

I looked up to see Cassie and Seth in the aisle.

"Cass! Seth!" I straightened up. "Great to see you."

They dropped into the seats next to us. Seth looked wistfully at me and Devlin, and tentatively stretched out his arm, as if he'd like to put it around Cassie's shoulders. Then he flushed and hurriedly withdrew it. I felt a pang of pity for him. Seth, like many men, longed to capture Cassie's heart. The only difference was, he'd suffered for years in silence—ever since the time we'd all met as freshers in our first week at Oxford, actually—and despite yearning to tell her, he was too shy to express his feelings. Which left me awkwardly in the middle. Sometimes I was so frustrated by the stalemate that I wanted to tell Cassie myself, but I knew it was none of my business, really. So now I gave Seth a sympathetic smile behind Cassie's back and said quickly, to distract him:

"Seth—you'll be pleased to know that they're repeating the magician act."

"Oh really? That's brilliant."

"Are they letting him use the liquid nitrogen again?" said Cassie, raising her eyebrows. "I would have thought... given that it was used to commit a murder... Seems a bit bad taste?"

"Albert insisted that he needed it for the special effects—that his act just wouldn't be the same—and you know how Monty Gibbs doesn't care about being PC."

"He did agree to precautions though," said

Devlin. "I've got one of my men backstage, standing guard next to the cauldron, to make sure no one else 'falls in'."

"I doubt anyone would try to use the liquid nitrogen as a murder weapon again anyway," said Cassie. "Not that I'm expecting another death... are you? Is that why you're here?" she looked curiously at Devlin.

"No, I just thought watching the contestants perform might help me understand them better, and besides, it was an excuse to spend a bit of time with Gemma."

"Yeah, but—"

"SHHH!" said Seth suddenly. "It's starting!"

I noticed that the lights were dimming and the din of conversation in the audience slowly died down. There was a drumroll, then a disembodied voice came over the speakers:

"Welcome to the continuation of the Semi-Finals for From Pleb to Celeb*, the show where we turn nobodies into somebodies!"*

I winced at the dreadful slogan and watched as the curtains parted and the three judges walked out on stage. It was still a shock seeing my mother up there with Stuart Hollande and Monty Gibbs, and she was a stark contrast—in her cashmere twinset, demure pencil skirt, and pearls—to the other two judges in their trendy designer jeans and badly fitting Armani suit, respectively. She looked like someone who had been on her way to the Queen's

Garden Party and somehow got lost and ended up here. But I had to admit, she handled it all with amazing aplomb, showing no nerves or insecurity about her image, and waving to the crowd as graciously as Her Majesty herself. A roar of appreciation and applause greeted her wave and I even heard a chorus of "Evelyn Rose! Evelyn Rose!"

"I don't get it," I whispered to Cassie. "My mother is like the worst stereotype of the 1950s housewife... but everyone seems to love her. How come?"

"Maybe it's because she's a refreshing change," said Cassie with a chuckle. "Everybody's fed up of these self-obsessed, B-list celebrities who just spout insincere crap, like 'you *owned* that song, darling'... it's nice to see a judge speaking honestly, without trying to pose for the cameras or boost their image with the public—you know? I mean, your mother's comments to the contestants are so old-fashioned and politically *in*correct, it's almost hilarious. Last time, she told that hip hop kid he'd have a great career ahead of him, if he could just cut his hair shorter and wear a belt so that his jeans didn't keep falling down. And she also told the plumber chap that he really needed to find a wife because at fifty-four, he was getting on and needed a woman in the house to look after him properly."

"Oh God, she didn't," I said, putting my face in my hands.

"Yeah, but memes of her comments are going

viral on social media, you know? I even heard that one of the breakfast TV shows has done a special segment about her, raving about how she's bringing back old-fashioned values to British broadcasting."

I shook my head in disbelief and wondered what my father thought. He was away at an academic conference, otherwise he would have been here tonight, although I couldn't help thinking that the gentle, absent-minded Professor Rose would probably have been bewildered by it all. On the other hand, after several decades of being married to my mother, he was probably used to being bewildered!

The sound of music blaring on stage reminded me that the show was beginning. Then, to my surprise, the disembodied voice rang out again, this time in sober tones:

"Before we begin our show tonight, we'd like to take a moment to acknowledge the loss of one of our most talented contestants. We are all devastated by Lara King's death and we know that you will miss her terribly. However, we know that as a consummate professional, she would have understood—better than anyone else—the old adage: the show must go on. And in honour of her memory, we will begin tonight's show with a short tribute to Lara and some of her finest moments..."

A screen dropped down on the stage and began playing a compilation of footage of the dead woman, from her singing on stage to relaxing backstage, and even a saucy clip of her getting undressed in the dressing room, unzipping her dress and showing a smooth expanse of bare skin which broadcast her lack of underwear.

There was an appreciative murmur from the audience and I wondered cynically if Monty Gibbs had decided to listen to his producers after all about making some kind of gesture towards Lara's death. Then I saw the little businessman turn around in his seat and scan the audience behind him, smiling with pleasure as he saw their rapt faces. It was just as well that it was too dark for most people to see his expression, otherwise they might have been shocked at how cheerful he looked about Lara's death.

Again, that uneasy thought crossed my mind and I wondered about Gibbs's morals. He was notorious for being insensitive to taste and political correctness... but what about justice and ethics? Would he stoop to murder to boost the publicity for his show? I knew that in the week since Lara's death, the ratings for *FPTC* had gone through the roof. Even with filming stopped and no new episodes to broadcast, the re-runs had still drawn tens of thousands of viewers, and there were already syndication offers from US channels and other networks around the world, even though the show hadn't finished yet.

I glanced at Devlin and wondered if I should voice my thoughts, but he was watching the stage with a broad grin on his face as Albert the magician came on, and I felt bad spoiling his mood. There would be time enough to tell him about my suspicions later—I would let him enjoy the evening first.

Leaning back in my own seat, I settled down to watch Albert's performance. Because this was his second attempt, the young student seemed less nervous than usual and even managed not to stammer as he introduced himself.

"Now, Albert—you live on a council estate on the outskirts of Gloucester, is that right?" asked Stuart in a tone that was obviously done to milk drama for the cameras. "I understand that you've had a tough childhood... your mother was a single mum?"

Albert flushed. He looked down and shuffled his feet. "Yeah... it wasn't easy."

"And your mother... Is she in the audience tonight?" Stuart turned around to look at the rows of seats behind him.

"No," mumbled Albert. "She couldn't make it."

"Oh, but I'm sure she's *very* proud of you," gushed my mother. "You're such a fine young man—I'm sure you're a testament to her care and upbringing. And I'm sure she must have made home-cooked meals for you while you were growing up? I know parenting is so different nowadays and there is so much emphasis on education and social stimulation, but really, I think home-cooking is one of the most important factors in raising a healthy child and I'm *sure* your mother would have baked you wonderful cakes and buns—"

Albert looked even more embarrassed. "Yeah... er... I've got some of her scones with me."

"Oh, how delightful! My daughter, Gemma, has a tearoom that sells scones and they're so popular—"

I looked up in horror. *Oh God. Why is she bringing me into this?*

"—and she bakes them fresh every day—well, when I say 'she', I really mean her pastry chef, Dora, because Gemma just cannot bake. Heaven knows, I've tried to teach her, but she can't seem to master the technique. I think it's a dreadful shame that girls nowadays can do all these high-flying executive jobs but cannot make a good home-cooked meal or bake a cake from scratch. Really, these are essential skills that every woman ought to know—"

"Please... somebody shut her up!" I moaned, cringing in my seat. My friends, though, seemed to find it amusing, and when I glanced at Devlin, even he was chuckling.

"Devlin—do something!" I pleaded.

"What do you want me to do?" he asked with a laugh. "Arrest her for being anti-feminist?"

"It should be a crime to embarrass your daughter on national TV," I said, scowling.

Finally, to my relief, Stuart interrupted my mother and said smoothly: "Yes, very true, Evelyn, very true... and I'm sure Albert's mother will be watching at home and cheering him on. Now, let's sit back and enjoy a bit of magic, shall we?"

The lights dimmed except for those lighting the stage; Albert walked over to his props and began his routine. The act wasn't particularly exciting or original—it was a medley of standard magic tricks, given a slight "fantasy" spin to match his wizard costume—and I was surprised that Albert had come so far in the contest. *Perhaps he'd always got the pity vote*, I thought. It had seemed like the judges were going for that angle, by playing up his disadvantaged background and difficult childhood. People loved an underdog. Besides, Albert projected an air of wounded vulnerability—like a small animal cowering in fear—which made you instantly want to help and protect him.

The white fog from the liquid nitrogen, which flowed out from the wings and blanketed the stage, did help to lift his act, giving the whole stage a mysterious ambience. In fact, it was so thick at ground level that it obscured everything up to Albert's knees and made him look almost as if he was floating as he moved across the stage. And the rising plumes of vapour helped to hide his occasionally clumsy sleight-of-hand. When he performed his climax—a classic disappearing act where he sat in a chair and covered himself with a sheet, then reappeared several minutes later out of the white fog on the other side of the stage—I was unexpectedly impressed and joined the rest of the audience in applauding him with gusto.

"So was it worth watching it again?" I leaned across and asked Seth, when Albert had left the stage.

"Yes, although I thought there'd be a lot more, but we didn't actually miss much last time. We'd just got to that big disappearing trick when we heard you screaming. So the only thing we didn't see was the ending."

"Yeah, you know, for a few minutes, I thought your screaming *was* part of his act," said Cassie.

Before I could reply, the disembodied voice rang out again:

"And now, here's a treat for all the dog lovers in the audience... let's welcome Trish Bingham and her canine dance partner, Skip the collie!"

The crowd cheered dutifully as Trish walked on stage, with Skip trotting at heel next to her. Trish was dressed in a cowboy costume and Skip had a matching bandana around his neck. I had to admit that they looked very good and I could hear the *aww*s already starting from the audience behind me.

Stuart Hollande, as usual, assumed the lead judge's role and did the introductory spiel, asking Trish why winning the contest was important to her.

"I just want to win," she said, unsmiling.

"Ha-ha... of course... I suppose you have big plans for the prize money?"

"No, not really."

"Oh." Stuart looked a bit taken aback. "Um... then I suppose you're looking to make a name for yourself and Skip—maybe get a gig performing around the country?"

"No, I just want to win," said Trish again.

Stuart blinked. "Oh... er... right."

"Yer like me," said Monty Gibbs with satisfaction. "We just like ter win, right? In everything."

Trish didn't respond and, after another awkward silence, Stuart hastily invited her to begin. We all watched as the woman and dog took up their positions in the centre of the stage. Then, as the opening strains of country music filled the auditorium, the duo began to move. Trish bowed low and the collie mimicked her, dropping into a classic canine "play-bow" pose. Then he twisted his body around and reversed through Trish's open legs, before springing up onto his hind legs.

"*Oooo-oooh!*" cried the audience, delighted.

Trish uncoiled a length of rope from around her waist and pretend to lasso Skip, while the collie leapt over the swinging rope, nimbly evading it. Then at a command from Trish, he grabbed the rope in his teeth and backed away from her, tugging hard as he did so. Trish pulled back and the two of them circled in an exciting tug-o-war, before letting go of the rope simultaneously to spin around together.

"*Aaaaw!*" cried the audience. "*Ohhh!*"

They were a great team. The dog and woman moved in perfect sync to the music as they twirled and weaved, marched and skipped around the stage. It would have been nicer if Trish had cracked a smile at least once, but Skip's bright-eyed enthusiasm more than made up for his owner's sullen demeanour. When they performed their final twirl and finished with a bow to the judges, the audience erupted in cheers and applause.

"I hate to say it but she was pretty good," commented Cassie as Trish led Skip off the stage. "I think, now that Lara's gone, it's going to be a close race between her and Gaz for the second spot."

I was about to answer when the voice came over the speakers again and my heart beat faster as I heard the announcement.

"It looks like it's raining cats and dogs on From Pleb to Celeb tonight! Straight on the heels—oops, I mean paws—of Skip the collie, we have a little feline competing for the limelight. Let's put it together for Cheryl Sullivan and her special feline friend, Muesli!"

CHAPTER SIXTEEN

I sat up straighter as Cheryl walked on stage, leading Muesli on the leash. My little tabby cat paused in the glare of the footlights and pricked her ears at the sound of the audience whooping and clapping. I watched tensely, wondering how she was going to cope with all the noise and lights. Muesli was probably the most confident cat I knew, but still, most cats would have been terrified. And although she had gone through the moves during the rehearsal yesterday, nothing could have replicated the noise and energy of the crowd tonight.

Muesli peered around, her tail twitching from side to side, and lifted one paw, as if preparing to bolt. Cheryl bent down quickly and stroked her, saying something reassuring, and I saw Muesli relax as the audience slowly quietened down.

"*Meorrw?*" she said, her voice carrying clearly into the audience.

"Awww...." came the response from the crowd.

I grinned to myself. If the contest was judged only on the "cute" factor, Cheryl would be heading for top spot. There was even more "awwing" as people watched Muesli trot over to the little stand that had been erected for her in the centre of the stage and jump into the basket. Cheryl smiled and went through her pretence of conversation, asking if Muesli wanted to hear a story, and my little cat responded on cue with a chirpy "*Meorrw!*" in all the right places.

The audience literally melted and I felt inordinately proud of my little cat. I began to relax as well, and watched, beaming, as Cheryl picked up the puppets and started her song. But she hadn't sung two verses when Muesli suddenly sat up in her basket. The little tabby looked out into the audience, her pink nose twitching as she sniffed the air. Then, before anyone could stop her, she sprang out of the basket and ran out to the front of the stage.

"*Meorrw?*" she cried, peering out into the audience.

Cheryl faltered, then tried to pretend that this was all part of the act as she continued singing and manipulating the puppets. I hesitated, not sure whether I should call out to Muesli to try and reassure her, or whether that would just make things worse. The little cat paced back and forth for a moment, then she gathered herself and leapt from the stage. There was a loud gasp from the audience, then an audible sigh of relief as Muesli landed on the judges' table.

"Wot the—! Oi... get off!" spluttered Monty Gibbs, waving his hand at Muesli.

"Oh, Muesli...!" cried my mother.

She reached for the little tabby cat, but Muesli evaded her hands. Instead, she trotted down the table, past a bemused Stuart Hollande, and took another leap, this time landing in the central aisle. People were starting to point and laugh now, and several leaned out of their seats calling: "Here, kitty, kitty, kitty..." Others were coming down the aisle, bending and attempting to catch her, whilst a few yelled for someone to call the RSPCA. It was absolute mayhem and no one was paying any attention to Cheryl on stage anymore.

I tried to get out into the aisle but found that with my seat in the centre of the row, I was wedged in by several people on either side and would have to climb over them. I stretched up as tall as I could and tried to make myself heard above the din, calling "Muesli! Muesli!" but my voice was drowned out by all the other people in the audience shouting at my cat. She was wandering up the aisle now, crying "*Meorrw? Meorrw?*" as she searched for a familiar face.

Then Devlin called out suddenly in his deep baritone: "MUUUUESLI!"

The little cat stopped, then whirled and trotted back eagerly in our direction. Devlin called again and she jumped up onto the seat backs, then—balancing nimbly—she clambered across the rows. There was a cheer from the crowd as she reached us and I scooped her up. But she squirmed in my grasp and stretched towards Devlin instead. I shook my head and laughed. I should have known. Devlin was probably Muesli's most favourite person in the whole world. Perhaps she had smelled him while she was on stage and that was why she had come down: to look for him. Now she purred happily as he held her against his chest.

Several members of the crew were hurrying through the audience, trying to get people to return to their seats, but everyone was too keyed up now and people gathered in small groups, talking excitedly. Finally, the voice came over the speakers again and said:

"Ladies and gentlemen... er... we'll take a short break now. There will be a twenty-minute interval."

Slowly, the auditorium emptied as people wandered out into the lobby to stretch their legs and get refreshments. I looked towards the stage where Cheryl was standing forlornly, and felt a stab of guilt. Maybe, if Devlin hadn't been sitting at the front of the audience, Muesli wouldn't have smelled him and run off like that...

I found Cheryl backstage ten minutes later and hurried over, Muesli held firmly in my arms. The nursery teacher smiled in relief when she saw us.

"Oh, I'm so glad you got her! She wasn't hurt, was she?"

"No, Muesli's fine," I assured her. "In fact, she seems to have enjoyed her little adventure. I was stopped by so many people wanting to pat her— that's why it's taken me so long to come backstage."

I put Muesli into her carrier, then turned to see Cheryl packing her puppets into her chest.

"Aren't they going to let you do your act again?" I asked.

She gave me a sad smile. "There's no point, really. I didn't think it was worth trying again."

"I'm so sorry about Muesli—" I started to say but she cut me off.

"No, no... it was my fault, really. It was silly of me to think that I could expect a cat to cope with all that noise and distraction." She gave a self-deprecating laugh. "I don't know what I was thinking, planning a routine with a cat on stage." She looked enviously at Trish and Skip on the other side of the Waiting Area and said with a sigh, "There's a reason why performing acts always use dogs."

"You could do your act without Muesli," I ventured.

"No, no, the feline partner is what makes it special and charming. Without Muesli, it would just be a middle-aged woman singing a silly song. Anyway..." She sighed. "This whole thing has made me realise that maybe this isn't what I want to do after all."

"Really? But I thought—"

"I don't think showbiz is for me. What I enjoy is using song and puppetry to tell stories—and seeing the little children's faces light up."

"Well, you can do that, even without winning the contest," I said. "There's a big demand for children's entertainers nowadays and I think you'd be fantastic. I'm not a child and I found your performance totally captivating—and not because of the cat," I added quickly. "It was *you*. Don't sell yourself short, Cheryl. You're a great entertainer and you've got a lovely voice."

"Th-thank you." She looked surprised and touched by my praise.

"Why don't you print up some leaflets and distribute them locally—see if people might like to hire you for birthday parties and things like that?"

She looked doubtful. "I suppose... I'd have to get permission from work first though."

"Permission?"

"The nursery I teach at is part of a very exclusive private school and they have strict rules about staff behaviour and activities. One of the other teachers was recently dismissed, and although officially they said it was because they were consolidating positions, everyone knew it was because they found out that she was hosting 'girls-only parties' in her home."

"Girls-only parties?"

She gave me a look. "You know, when you get a bunch of girlfriends around and one of those companies sends a rep with a box of sexy lingerie and adult toys for you to all look at and buy. It's really popular for hen nights and events like that. The person hosting the party usually gets a small commission."

"But surely it doesn't matter what your colleague does in her personal life, unless it affects her teaching?"

Cheryl shrugged. "Those are their rules. They are a Catholic institution and very intolerant about certain things. They pay really well though—almost double the usual rate—so people put up with it." She brightened. "They've been very understanding, though, about me entering this contest and have even given me extended leave, so maybe you're right. After all, moonlighting as a children's entertainer is different to selling sex toys on the side." She smiled at me. "Thanks for the suggestion. You've made me feel much more positive now about the whole thing."

"Well, good luck... and I hope you'll come and see us at my tearoom sometime," I said with a warm smile.

"Oh, definitely," she promised. "I live in Burford, just by the church, so that's not far from your tearoom." She reached out and stroked Muesli through the bars of her carrier, saying with a smile: "And, of course, I have to visit my second favourite tabby cat!"

***

After making sure that Muesli was settled in her carrier, in a safe corner of the Waiting Area, I headed back to rejoin Devlin and the others. But as I was about to enter the auditorium again, I spotted the sign for the toilets. I glanced at my watch: there were still several minutes of the intermission left, and for once the queue outside the Ladies didn't look too bad. Quickly, I joined the end of the line. There was a group of three women standing in front of me and from their accents, it sounded like they had come down from Birmingham especially for tonight's show.

"—didn't think mooch of Trish's act, did you?" said one of the women with a sniff.

"Same old routine she always trots out," said another woman. "I thought she'd prepare sumthink' really special for the show—else I wouldn't have bothered to come down to watch. But no, it's the same old boring moves... she hasn't even bothered to change the order! It's like she just marches around, doink' the same things, whatever the music. I could've watched her doink' that at the club on a Monday evenink'."

"Her reverse spins were dead sloppy too," said the third woman. "My Bella could do them much better—and it only took me, loike, two sessions of clicker training to teach 'er. I saw Trish down at the club trying it with Skip for weeks."

"Her timing's all wrong, that's what... I've watched 'er. She rewards too slowly. Doog doesn't make the connection," said the first woman.

"Did you tell her?"

"Are you kidding? That woman's a loose cannon. I'm not going anywhere near 'er if I can help it."

"What d'you mean?"

"Didn't you hear what 'appened at the obedience cloob show last month?"

"You mean, when that poodle attacked that Great Dane?"

"No, that was the weekend before. This was the Championship Class C... with the joodge from Australia."

"Oh... yeah?"

"Yeah, well, Trish lost to this new girl and her Labrador—really good 'andler, she was, this girl; they'd only just started six months ago, can you believe it, and they'd blazed right through Novice class and Class A and B—and they were definitely the best in the ring that day. But my God, Trish went berserk when the joodge announced the winner! Joomped on the other girl and really started going for 'er. They needed two people to pull 'er off."

"Bluddy hell! Was the girl all roight?" said the

third woman.

"Yeah, she was loocky—got a nasty bruise on 'er jaw and a couple of scratches but nothing too serious."

"I'm not surprised, to be honest," said the second woman. "I've seen Trish at shows before: she's a bluddy awful loser. I always feel sorry for those competink' against her—I keep well away from her."

"Did this girl report her for assault?" asked the second woman.

"No... Trish apologised and this girl decided to droop it."

"I would have reported her," said the third woman. "The authoritays ought to know if she's getting aggressive. It's loike that with the dogs, you know? You report them to the dog warden."

"Yeah, well, what if Trish finds out that you snitched on her?" asked the second woman. "I wouldn't want to stand too close to her the next time we're trainink' at the club."

"Still, you know that—" The first woman broke off suddenly as she caught my eye and realised that I was listening avidly to every word.

I flushed and looked hastily away, pretending to check the time on my watch. The women eyed me suspiciously, then turned their backs on me and changed the subject. I was relieved that the line had moved forwards enough that they soon disappeared into the toilet, and I made sure that I lingered long enough in my cubicle that they would be long gone by the time I came out. All this meant that I was really late getting back to my seat. In fact, the auditorium was already dark as I scurried down the aisle and squeezed apologetically past several people already seated in our row, until I made it back to my seat between Cassie and Devlin.

"I thought you'd decided to abscond," he joked. "Muesli all right?"

"She's fine," I whispered.

I started to tell him what I'd overheard, but at that moment music blared from the speakers, drowning out any attempt at conversation. I gave up and sat back; I could tell Devlin later. Still, as the twins appeared and began their singing and tap-dancing routine, I found myself struggling to keep my mind on the act on stage. Instead, my thoughts kept returning to the conversation I'd just overheard.

A lot of it, I had to admit, just sounded like sour grapes. But regardless of that, those women obviously trained at the same dog club as Trish and knew her well. They certainly weren't making up the stories of her behaviour at other competitions. *So Trish Bingham has a history of assault and is known for being a bad loser...* I mused. And now she was competing in something ten times more important than some local dog obedience show. How far would she go to remove a threat to her winning?

CHAPTER SEVENTEEN

I was so immersed in my speculation about Trish that I barely noticed the twins' routine, but I snapped out of my thoughts with a jolt when I heard the voice over the speakers say:

"And now, for something a little bit different... A group who shows that age really is just a number. Please welcome the Pussy Puffs—er, sorry, I mean, the Herb Girls!"

The audience erupted into laughter as the Old Biddies and June Driscoll trotted on stage. They might have changed their name but they'd obviously decided to stick with their white satin, rhinestone-covered Elvis outfits. They looked unfazed, however, by the crowd's reaction, and stood together with such dignity that the jeering soon faded into a respectful silence.

"So... um... Herb Girls!" said Stuart Hollande

brightly. "We're delighted to have you on the show. It's quite something to have senior citizens in the competition. In fact, this is the first time in the history of talent shows, I think, that there's been a band where the average age of its members is eighty yea—"

"Yer 'ear that?" cried Monty Gibbs, shaking a fist. "This is a first in British television! We are leadin' the way. Yer might be shrivelled ole prunes, right, like this lot 'ere, but yer can still be a star!"

"Er... right, thanks, Monty," Stuart cut in hastily. "Now, let's see if the Herb Girls would like to say a few words before they begin their performance. Er..." He glanced down at his notes, then looked at Mabel expectantly. "Um... Parsley, is that right?"

"I'm Parsley!" squeaked Ethel. "She's Tarragon... and that's Chives," she added, pointing at Florence.

"And I'm Dill," said Glenda. "Not Fennel, mind— make sure you don't confuse the two, although they do look very similar. But dill tastes so much nicer, I think, especially with a bit of grilled salmon or when you're making pickled cucumbers, don't you think?"

"Oh... er... right," said Stuart, looking totally bemused. "Um... so what inspired you to form a 'granny band'?"

"I think Borage should answer that," said Mabel, indicating June next to her.

The widow stepped forwards and said in a quavering voice, "It's for my husband, Bill, who passed away last year. I hope to win the prize and use the money to promote B.E.A.S.T., his support group for those with bushy eyebrows, and continue the work in his memory."

Laughter erupted in the audience and, for an awful moment, I thought Stuart was going to ask her for more details, but to my great relief, he must have received a signal from backstage about keeping to the schedule because he touched the concealed microphone in his ear, nodded, then turned back to the stage and said:

"Right! That's... er... very touching. So without further ado—let's hear it for the Herb Girls!"

The crowd whooped and cheered, more out of reflex than anything else, I think. But when the music started and the five little old ladies on stage began swaying and bobbing to the rhythm, the crowd began to cheer in earnest. Armed with fresh blue rinses, brand-new orthotics, and extra-thick support tights, the Old Biddies and June performed their number with gusto. Okay, so they sang completely off-key and forgot half their lyrics, but there *was* something very endearing about them and the audience seemed to share my feelings, giving them thunderous applause when they finished.

As the clapping died down, Stuart turned to my mother and said: "So, Evelyn... what did you think of our peppy pensioners? Do you reckon they're good enough to go through to the Finals?"

My mother frowned. "Well, the thing is, Stuart... I can't really judge them, can I? Mabel, Glenda, Florence, and Ethel are personal friends of mine—"

"Shh!" hissed Monty Gibbs. "Who said yer know them, eh? Just pretend!"

My mother shook her head firmly. "No, that would be wrong. It would be a conflict of interest."

Gibbs went very red in the face and started to say something, but Stuart cut in hastily:

"Uh... right, so... I think your opinion is probably the same as mine, Evelyn. These gorgeous grannies have really given the younger contestants a run for their money! I think they deserve a chance to perform in the Finals, for sheer gumption, if nothing else... Monty? What say you?"

Monty Gibbs was still giving my mother dirty looks, but he gathered himself with an effort and said:

"Uh... yeah! Yeah! Blimey, 'course they deserve ter go through, mate! It's all dahn ter the public vote though..." He turned towards the main camera and jabbed a finger at it. "So all yer people watchin' on yor telly at 'ome—make sure yer vote t'night when the show's over!"

There was only one act left: Gaz and his impressions, and I could feel a sense of anticipation from the audience. After this, the phone lines would be opened for voting and the two finalists would be decided. So far, based on the audience's reaction, it looked like the twins were in the lead, with Trish a strong contender for second place, and the Old Biddies not far behind. Of course, that could all change if Gaz wowed the audience...

The handsome comedian strolled on stage, looking very trendy in a bright collared shirt and designer jeans. He also looked slightly irritable, rubbing a hand along one cheek, and—recalling what he had said to Cassie at the pub last night—I wondered if he had just been mobbed by the make-up artist for a last powder touch-up.

"Gaz... good to see you," said Stuart with a warm smile. "You're our final act tonight but I hope you'll live up to the saying of saving the best for last?"

"Yeah, I... I've got a great show planned..." Gaz trailed off, scratching harder along his cheek. I noticed that a red rash was starting to show on his face. He scratched at his nose, then fiddled with his collar. "I'm... uh..." He broke off again and began scratching in earnest, using both hands.

Devlin frowned and said: "Something's wrong..."

Gaz scratched furiously at his face and neck, looking like he was trying to rip his skin to shreds. He twisted and contorted, trying to reach a spot behind his ear, all while cursing violently. A murmur of concern rippled through the audience as they realised that this wasn't part of the act but a man really in distress.

Devlin stood up suddenly and shouted: "He needs help! He might be having an allergic reaction!"

The next moment, several members of the crew rushed on stage to help the stricken man and they hustled him into the wings, out of sight. The judges also sprang up from the panel and rushed backstage through their private entrance. Devlin excused himself and pushed past the other people seated in our row, climbing out into the aisle and hurrying out of the auditorium. I followed hard at his heels, whilst behind us, the audience erupted in a babble of confused shouts and questions. We rushed through the doors connecting the lobby to backstage and arrived in the Waiting Area to find Gaz surrounded by judges, crew members, and other contestants. Everyone was talking at once and people were milling around in panicked confusion.

Gaz was still scrubbing manically at his face. "I need a shower," he moaned. "I need to get this stuff off me!"

"Has someone called the ambulance?" Devlin demanded.

"Yes, sir... it's on its way," his constable spoke up.

"Do we 'ave a shower 'ere?" yelled Monty Gibbs.

"No, sir..."

"What about the kitchen sink?" suggested Stuart.

Then Mabel spoke up, her booming voice cutting through the din. "Young man—" She jabbed a finger at one of the crew members. "Go and bring one of the bottles you use to refill the water cooler."

"The... the water cooler?"

"Yes, the big 15L bottles. Well, don't just stand there—be quick about it!"

The young man hesitated, then rushed off, returning a moment later lugging one of the giant plastic refill bottles for the water cooler. Gaz grabbed this and upended the whole thing over his head, sloshing water over his face and body. A few minutes later, he stood dripping from head to toe, with a puddle forming around his feet.

"Is it better?" my mother asked anxiously.

"Yeah, a bit," panted Gaz. "It's not itching so badly."

Florence and Ethel handed him their embroidered handkerchiefs, whilst Glenda fished in her handbag and pulled out a large tube of cream.

"Put this on your face, dear... It's aloe vera cream. It will soothe your skin."

Gaz mopped his face dry, then did as he was told, grimacing as he spread the cold cream over his skin. A few minutes later, though, he gave a small sigh of relief and I noticed that the red rash seemed to be lessening.

"Thanks... I... I feel better now."

"That was quick thinking, Mrs Cooke," said Devlin, nodding approvingly at Mabel. He stepped forwards and everyone fell back, responding to his air of authority. "Are you allergic to anything, Mr Hillman?" he asked Gaz.

The comedian shook his head. "Nah. Never had a

problem eating peanuts or shellfish or anything like that."

"When did you first notice the itching?"

"I dunno... Think it was just as I was walking on stage."

"Did you put something on your face just before you went on stage?"

"No... but *Sharon* did!" Gaz pointed accusingly at a woman in the crowd. "Bloody powder—come to think of it, I started itching as soon as she put it on."

The woman shook her head in confusion, her eyes wide. "But... but it's just face powder... We've used it before and there's never been any problem..."

"Can I see this powder?" asked Devlin.

The woman rummaged in a large bag slung over her shoulder and took out a small, flat box. I gasped as I recognised it.

"That's the powder that Trish was holding yesterday!" I blurted.

Everyone turned to look at me, then swung their heads to stare at the dog walker. She flushed and took a step backwards.

"What are you saying, Gemma? Did you see Trish tampering with this box of powder?" asked Devlin. He took the box from Sharon, being careful to use a handkerchief to wrap around it, so as not to leave any fingerprints.

I hesitated. "Well, not exactly... I just happened

to walk into the dressing room and Trish was in there. She was fiddling with something at one of the dressing tables and she was really... uh... defensive when she saw me. She left in a hurry but I noticed that there was some spilled powder on the table where she had been, and a small, flat box which wasn't with the others." I indicated the flat box in Devlin's hands. "It looked exactly like this."

Gaz narrowed his eyes at Trish. "It was you! You did it to sabotage me!"

"No! She... she's lying! I never... It wasn't me!" cried Trish, shaking her head vehemently. "I swear, I never touched that box—"

"Wait—this box isn't—" Sharon started to say but Gaz interrupted her.

"I know it's you! You were worried I'd beat you in the voting tonight and you wanted to make sure that you eliminated the competition. You probably murdered Lara too, you bitc—"

"Mr Hillman." Devlin's calm voice cut across Gaz's shouting. "I must ask you to desist from such behaviour and leave the charges of guilt to the police. I will have this box of powder tested for fingerprints and that will easily confirm if Ms Bingham has touched it or not. In the meantime, I would like you to accompany me to the station to answer some questions—after you've been checked over by the paramedics when they arrive. And you too, Ms Bingham," he added to the pale-faced Trish.

Sharon started to say something again, but she

was cut off once more, this time by Monty Gibbs.

"Wait—wot about the show?" demanded the businessman. "Gaz ain't done 'is act."

"Surely you can't expect him to go on stage and do his act now?" said Devlin incredulously.

"We 'ave to finish the Semi-Finals show," said Gibbs stubbornly.

"As far as I'm concerned, the show tonight *is* finished," said Devlin. "This was potentially a malicious act of sabotage which could have caused serious harm. I need to get a Forensics team in here and I also need to question those who were in the vicinity."

"No! No, yer can't put the mockers on the show!" shouted Monty Gibbs. "Do yer realise 'ow many people are watchin' us tonight? Do yer realise wot the commercial spots cost? Not ter mention me syndication deal... This is me show and I'm not 'avin' yer shut us dahn again, guv!"

"And this is my murder investigation, Mr Gibbs," said Devlin coolly. "I'm not having you put people in danger simply to line your pockets. Now, you can either step aside and let me do my job—or I can have my men escort you off the premises."

Devlin hadn't raised his voice but there was no mistaking the gravity in his words. Monty Gibbs spluttered furiously, his face turning the colour of a beetroot. But after a moment he seemed to deflate, and he stepped back in a gesture of acquiescence.

Devlin added, in a more conciliatory tone: "We

don't know what substance affected Gaz—it may still be contaminating the area backstage or even on stage. I'm sure you wouldn't want to risk any member of the audience becoming affected as well. It would be best if you cleared the concert hall for everyone's safety."

A look of horror crossed Monty Gibbs's face as he considered the litigation potential of such a situation, not to mention the negative publicity, and suddenly he couldn't cooperate with the police fast enough. Within half an hour, the auditorium and backstage had been cleared, and Trish and Gaz were in a police car, on their way to the station to be questioned.

I accompanied Devlin out to his black Jaguar as he prepared to follow them. He opened the driver's door and gave me a rueful look.

"I'm sorry the night's ended like this, Gemma."

"It's all right—I understand," I said, reaching up to give him a quick hug. "I just feel bad for you, having to go back to work now. I hope you're not stuck there too late."

Devlin sighed, rubbing the back of his neck. "I think it's going to be a long night, whatever happens. I'll ring you tomorrow morning and let you know."

He leaned forwards and gave me a brief, hard kiss, then he got into his car and, with a powerful growl of the engine, swung out of the concert hall car park and was gone.

CHAPTER EIGHTEEN

True to his word, Devlin rang me early the next morning. I had been pottering around aimlessly at home, wondering what to do with myself. With the show on hold again, I didn't have any catering to provide, but since things could also resume at any time, I was loathe to reopen the tearoom. It was a frustrating limbo state to be in and I pounced on my phone when it rang, eager for some news.

"Hi, sweetheart," said Devlin in a tired voice.

"Gosh, you sound absolutely knackered. When did you get to bed?"

"I don't know... sometime in the early hours. It wasn't actually as bad as I'd expected. I thought I'd be there all night."

"So what happened? Have you arrested Trish?"

"Well, first I'd need to find something to arrest her for."

"What do you mean? What about the sabotage attack on Gaz?"

"She was telling the truth about that. Her prints weren't on the box."

"But... but I definitely saw her—"

"She admitted to being in the make-up room, yes. She said she was trying on some of the stuff and she was embarrassed when you saw her. But she denies tampering with anything. And Sharon the make-up artist's testimony bears that out. She came to find me last night before I left the concert hall and told me that the powder she used for Gaz wasn't from any of the dressing tables. It came from the bag of stuff she carries around with her for last-minute touch-ups."

"Oh." I felt a stab of guilt for accusing Trish when she'd had nothing to do with the box that had been tampered with. Then I gave a despondent sigh. "If the bag was out in the Waiting Area, anyone backstage could have had access to it. And with how busy things are, it would have been easy to tamper with the box without anybody noticing. You're back to too many possible suspects! By the way, what *was* in the powder?"

"Forensics haven't isolated all the ingredients yet, but it looks like some kind of itching powder— the kind that you can easily buy to play pranks on people."

"Ugh. I can't believe people would play pranks using this stuff! I mean, Gaz looked like he was really suffering. How is he, by the way?"

"He's fine. No permanent damage done. From what I hear, most itching powder is fairly harmless in the long run, although it's not pleasant during the attack, of course."

"So I suppose you've let Trish go?"

"Well, she was never under arrest anyway. And there's no reason to detain her further. She denies having had anything to do with this powder incident and the evidence seems to back her up."

I sighed. "It would have made so much sense if it had been her though…"

"What do you mean?"

"Because it's the kind of thing I can see her doing. She's *really* competitive—I mean, seriously, she's the type that just *has* to win, at any cost. And she's already got aggressive with a fellow competitor once." Quickly, I recounted the conversation I'd overheard in the queue for the ladies' toilets.

"Hmm…" Devlin was silent for a moment. "Well, that does sound suggestive, but the fact remains that unless I have concrete proof tying Trish to the murder or even to this attempted sabotage, she is no stronger a suspect than any of the others."

"But we've ruled out most of the others now, haven't we?" I asked. "I mean, who else is left?"

"I wouldn't say that we've ruled them out. Nicole still hasn't got an alibi for the time of the murder, and she has a strong motive. Cheryl also hasn't got an alibi, although—to be fair—she *doesn't* seem to have a motive either. The Old Biddies are obviously out of the question and their friend, June Driscoll—well, she was with them, so I suppose they could vouch for her. That leaves only Gaz. And after last night, I'm more inclined to think of him as a victim."

"Maybe that's what he wants everyone to think," I said suddenly. "Maybe he set up the whole thing to divert suspicion away from himself."

Devlin laughed. "Gemma, two minutes ago you were convinced that Trish was guilty, and you felt sorry for Gaz... and now you're saying he could have done it to himself? He'd have to be a bloody masochist, if he did. That was a pretty unpleasant experience to go through—"

"You said yourself that itching powder has no long-term side effects."

"No, but that's like saying yanking your nose hairs out, one by one, has no long-term side effects. You still wouldn't find many people who would voluntarily do it! Besides, what would his motive be? He has the least connection with Lara."

"That's what you think. Actually he and Lara got to know each other pretty well... in the Biblical sense of the word."

"What? Where did you hear that?"

"The Old Biddies."

"How would they—"

"Backstage gossip. They got chatting to a girl who overheard Lara boasting on the phone about the night of passion she'd spent with Gaz."

Devlin whistled. "My boys never dug this up."

I laughed. "Your boys need to come and take lessons from the Old Biddies."

"So Gaz and Lara were an item?"

"Well, I wouldn't go that far. From what the Old Biddies said, it sounds like they had a one-night stand."

"How do you know their information is reliable?"

"We asked Gaz himself."

"You what?"

"He happened to walk into the pub the night I went out for drinks with Cassie and then the Old Biddies arrived straight after him—they were tailing him, you see—"

"They were *what*? Never mind..." Devlin sighed. "I don't think I want to know."

I grinned. "Well, they came over to join us and they told us what they'd found out. Then Mabel and Cassie got into an argument about whether you could trick someone into lowering their guard and blurting out the truth, just by chatting to them... and Cassie decided to try it with Gaz. Oh my God, Devlin—she was brilliant! Seriously, I wish you could have seen her. Mata Hari herself couldn't have done better. In less than five minutes, she'd got him to admit to the whole thing."

"She just asked him outright and he told her, just like that?" asked Devlin incredulously.

"No, well... she sort of softened him up a bit first. She got all flirty and stroked his ego... and you know Cassie's so gorgeous, with that perfect hourglass figure and her hair, all long and sexy... what man could resist?"

"Well, personally, I prefer a slim, athletic figure with a cute short bob, myself."

I blushed and laughed. "Thanks... although I don't know how much longer I'm going to have that slim, athletic figure if I keep running a tearoom."

"So Gaz told you all about him and Lara?" said Devlin, returning to the subject.

"Yes, although he insisted that it *was* just the one night and that he had no reason to kill Lara."

"Well, he could hardly say anything else," said Devlin dryly. "What else did he say? Anything about the other suspects?"

I hesitated. I knew I should tell Devlin what Gaz had said about Cheryl's past career and the chance that Lara might have been blackmailing her, but I found my tongue strangely paralysed.

"Gemma?"

"Um... yeah, I'm here... er... I was just thinking..." I took a deep breath. "No, he didn't say anything else."

For a moment, I thought Devlin was going to challenge me. He had an uncanny ability to guess my deepest thoughts and if we had been talking face to face, he would probably have known that I was lying. But luckily for me, the phone must have provided some buffer, and to my relief, he didn't pursue the subject. Instead, he said:

"By the way, Gemma, do you remember if you were serving scones on the day of the murder?"

"Scones?" I was a bit thrown by the seemingly random question. "Yes... why?"

"Oh, nothing... Forensics found some crumbs on Lara's clothing, which they were uncertain about the identification of. From the texture, they didn't think it was bread or cake—and I suggested it might be pieces broken off from a scone. I thought—since you found her body—the crumbs might have dropped off your clothes when you bent over her."

"Probably," I said. "To be honest with you, that whole day is still a bit of a haze in my memory. But yes, I would have brought some scones in—Monty Gibbs really likes them so I always include them in the catering order every day. He often checks the deliveries in person and helps himself to a daily stash, which he keeps with him and eats throughout the day... By the way—I don't suppose Monty Gibbs is likely to be a suspect?"

"Gibbs? Why do you ask that?" Devlin sounded surprised.

"It's just... he seems very—" I broke off. "Oh, it's probably a silly idea."

"I like your silly ideas," said Devlin. "Go on, tell me."

"Well... I just wondered how far Monty Gibbs would be willing to go to... to boost the viewing figures for *From Pleb to Celeb*."

Devlin drew a breath. "You think he'd resort to

murder to create publicity for the show?"

"He just seems so... so cold-blooded and calculating about it all! He's got this roving camera crew that goes around filming contestants—you know, like a reality-TV programme—and they only seem to care about getting good footage, at any cost. They never stepped in, you know, when Lara and Nicole were fighting, and they were even getting excited about filming in the ambulance if one of them got badly hurt! And the producer girl wasn't even repentant when I called her out," I added indignantly. "She just started lecturing me about 'good TV'. In fact, Monty Gibbs himself gave me a long spiel about why they were justified in massaging the truth to create good entertainment. He was trying to set up this sob story about Albert's deprived childhood and when I objected, he got all superior about it. He seems to think it's perfectly acceptable to manipulate the audience through faked drama—"

"Gemma, that is, sadly, what a lot of TV is nowadays. It's all about selective shooting and editing, to present a certain story or angle that the producers want the audience to believe."

"Well, I'm not having my baking used in some sordid soap opera drama!" I said hotly. "And if Monty Gibbs is willing to do all this to promote the show, what else is he willing to do?"

"Murder is a bit different to creative editing," said Devlin. "In any case, Monty Gibbs was sitting at the judges' table, in full view of the audience the entire time. So he has a rock-solid alibi."

"Well, maybe he didn't do the murder himself..." I muttered.

Devlin laughed. "Gemma, now *you're* getting into the realms of make-believe! If it wasn't for the fact that he has an alibi, I would agree with you that Monty Gibbs could be a viable suspect. But I think it's pushing things too far to suggest that there's some kind of mass conspiracy backstage, where Gibbs has got his entire crew ready to do murder for him."

"Oh, all right... I suppose that's a bit far-fetched," I said grudgingly. "Still, if anyone is likely to have my scone crumbs on him, it's Monty Gibbs!"

***

After I hung up, I sat on the sofa for a long time, lost in thought. Devlin had told me that the police had reopened the concert hall and the crew had been allowed back to continue preparing and filming as normal—although I knew that nothing much would happen until the votes had been counted and the two finalists decided. The phone lines had been open until midnight last night and I was sure that Monty Gibbs would follow the original plan of announcing the results in a special show tomorrow evening. In fact, I wondered cynically if the diminutive business mogul would put on an extra-long show, with lots of filler performances, just to drag it out as long as possible before he announced the finalists. It would be one way to keep people hooked as they waited for the results, and keep his viewing figures up.

On the sofa next to me, Muesli stretched luxuriously in her sleep, then opened one green eye to look at me drowsily.

"*Meorrw?*"

"It's about time you got up, sleepyhead," I said, reaching out to give her a chin rub. "You've been napping ever since this morning!"

With the coming of the chilly winter weather, Muesli had taken to getting up for breakfast and then retreating straight back to her cosy nest of blankets on the sofa, where she slept away most of the day. This was fine, except that come evening, she was usually full of beans and driving me crazy, zooming around the house, bristling with energy. When I had been able to take her into work with me, it wasn't too bad as she was kept awake and distracted by the busy atmosphere of the tearoom. But with the Little Stables being shut the last few days, Muesli had been left mostly to her own devices at home. After several disturbed nights listening to my little cat galloping up and down the stairs at 2 a.m. while she let off steam, I had vowed to try and keep her awake during the day so that she would be tired at night.

This morning, however, I'd taken one look at the

little tabby, curled up so snugly in her blankets, her face tucked against one white paw, and I hadn't had the heart to wake her. Besides, she was probably exhausted after her escapades at the Semi-Finals last night, and needed a bit of extra sleep to recover. The memory of Muesli's adventures last night made me think of Cheryl and I felt a stab of guilt for not telling Devlin what Gaz had said about the nursery teacher. What was I doing, withholding information in a murder investigation? Besides, it was only a matter of time before the police dug up the truth about Cheryl's past and then Devlin would be furious that I'd hidden information from him. In fact, I was surprised that they hadn't uncovered it already, but with so many suspects this time, the CID team had probably been spread a bit thin and hadn't made as much progress as they normally would have.

Well, why don't I help them out? I sat up at the thought.

Gaz had mentioned a shop on Cowley Road—an adult store, no doubt, where vintage copies of porn magazines were sold. I could pop in there and check first—make sure he was telling the truth—before saying anything to Devlin. That way, I wouldn't be stirring up a hornet's nest and possibly humiliating Cheryl for nothing, if Gaz turned out to be lying or even just mistaken.

Getting up from the sofa, I gave Muesli a last pat, then grabbed my bicycle and headed off.

CHAPTER NINETEEN

Cowley Road was an area with a reputation as the multicultural, bohemian, and slightly seedy heart of Oxford. It ran southeast out of the city, past Magdalen College, one of the stalwarts of the iconic Oxford skyline, to the industrial suburb of Cowley. Home to a diverse mix of ethnic groups— from Jamaican to Pakistani, Italians to Greeks, Turks to Russians—as well as a large student population, the road was filled with quirky shops and unique restaurants serving eclectic cuisine. It was also the hotbed for Oxford's music scene and its colourful annual carnival was a big part of the local calendar.

If Oxford had a red-light district, it would probably have been here... and it was here that I found the store Gaz had mentioned. I stood outside

For Your Eyes Only, shifting my weight uncomfortably and trying to work up the courage to go in. It sounded silly, I know, but I had never been in a sex shop before, and I was embarrassed. The discreetly covered windows which shielded customers from prying eyes in the street should have reassured me, but they only made me more nervous as they gave me no clue as to what I might encounter inside.

Then I felt a tap on the shoulder and I jumped in surprise. Whirling around, I found myself staring at the Old Biddies.

"Hello, dear... how nice to see you here!" said Ethel.

"We were coming down the street and I said, 'That looks like Gemma,' and I was right," said Mabel, nodding with satisfaction.

"You're looking a bit thin, dear—are you sure you've been eating properly?" asked Florence, her plump face creasing in concern.

"Yes, you mustn't get too stringy, you know—men like to have some flesh to hold on to," said Glenda.

"Wha-what are you doing here?" I asked faintly.

"We're following a lead," said Mabel importantly. "You see, after what happened to Gaz last night it seems that *he* can't be the murderer after all. But we remembered what he'd said about Cheryl—"

"It was a clue!" said Florence.

"And I remembered the name of the bookshop he

mentioned," said Ethel proudly.

"So we decided we'd come and find it!" finished Glenda.

Ethel peered up at the shop next to us. "That's a very strange-looking bookshop, isn't it? Why are all the windows covered up?"

"Er... it's not a bookshop exactly," I said.

Mabel marched up to the discreet sign by the front door, accompanied by the other Old Biddies, and, reluctantly, I followed them.

"Hmm... 'Adult entertainment store'..." Mabel read out loud.

"Ooh—that means sex shop!" squealed Glenda. "How exciting! I've always wanted to see inside one of those."

"But why would Cheryl be in a book in a sex shop?" asked Ethel, still looking confused.

Florence patted her arm. "That's because she probably posed for nude photos, dear. You know, the kind that men like to look at when they're feeling fruity."

I was a bit taken aback at how matter-of-fact she seemed about it. Perhaps it had been naïve of me, but somehow I'd expected little old ladies to be scandalised at the thought of pornography.

"Yes, that's what Gaz was implying—that Cheryl used to work as a glamour model and he found out when he recognised her in the pages of a vintage men's magazine," I explained to Ethel.

"I'm sure she wouldn't want anybody to know

about it now," said Florence. "She would be mortified!"

"But Lara knew about it, because Gaz told her," said Glenda.

"Which means Cheryl could have murdered Lara to stop her blackmailing her about her guilty secret," said Mabel triumphantly.

"Hang on, hang on—that's a bit of a leap," I protested. "We don't even know if Cheryl knew that Lara knew... or if Lara was trying to blackmail her... And even if she had been, that doesn't mean Cheryl murdered her! Come on, it's not as if this was some kind of state secret—even if Lara was silenced, Gaz still knew about it... and there would be other ways to find out. I'm sure the police would have dug it up eventually if they did a bit more research into Cheryl's past."

"Well, if you didn't think that Cheryl might be guilty, why did you come here then?" asked Mabel.

I paused, stumped. She was right. "I... I'm just double-checking, that's all," I said weakly. "We're not even sure if Gaz is telling the truth. I wanted to make sure that there really *is* a picture of Cheryl in the magazines in the first place."

"Well, why are you dawdling then?" asked Mabel.

Without waiting for me to reply, she opened the door and marched into the shop, followed by the other three. I hesitated for a moment, then sighed and hurried in after them. I found myself inside a cluttered store, filled to the brim with sex toys, lingerie, bondage equipment, lubricants, condoms, and an assortment of strange-looking objects that I had no idea what they were for (and probably didn't want to know).

A young woman wearing a hideous black leather corset came hurrying up as we entered, but she faltered as she saw the Old Biddies.

"Can... can I help you?" she asked.

"Just browsing," I said brightly.

She goggled at the Old Biddies tottering past us. "Uh... are they just browsing too?"

"Yes, they're... er... they're with me," I mumbled, hurrying after the four octogenarians.

The girl hesitated, then retreated behind her counter, although she continued to watch us suspiciously over the tops of the shelves as we wandered around the store. I was hoping to find the rack of erotic magazines, look through the vintage issues, and get out as soon as possible, but I hadn't banked on the Old Biddies' avid curiosity. They seemed to want to pick up every item on the shelves and examine each one in excruciating detail.

"What do you suppose this is for, Florence?" asked Glenda, holding up a piece of lurid pink silicone.

"It looks a bit like a banana," said Florence thoughtfully.

"But you put batteries in it," said Glenda, unscrewing the end to show us.

"Maybe it's a kind of torch," suggested Ethel. "My

Eveready torch unscrews at one end, just like that. Does it take 9V batteries too?"

"The quality of products in this place is really quite poor," said Mabel with a disdainful sniff. She held up a pair of black panties. "Look at this pair of knickers—there's a huge hole right in the middle! And this pair! And this pair!" She rifled through the rack. "All of these have holes. I would have sent them all back to the manufacturers, instead of having the audacity to sell them in the store. And for so much money too! Disgusting!"

"Oh, look—they even sell shortbread biscuits in here," said Florence, who had wandered down the aisle. She held up a tin labelled *Dunking Dickies*.

Ethel peered over her shoulder. "Well, whoever was using the cookie cutter wasn't very good with it," she said. "All the biscuits look like penises."

"What do you suppose this is for?" asked Glenda, holding up a life-sized rubber foot.

Oh help. In my wildest dreams, I never imagined I would have to go into a sex shop with the Old Biddies. I grabbed the rubber foot from Glenda and shoved it hastily back on the shelf.

"Look... can we just... move on? I think the magazines are over there."

I hustled them over to a wall of magazine stands and left them discussing the improbable proportions of the busty girl on the cover of *Penthouse* while I hunted through the section marked "Vintage Porn". Remembering the dates that

Gaz had mentioned, I rifled through the issues from the '80s, taking out several and flicking through them quickly. My heart sank as I realised how many more magazines were arranged on the racks in front of me. How was I ever going to go through them all?

Then, just as I was about to admit defeat, the magazine I was holding opened onto a large centrefold depicting a young woman clad only in a black velvet choker and a pair of stiletto heels. I stared down at the faded photo. She was thinner and more fresh-faced, with artificially bright blonde hair that was obviously coloured from a bottle, but there was no denying that it was Cheryl Sullivan.

I felt a stab of disappointment. A part of me had still hoped that Gaz was lying. I thought uneasily of what Cheryl had told me about the strict Catholic school where she worked. If her colleague had been fired simply for hosting sex toy parties in her home, what would happen to Cheryl if the school found out about her past in pornography?

It's not even as if there's any way to pass this off as something else, I thought, looking down at the picture again. With her suggestive pose and inviting expression, there was no doubt that Cheryl was happily flaunting her naked body for the camera.

But what I had said to the Old Biddies was true, I reminded myself. Just because Cheryl was ashamed of her past didn't mean that she would murder someone to hide it. And she couldn't hide it, anyway. That was the whole point. Killing Lara wouldn't have kept her secret safe—it would be easy enough for anyone to find out the truth if they just did a bit of digging. (In fact, I was surprised that none of the tabloid papers had unearthed this yet.) Still, I knew that people weren't always logical, especially scared, desperate people. More than one murder had been committed for the flimsiest of reasons, simply because people had panicked.

"What have you found, dear?" asked Mabel as the Old Biddies came over to join me.

Ethel's eyes popped out as she saw the picture of Cheryl. "Oh my goodness, she hasn't even covered her front bottom!" she squeaked.

"Is that really Cheryl?" said Glenda, leaning over to peer closely at the page.

"HEY! What are you guys doing?"

I looked up to see the shop assistant glaring at us.

"Those magazines are for buying, not reading in the store. Are you in here just to sneak a look at free porn?" she demanded.

"Oh no... no!" I said, shoving the magazine back on the rack and grabbing something at random from the shelf next to it. I hurried to the counter. "Here... um... I'm buying this."

The girl looked mollified. "Cool. I haven't tried this model of the Randy Rabbit, but I hear it's really good."

"The Randy what—?" I looked down in horror at the box I had just handed her. It held an enormous purple vibrator. "Oh! Actually... um... I don't... I'm not sure—"

"Don't worry, you won't regret it," said the girl earnestly, opening the box. "It's got all these different settings, see? Rotating, pulsing—"

"That's—that's great!" I cut in, my face flaming as I noticed that a couple had just walked into the store. *Oh my God, I hope it's not one of the regulars at the tearoom!* I thought, turning so that my back was to them.

"Now, would you like it gift-wrapped?"

"Uh... no, no... that's fine... In fact, never mind the box," I gabbled, grabbing the vibrator and stuffing it out of sight in my handbag. "I'll just pay for it, okay?"

I stood in an agony of embarrassment as she put the sale through. The Old Biddies came to stand next to me and I braced myself for Glenda to start asking "What do you suppose this is for?" again— but thankfully, she and Florence seemed to be preoccupied examining the sexy lingerie displayed by the counter. As the girl was handing me the receipt, a man in a business suit came into the store. He cast a shifty look around, then leaned over the counter and said out of the corner of his mouth:

"I'm looking for a blow-up doll. You got any with extra-large breasts?"

Before the girl could reply, Mabel said in her booming voice: "They're over in the cabinet by the far wall, young man, although I must say, I find it quite preposterous that you should be requesting a specific breast size. Back in my day, girls made do with the size of breasts that they were born with—none of this 'boob job' nonsense—and men knew better than to reveal their preferences in public. They behaved like gentlemen and—"

"Uh... yes, right... well, we'd better be going now," I said, grabbing Mabel's arm and hauling her out of the shop, leaving the man looking slightly shell-shocked behind us.

"Goodbye!" said the other Old Biddies, waving to the girl behind the counter as they tottered out after me and Mabel. "Thank you for a lovely time!"

CHAPTER TWENTY

Once I'd seen the Old Biddies safely onto a bus, I climbed onto my bike to head home. But as I was about to push off, I changed my mind—the thought of sitting alone in the house didn't appeal to me—and instead, I headed northwest out of Oxford and cycled to Meadowford-on-Smythe. Arriving at the little stone bridge which crossed the stream just outside the village, I dismounted and wheeled my bicycle slowly up the High Street, enjoying the sight of the pretty little shops and winding cobbled lanes which made Meadowford such a popular tourist destination. Even on a wintry day like this one, the village looked quaint and picturesque, with the grey clouds adding drama above the thatched roofs of the traditional Cotswolds cottages.

I parked my bike outside the tearoom and let myself in, shutting the door behind me and leaning on it with a happy sigh. *Ahhh...* The Little Stables wasn't open, of course, but somehow, even without the hum of customer conversation and the comforting smell of fresh baking, it still had a cosy, welcoming atmosphere, a sense of peace and security. And after the havoc in the sex shop, I was glad to get back to my little haven.

Still, I knew that I was only putting off the inevitable. I needed to call Devlin and tell him about Cheryl. It was important information and she was still a suspect in a murder investigation, no matter how much I liked her. Reluctantly, I pulled out my phone and was just about to punch in Devlin's number when a knock on the door startled me. I opened it to find Cheryl Sullivan herself standing on the doorstep.

"Hi!" she beamed. "I was at a loose end this morning so I thought I'd take you up on your invitation to pop into your tearoom. I'd arrived here before I remembered that it might be shut, but then I saw the bike outside and thought I'd try on the off-chance—" She faltered, her smile fading as she saw my expression. "Is something wrong?"

I hesitated, then took a deep breath and said: "Cheryl, on the first night of the Semi-Finals, when I came back to the concert hall with Muesli, I searched for you but couldn't find you anywhere. Where were you?"

She looked bewildered. "What... what do you mean? I told you—I went out to the little car park behind the concert hall to look for Misty again."

"Did you see anyone? Talk to anyone? Did anyone see you?"

She flushed. "You're asking if I have an alibi for the time of Lara's murder, aren't you? Do you think that *I* might have murdered Lara?" she asked incredulously. "That's crazy! Why on earth would I want to kill her?"

"Because she found out about your shameful secret," I blurted.

Cheryl went very still. "My... my shameful... secret?" she stammered. "I... I don't know what you're talking about."

I mentioned the name of the magazine in which I had seen her picture at the sex shop. She blanched visibly.

"That... that was a long time ago," she whispered. "I was a student... I needed the money. We... we all make bad decisions sometimes, especially in our younger years—"

"But you thought that bad decision had been covered up and hidden safely away, didn't you? Until Lara raked it all up again. What did she do? Taunt you with it? Threaten to expose you to the press? Or to your school? That would have cost you your job, wouldn't it? Is that why you killed her?"

"NO!" cried Cheryl, looking horrified. "I didn't kill Lara! How could you—I would never—that's a horrible thing to say!"

"The truth is horrible sometimes."

"But that's *not* the truth!" said Cheryl. "I didn't kill Lara! I wouldn't have killed her even if she *had* been blackmailing me or whatever—but anyway, she wasn't! I don't know where you got that crazy idea from. I don't think Lara even knew about my past. And in any case, it wouldn't have mattered if she had told my school." She raised her chin. "I'd told them myself."

"You did?" I stared at her.

She nodded. "Years ago, when I went for the job interview. I didn't want it hanging over my head, like some guilty secret, so I told them everything. They were surprisingly understanding about it, actually. Maybe it's the Catholic belief in confession and forgiveness, but anyway, they gave me the position, in spite of my 'chequered past'. So you see, there was nothing that Lara could hold over me."

I didn't know what to say. She had taken the wind completely out of my sails. Not only did I now look a complete fool, I also felt like a narrow-minded, sneaking Judas.

I cleared my throat and said awkwardly, "Um... well..."

"I was wrong about you, Gemma," said Cheryl, two spots of angry colour in her cheeks. "I thought you were my friend—but friends don't go around behind each other's backs, prying into their past and then making nasty assumptions!" She lifted the gift bag she had been holding and thrust it at me. "Here. I brought this as a thank you for your help with my act." She handed me a hand-knitted toy mouse. "And I made that for Muesli. I was going to give it to her myself but you'd better take it since I doubt I'll be back."

Turning on her heel, she stalked down the street and out of sight. I stood miserably on the doorstep, holding the gift bag and watching her go. I'd never felt so small and ashamed of myself. How could I have got it so wrong? Then I straightened. Actually, I hadn't. My gut instinct had always been that Cheryl was innocent. I'd just let myself be swayed by the "evidence" to the contrary.

Sighing, I stepped back inside and shut the door. But now, the empty tearoom no longer seemed cosy and welcoming. Instead, the silence felt oppressive and all I kept hearing was Cheryl's voice saying over and over again: "*I was wrong about you, Gemma... I thought you were my friend... I was wrong about you, Gemma... I thought you were my friend...!*"

Impulsively, I let myself back out, jumped on my bike and headed back to Oxford. Not to my cottage though. Suddenly, for all her faults and exasperating habits, I wanted to see my mother. I cycled to the tree-lined streets of North Oxford, parked my bike outside my parents' elegant Victorian townhouse and hurried inside, only to stop short as I stepped into the sitting room. My mother had a visitor and my heart sank as I recognised the woman sitting next to her on the sofa. It was Grace Lamont.

"Hello, darling—how lovely! Are you staying for lunch?" trilled my mother.

"Er..." I hesitated in the doorway. The last thing I wanted to do was have lunch with the scary editor of *Society Madam* magazine. But my brain struggled to come up with a realistic excuse on the spur of the moment and the long pause meant that if I declined now, it would have been obvious why. "Um... yeah, I'd love to have lunch with you."

Grace shifted irritably in her seat and said: "I do abhor the way young people say 'yeah' these days. So sloppy and uncouth! The word is 'yes'—a nice, firm affirmative, with no slurring or distortion of the vowels."

Bloody hell. Lunch with this woman was going to be torture. My mother had always been pretty strict about manners and etiquette, but Grace made her look like a slovenly '60s hippy. I went to wash my hands before the meal—one of the edicts drummed into me from an early age—and then sat down with some trepidation opposite Grace at the dining table.

My mother had prepared a simple meal of salads and cold meats, accompanied by soft bread rolls, for which I was grateful as it involved fewer fancy utensils and less effort for me to remember which knife or fork to use on what first. But even as I reached for a bread roll, I hesitated. I knew you definitely didn't bring the whole roll up to your face and take a bite out directly, but were you supposed to break the bread roll open with your hands? Or slice it into two halves with the bread knife? Which was the correct etiquette? Suddenly, I couldn't remember.

Surreptitiously, I watched Grace, but to my dismay, while she accepted helpings of salad and cold roast chicken, she declined the basket of bread rolls. *Bugger.* She was probably avoiding carbs or something. I looked to my mother for guidance, but she had just left the table and gone into the kitchen to bring out something else. I was left holding a bread roll aimlessly in front of me, like a squirrel posing with a nut.

I saw Grace raise her eyebrows at me and hastily put the bread roll down on my side plate. To stall for time, I grabbed a nearby platter and made a performance of helping myself to some potato salad, saying brightly:

"So... um... are you doing interviews with any of the other judges from the show?"

"No, but I shall be including a special feature on some of the contestants in the next issue," replied Grace. "Your mother has been telling me about several of the performers who have quite interesting backgrounds. While *Society Madam* does focus on home-making, fashion, and etiquette, we do also like to include human interest stories from time to time. And given the enormous amount of national interest in the show, I think our readers might enjoy some coverage of the performers."

"Yea—yes, I noticed several newspapers and

magazines have been doing stories on the contestants."

"Well, naturally, we would not publish the type of dreadful sensationalist stories that are favoured by the tabloid papers," said Grace haughtily. "We aim to provide thoughtful, intelligent editorial, with a focus on family values. Thus, I would like to interview the mother of the twins about the challenges of bringing up child prodigies, for example. And the plumber, Mr Ziegler, seems an interesting man. According to your mother, his family came over to England from Germany during the Second World War."

"Oh yes," said my mother, returning from the kitchen with a tureen of soup which she set down in the middle of the table. "I was chatting to Mr Ziegler and it was fascinating listening to his stories of how his grandparents escaped the Nazis and made their way across France, to safety in England. They had two young children with them—one of them was Mr Ziegler's father, who was only six at the time—and it sounded like the most harrowing journey."

"And once they arrived here, there would have been challenges settling into their adopted country... but despite these difficulties, I believe Mr Ziegler's father grew up to become an outstanding member of the community?" said Grace, looking at my mother for confirmation.

"Yes, apparently he started as a factory

apprentice but was quickly promoted to foreman and was even elected leader of the local factory workers' union. But sadly, he died rather young, of lung cancer, and Mr Ziegler's mother had to bring him up as a single mother."

"Indeed?" said Grace, looking pleased at this additional drama for her feature. "That cannot have been easy in the 1960s. Hmm... yes, a most heart-warming story. And Mr Ziegler himself—he seems to have overcome his difficult childhood with a single parent, to establish a successful plumbing business?"

"He told me that his grandfather was actually a plumber back in Germany, so he says he is proud to be continuing the family tradition," said my mother with a smile. "And he is also continuing the family tradition of yodelling—another thing which his grandfather excelled at back in Bavaria."

"Very commendable, very commendable," said Grace, nodding. "It is a shame he's likely to be eliminated from the competition."

"Yes, it is so hard when you're judging," said my mother with a sigh. "One is supposed to judge them purely on the merits of their performance, and yet it is so difficult to be critical when one knows their background and how deserving they are of having a chance to win."

"Maybe that's why the other judges don't get too close to the contestants," I suggested. "That way, they don't have to feel bad when they have to pick favourites."

"I think it is very good of your mother to take so much personal interest in the contestants," said Grace, frowning at me.

"Well, really, it's very hard not to," said my mother. "They all have such heart-breaking stories. That boy, Albert, for instance—he's from a single-parent family too, did you know that? Oh, it was the most dreadful thing: his father left them for his mistress and then died in a car crash, so they were left completely alone. They were forced to move into council housing and it sounds like Albert's mother became very depressed. He told me that he started doing magic tricks to cheer her up."

"Ahh..." Grace smiled with satisfaction as she saw another feel-good story developing. "A wonderful son supporting his wounded mother. Yes, yes, I must include Albert in the feature. I wonder if his mother would be prepared to come to Oxford for a photo-shoot with her son? If not, I can send a photographer up to them... Now, what about that girl who plays the piano? She appears to be a demure, lovely lady."

"I'm afraid I don't know very much about Nicole—she seems very shy and she keeps to herself," said my mother, finally picking up her bread roll.

I watched avidly as she broke off a bite-sized piece, applied a dab of butter with the bread knife, then popped it into her mouth. *Aha!* I started to follow suit, then was distracted as I heard Grace Lamont say:

"—believe she is a podiatrist, isn't she? And I noticed her listed as 'Mrs' in the directory but I don't recall seeing her husband in any of the show footage. I would have thought that he would be coming to watch the performances, to support his wife. Perhaps I will ring Nicole and ask her about her husband. It would be nice if we can do a more romantic piece to balance the other two—"

"Oh no, don't do that!" I said before I could stop myself.

Grace looked at me in astonishment. "I beg your pardon?"

"Sorry... it's just... it's probably not a good idea to ask Nicole about her husband."

"And why not?"

"Well..." I shifted uncomfortably, feeling like I was betraying a confidence. "Nicole's husband had an affair and left her recently, and I think she's still very sensitive about it."

"I see..." Grace paused, then her eyes gleamed. "Well, we can change the angle of the piece! We will feature her as a strong woman, triumphing against a bitter situation. Perhaps her motivation for going on the show was simply to thumb her nose at her husband... yes, that would make an even better story than the romantic angle."

"No, no... I really don't think Nicole would like that," I protested. "Why don't you leave her out of the piece? You've got more than enough stories with the other contestants—"

"Oh, no, this is a prime piece of melodrama—far too good to leave out. It is just the sort of thing that readers love and will do wonders to boost circulation."

I looked at the woman with a mixture of surprise and distaste. So—for all her posh mannerisms and holier-than-thou attitude, Grace Lamont was really no better than Monty Gibbs: a newspaper hack out for a sensationalist story! And for all my dislike of the pushy businessman, at least he was honest about it, whereas Grace was a big hypocrite.

"I think you should have the decency to respect Nicole's feelings and not hound her for the sake of a story, whatever the angle," I said, more sharply than I intended.

Grace Lamont gasped in outrage and my mother looked horrified.

"Gemma!" she cried.

"I'm sorry," I said stiffly. "I think good manners and good taste apply to more than just using the correct fork at the table. The most important place it should be observed is in the way we treat others."

Grace bristled but seemed unable to think of anything to say in return. We sat in an awkward silence for a long moment, then my mother smiled brightly as she jumped on the tried-and-true British answer to every problem.

"Would anyone like a cup of tea?"

CHAPTER TWENTY-ONE

It was business as usual at the concert hall the next day. I was woken by a very early phone call from one of the show producers, asking me to provide the usual catering order. After a panicked call to Dora and a rush up to the tearoom to help her and Cassie prepare everything, I arrived at the concert hall mid-morning to find the place buzzing with even more tension and excitement than usual. The results of the votes were in, but the producers were tight-lipped, jealously guarding the results until they were to be announced live on stage that evening.

I found that I was wrong about Monty Gibbs milking the anticipation for the results and dragging things out. In fact, the show was planned to be shorter than normal. There would be a guest performance by one of Britain's newest rock bands, followed by a recap from the judges of each contestant, and then the two finalists would be announced.

Afterwards, Monty Gibbs had invited the entire cast and crew to his estate in the Cotswolds for an "after-show party". I couldn't help cynically thinking that Monty Gibbs didn't just have aspirations to be a TV judge; he obviously also fancied being one of those celebrities who hosted glamorous parties after awards ceremonies like the Oscars.

Much to my surprise, I was included in the invitation, and since I had no other plans for the evening, I decided to accept. My mother, as one of the judges, would be there and I could get a lift with her, going straight from the concert hall to Gibbs's estate after the show. That only left me the issue of finding someone to feed Muesli her dinner and finding something to wear.

A phone call to Cassie solved the former problem and the Old Biddies came up with a suggestion for the latter:

"Ask Sharon, dear—she's the head make-up artist and wardrobe lady," advised Mabel. "I noticed that they have a rack in the dressing room filled with dresses of various sizes. They must have been there to provide different options for Nicole, Cheryl, Lara, and—well, Trish was usually in a costume of her own, so she didn't need a gown for her performance. Anyway, I'm sure there will be something on that rack in your size, that you could borrow for the evening."

I was doubtful but when I did approach Sharon, I was pleasantly surprised.

"Oh yes, I think I've got something that would suit you perfectly," said the woman, looking me up and down. "You're a size ten, aren't you?"

"Yes, usually, although sometimes I prefer a twelve, just to have a more relaxed fit."

Sharon laughed. "Darling, these are evening gowns we're talking about, not weekend pullovers. You want them to hug your figure, not be swimming around it."

The dress she had in mind turned out to be an elegant gown in a deep-burgundy velveteen fabric which draped softly to give my boyish figure the illusion of curves. The colour made my complexion beautifully creamy and my dark bob of hair look extra glossy. In fact, I looked so good in it that I considered buying the dress from her after the party!

"This is gorgeous!" I said, standing in front of the mirror and smoothing the dress down over my hips.

"Mm..." said Sharon behind me, with a pin clamped in her mouth. She was busily nipping and tucking something at the back of the bodice. "I just need to tighten this a bit—it'll only take a minute... By the way, have you got any make-up with you? You'll want to get dolled up a bit, wearing a dress like this. It'll look odd if you're barefaced. If you haven't got anything, you're welcome to use the things here." She gestured to the row of dressing tables next to us, each holding a collection of creams, powders, eye-shadows, and lipsticks.

"Oh, thanks... that's really kind. I might take you up on that—although I don't tend to wear much make-up usually."

"If you just want a light, natural look, I've got a great palette in my make-up bag, together with some tinted lip gloss and a nice loose powder that I use for last-minute touch-ups—oh, not the one that I used the other night," she added quickly. "Don't worry, I opened a fresh box."

"I didn't think you'd be using that," I assured her. "Anyway, I would have thought that the police would have taken that box for analysis."

"They have. Although they haven't found anything useful, from what I've heard—other than the fact that it had been tampered with." She made a face. "Apparently someone had added itching powder to the box—what a horrible prank!"

"Do you think that's what it was?"

"Well, what else could it be?"

"I thought it could be connected to the—" I broke off and smiled. "No, you're probably right."

A look of understanding dawned on her face. "Oh, you still think Trish did it to sabotage Gaz's performance? But I thought the police checked and her fingerprints weren't on the box."

"No, you're right. And anyway, Devl—I mean,

Inspector O'Connor said that you told him the powder you use for last-minute touch-ups isn't from this room, so it couldn't have been the box that I saw Trish holding."

"Yeah, I keep the last-minute stuff separate. Like I said, it's mostly lighter, more natural colours—just to stop shine and retouch lip gloss—that kind of thing. We have another make-up artist who does the contestants when they're dressing in this room and she uses the stronger colours that we have in here."

"So whoever tampered with the box had to have done it outside, in the Waiting Area, when nobody was looking..." I mused.

"That's what the inspector said. But the thing is..." She frowned. "I've been racking my brains trying to remember and I'm sure I didn't leave the bag unattended. And anyway, I was touching up the granny band before I did Gaz and they were all fine, weren't they? None of them were itching."

"Yes, which means that the tampering was done between the time you did them and then did Gaz. Are you sure you didn't put the bag down somewhere, even for a minute?"

She nodded. "I always carry it slung across my body, like this—see?" She demonstrated. "The only time I take it off is when I'm doing a contestant. Then it's easier to have it next to me, to reach for things." She screwed up her face in thought. "But I remember... I did each of the old ladies... they were all fairly quick and easy; they have lovely skin, actually—none of the usual liver spots or blemishes you have to worry about... oh, except for June: she's got some spider veins on one cheek that she's quite sensitive about so I had to add some extra coverage on that and I did her last. And then I popped to the loo—but the old ladies were watching my make-up bag for me—and then I came back and retrieved my bag and it never left my body, until the time I did Gaz." She shook her head in confusion. "So I just can't understand when anyone could have had the opportunity to tamper with the powder?"

"And are you *sure* the Old Bid—I mean, the old ladies were watching your bag?"

She nodded again. "Yes, I left it right next to June and she promised to keep an eye on it for me."

An uneasy thought struck me, but before I could question her further, one of the crew popped their head in the doorway with a message from Monty Gibbs asking about today's delivery. Hurriedly, I changed back into my normal clothes, left the gown with Sharon for alterations, and went to find Gibbs.

The rest of the day passed in a whirl of activity and before I knew it, it was time for the show. I was glad; it had been an awkward day from a social point of view. Trish had been even more unfriendly than usual: from her resentful looks, it was obvious that she blamed me for her visit to the police station. Cheryl gave me the cold shoulder as well, refusing to look at or speak to me, and I felt filled with guilt and remorse again for doubting her. Gaz moped around, a shadow of his former cheerful self. Although it hadn't been his fault, the fiasco with the itching powder had cost him dearly, since there hadn't been any opportunity for him to perform again before the voting lines closed at midnight. He would have to rely on audiences remembering his earlier performances and hope that his charm and talent had stayed strong in their memories. But from the sullen look on his face, it was obvious that he didn't think much of his chances.

The rest of the contestants all seemed strangely subdued as well—even the Old Biddies were less chatty than usual, remaining in a huddle in a corner of the Waiting Area with their friend June. I was relieved when the curtains finally went up and the familiar voice intoned:

"Welcome to From Pleb to Celeb, *the show where we turn nobodies into somebodies!*"

I stood in the wings and watched the performance by the guest rock band. But like the rest of the audience, I only paid half-hearted attention, impatient for the real focus of the show. The atmosphere was thick with anticipation by the time the judges began calling each contestant on stage, while providing a recap of their strengths and weaknesses. Finally, they all stood in a line, waiting nervously for the results, and I found that I was digging my fingers into my palms as I waited for the announcement.

Stuart Hollande stood and held up a large gold envelope to show the audience. There was a tense silence as he slowly peeled back the flap and drew out the card within.

"And the finalists are..." He smiled at my mother and held the card out to her. "Actually, Evelyn, I think you should do the honours."

"Oh...!" My mother stood up, slightly flustered. But she quickly composed herself, took the card, and read out loud in her clear, well-modulated voice: "Molly and Polly... and the Herb Girls!"

There was wild cheering from the audience and even wilder celebration on stage as June Driscoll gave a shriek of delight, then hugged each of the Old Biddies in turn. Mabel, Glenda, Florence, and Ethel looked slightly stunned, and I was surprised too. Okay, the granny band might have been a great novelty but even I had to admit—despite my affection for the Old Biddies—that their singing was atrocious. Could they really have beaten Trish and Skip, with their crowd-pleasing routine?

It was obvious that the dog walker was sharing my thoughts. While the other contestants conjured up strained smiles to hide their disappointment, Trish didn't even bother. Scowling ferociously, she snapped her fingers at Skip, then stomped off stage, the collie trotting obediently at her side. Her sudden departure left everyone at a loss and the applause petered out into an embarrassed silence.

Quickly, Stuart Hollande stepped into the breach with his usual smooth charm: "Er... right, well, congratulations to the finalists... and thank you to the rest of the contestants. You have all been marvellous—to have come this far in the competition is a great achievement and I know that the other judges will agree with me when I say that you are all winners in your own right!"

The audience cheered again and applauded enthusiastically.

"Yeah, and I'm not just sending them packin', right?" Monty Gibbs piped up, seizing his microphone and standing up in his chair so that everyone could see him. "They are all invited ter me estate for an after-show knees-up! Because we're not like uvver TV contests, yer know—we don't just chuck the losin' contestants out and forget about them—we treat them wiv consideration and give them a grand send-off!"

"Er... yes... right... thanks, Monty. Very generous of you," said Stuart with a pained expression. He cleared his throat and addressed the audience again: "But don't think it's all over—the real excitement is just beginning. The two finalists will be battling it out in the next episode of the show— so make sure you don't miss it!"

"And we'll be showin' footage from the after-show party!" added Monty Gibbs. "Yer'll see wot the contestants were eatin' and drinkin'. I've called in a chef from one o' those Michelin-starred restaurant ter provide the food—"

"*Thank you*, Monty, that's great," said Stuart through gritted teeth. "And now, we'll bid you all goodnight and see you in the next episode."

He looked relieved as the *FPTC* theme music blared from the speakers, and the curtains dropped, signalling the end of the show.

CHAPTER TWENTY-TWO

As the audience filed out of the auditorium, there was a noisy confusion backstage as members of the crew rushed around, dismantling equipment and moving props, and the roving camera team prepared to follow the contestants to the party.

I'd planned to get a lift with my mother, but somehow I found myself being herded with the rest of the contestants onto a hired coach bound for Gibbs's estate. Deciding it was easier to go with the flow, I settled into a seat at the back of the coach and wished that Devlin could have been there. For one thing, I'd have loved him to see me in the burgundy gown, and for another, it would have been less lonely. But he'd had a development on another case and would be busy following up a lead this evening.

In the interests of security, though, Devlin had sent one of his detective constables to provide a police presence backstage during the show and I assumed that the young officer would be coming along to the party too. I craned my neck, scanning the seats in front of me. I couldn't see him, but I did see Trish in a seat by a window, with a black-and-white plumed tail peeking out from the side of the seat next to her. I was surprised. After her fit of temper on stage, I didn't think she'd want to come to the party.

Then a lanky young man, who was obviously a police officer despite being in plainclothes, climbed aboard the coach and walked down the aisle, looking for an empty seat. He stopped next to me and asked:

"D'you mind if I join you?"

"No, of course not," I said, giving him a friendly smile as I recognised him: he was the constable who had hovered anxiously around me the night I'd found Lara's body. He looked very young—probably a new recruit to the CID—and he had an eager, almost puppy-like interest in everything, which was rather sweet.

"My name's Darren," he said shyly. He cleared his throat. "Uh... I mean, DC Lester. Detective Constable Lester."

"It's okay—I know you're officially on duty, but I think we can be on first-name terms," I told him with a grin.

He relaxed slightly and returned my grin. "Thanks. I'm still finding my feet a bit."

"Well, you've been thrown in the deep end, haven't you, with this case?"

He laughed. "Yeah, just a bit. But I'm learning heaps. The guv'nor is brilliant—he's so patient and takes time out to explain things to me—and he's been a real sport when I make mistakes."

"I'm sure Devlin remembers what it was like when he was new," I said.

He looked surprised to hear me refer to his superior so casually. "Oh... er... do you know the inspector then?"

I laughed. "Yes, you could say that. I'm his girlfriend."

"Oh!" He blushed. "Sorry—I probably should have known that."

"No, why should you? Anyway, it shouldn't make a difference."

"But the guv'nor discusses his cases with you, doesn't he?"

I glanced at the other seats around me to make sure that no one was eavesdropping. "Er... well, not always, but yes, sometimes. Especially if I'm directly involved, like this one. Why do you ask?"

"It just means that I can relax with you a bit. It's nice not to have to worry about what I'm saying all the time. With the rest of the people here, I have to be so careful when I'm speaking, to make sure that I'm not giving away some confidential information...

and some of them can be real nosy. Like those grannies there..." He nodded to the Old Biddies, who were sitting with June Driscoll at the front of the bus. "Bloody hell, they never stop asking me questions about the case!"

I chuckled. "Actually, you can probably relax a bit with them too. Devlin knows them quite well. They're... er... well, let's just say they've got some experience with murder investigations and they've helped the police in the past. So they're not 'normal' members of the public."

The young constable looked bewildered. "They've got experience with murder investigations? How?"

I laughed again. "It's a long story. I'm sure Devlin will tell you about it some time. So..." I glanced around again. We were sitting at the back of the coach, with no one in the last row behind us. Across the aisle, Tim the hip hop dancer and one of the roving camera crew were deep in a discussion about various hip hop bands, whilst in front of them, Albert sat with another crew member, who was busy showing him something on his phone. In the seats directly in front of us, Sharon and one of the show producers were poring over call sheets and production notes, and in front of them, Gaz was doing a hilarious impression of Mr Ziegler, the Yodelling Plumber. The comedian had obviously recovered his cheerful demeanour and was yodelling (badly) at the top of his voice, whilst Mr Ziegler grinned good-naturedly in the seat next to him. The rest of the contestants were all sitting farther in front.

Everybody seemed engrossed in their own business, not to mention that Gaz was singing so loudly that I didn't think anyone could overhear us. Still, just to be safe, I lowered my voice as I asked: "Have there been any recent developments on the case? I talked to Devlin yesterday, but I wondered if anything new has come up since then?"

Darren followed my example, answering in an undertone: "Not really. Forensics delivered a couple of extra reports this morning: the full analysis on the ingredients in the powder that had been tampered with, some further analysis of the area around the crime scene, and the results of a tox screen done on the victim."

I raised my eyebrows. "You tested Lara's blood for poison?"

"And stomach contents and urine—it's standard autopsy procedure. The guv'nor wanted to double-check that someone hadn't used the liquid nitrogen to hide the real cause of death."

"I hadn't even considered that," I said, thinking of Devlin with admiration.

"Yeah, he's brilliant, the guv'nor. So sharp."

"And was it clear?"

"Yeah, no toxins. In fact, all the results for all the tests were pretty standard."

"What about those crumbs that you found?"

"Crumbs?" He looked puzzled for a moment, then

understanding dawned. "Oh, yeah... they were just flour, butter and sugar, egg, milk, vanilla extract, baking powder, and salt. The guv'nor thinks they're crumbs from scones that you served that day, which probably fell off your clothes when you found Lara."

I frowned. "I don't think they're my scones—I'm pretty sure we don't use vanilla extract in our recipe. Of course, Dora could have changed the recipe recently..." I brightened. "I'll tell you what: I'll give Devlin a sample of my scones for Forensics to compare."

Darren nodded, then he glanced around again, checking the seats around us. Gaz had stopped singing so the coach was quieter now and it was easier for others to hear us. He lowered his voice even more and added, "The other thing was: they found a rhinestone."

I stared at him, my pulse quickening. "A rhinestone?"

"Yeah, it was mixed in with some of the smashed bits of... er... her face and so they missed it initially. But it doesn't necessarily mean much on its own. Several of the costumes had rhinestones, including the cowboy outfit worn by Trish and the evening gown worn by Nicole..."

And the Elvis outfits worn by the Old Biddies and June Driscoll on the night of the murder, I thought. Again, the uneasy thought tugged at my mind but I couldn't bring myself to take it seriously. It just seemed too ridiculous.

"...besides which, there were rhinestones found on the floor all over the Waiting Area and the dressing rooms. They snag on things and drop off so easily," Darren continued. "So it doesn't really help to narrow the pool of suspects at all. The guv'nor says that's been the problem with this whole case, really: too many suspects, too many people with reasons to murder the victim and with opportunities to do it, and too many without alibis. When you've got one or two, it's easier to narrow it down, but when they all look equally guilty, you don't know who to focus on."

I smiled at his earnest, serious tone. "Sounds like a tough case to be starting your CID career on. You must find it very frustrating."

"Well, actually..." He gave me that shy smile again. "I was delighted to get assigned to this case... I mean, I'd never have had the chance to see backstage and all the stuff that goes on behind these TV contests. I used to love watching these shows on telly—you know, like *Britain's Got Talent* and *The X Factor*—and it's so cool to see behind-the-scenes, and get to know the performers a bit."

I laughed. "Who's your favourite contestant then?"

He furrowed his brow. "It's hard to pick a favourite. I really like that Yodelling Plumber chap. He's different, know what I mean? And Lara was great, of course. She really knew how to sing. The hip hop kid is pretty cool. And that boy who does the magician act—I'd love to know how he does some of his tricks." He glanced across the aisle at Albert, in the row in front of us. "Hey—he's over there. I'm going to ask him!"

"I doubt he'll tell you," I said, laughing. "Magicians never reveal their secrets."

Darren leaned forwards and tapped Albert on the shoulder. When the student turned around, he gave him a friendly smile and said: "Hey mate... I loved some of the tricks that you do, like that levitation one and the one where you disappeared from the chair. Any chance you could tell us how they're done?"

Albert didn't return his smile. "A magician never reveals the techniques behind their tricks."

"Aww, come on... I won't tell," Darren cajoled. "Just give us a hint."

"I would be breaking the Magician's Code," Albert said pompously, then he turned to face the front again.

I grinned as Darren sat back, looking crestfallen.

"Don't worry," I said. "I've got a friend who's interested in magic—I mean, like a real boffin—and he's studied all the tricks in detail. He was telling me the other day about the chair trick and I'm sure he'd know about the levitation one too. I can ask him, if you like."

"Oh, cheers!" said Darren. "That would be wicked!"

I looked at him quizzically. "Doesn't it spoil things if you find out how everything is done though? I mean, it takes away the mystique. Sort of like finding out Santa isn't real... Christmas is never as exciting after that."

"I suppose so," he said. "But I just love finding out how things work, you know? When I was a little boy, I was always taking clocks and remote controls and other things apart to see how they worked inside. It used to drive my mother mad." He chuckled. "I guess it's why I joined the CID—to find out how murders are committed."

"I always think the 'why' is more interesting than the 'how'," I said. "I mean, isn't that the key to solving the murder?"

"Not always—sometimes if you find out the 'how', you can then figure out who could have done it. But yeah, the 'why' is more interesting, I suppose, but it's so confusing sometimes. Like in this case... there are so many possible reasons!" He shook his head. "How would you even know where to start?"

"Actually, there's usually the same shortlist of motives for murder," I said. "Most people kill for gain, like money or power, or because they're scared of something or want to hide something, or in a passion—either jealousy or hate—or to protect someone they love, or even to get revenge."

"Wow." Darren looked at me admiringly. "You sound like one of our teachers at the police training centre."

I gave an embarrassed laugh. "Well, you learn a lot when your boyfriend is a detective—although it's all common sense, if you think about it."

"Which one do you think is the motive in this case?"

I shrugged. "If I knew the answer to that, I think I would know who the killer is!"

CHAPTER TWENTY-THREE

The journey from Oxford to Gibbs's estate probably took no more than forty minutes, although it felt like forever. There wasn't much of a view, either, since darkness had fallen, and the country lanes were poorly lit. By the time we arrived, my stomach was growling, and I was more than ready for the Michelin-starred meal that had been promised. Besides, it was nice to go to an event where someone else was catering for once.

Before we could eat, though, Monty Gibbs insisted on taking us on a tour of his estate. What had once been a large country manor had been completely renovated and modernised, with a swanky triple garage added to one side and a large glass-and-chrome extension on the other. The sprawling property also housed a private gym, sauna and heated indoor pool, a home theatre and music room, a den designed to look like a cross between an English gentlemen's club and a casino straight out of James Bond (complete with circular poker table and a roulette wheel), an underground wine cellar, and a private art gallery—all spread out in two opposite wings which overlooked a huge central courtyard that seemed to be brimming with replica Italian marble fountains and enormous potted plants. Beyond the courtyard, the manicured lawns swept away from the house into open landscaped gardens, with a winding path that meandered down to a man-made lake and private boathouse.

"Built o' modern block and steel frame but completely faced in original Cotswolds stone," said Monty Gibbs proudly when he mentioned his boathouse. "Two indoor slips in the wet dock and access ter the lake through big double doors on a cable-track system. All automated, right? And there's a dayroom up the stairs above the dockin' area. Not some mingin' little rat hole, know what I mean? It's all finished ter the top standards: underfloor 'eatin', Lutron lightin', built-in speakers, remote skylights, and slate tile floorin'. There's even a kitchenette and boozer, and a walk-in rain shower."

Thankfully, Monty Gibbs didn't insist on us trudging through the dark down to the lake to view all this splendour in person. Instead, we followed him gratefully back into the house. The interior of the manor was filled with expensive furnishings and a mix of antique and Scandinavian designer furniture. It was obvious that Gibbs had always insisted on the best that money could buy. It was also obvious that he had often just chosen the most expensive item, without any regard for taste or harmony, and the result was a hotchpotch that resembled a garage sale more than a billionaire's pad!

There were a lot of people in the house—it seemed like the party was already in full swing—and the foyer, hallway, and vast open-plan living room were filled with boisterous crowds of people talking, laughing, and air-kissing one another. I had no idea who the other guests were—I supposed that they were mostly business associates, although I did recognise some local politicians and minor celebrities in the crowd. Waiters in gloves and white jackets walked around holding silver trays and serving champagne and canapés, and a live jazz band provided mellow background music from one corner.

We left our coats with the attendant in the ante-hall, then wandered through to the dining room. As I followed the Old Biddies to the long central table laid out with a lavish buffet, I had to admit that Monty Gibbs had been as good as his word: there were platters filled with gourmet dishes of every description, from fresh oysters with lime to beluga caviar blinis, from black truffles and goats' cheese ravioli to baked lobster with garlic aioli...

"Oh my... everything looks so delicious!" said Glenda as she eyed the buffet. She tried to pick up a plate and also help herself to some napkins and cutlery, all while juggling her handbag awkwardly.

I watched Mabel, Ethel, Florence, and June all struggle in a similar fashion and felt like rolling my eyes. They would have had an easier time if they hadn't insisted on carrying those ridiculously old-fashioned handbags as favoured by the Queen, the boxy type that could only be held in the hands or dangled stiffly from the forearm.

A lady standing at the buffet next to us was obviously watching too, because she leaned over and said: "Why didn't you leave your bags with the attendant in the ante-hall? That's what I've done. They'll be perfectly safe there. That's why Monty hired a cloakroom attendant—so that people could offload their things and enjoy the party."

"That sounds like a good idea. Here, I'll take them for you," I offered, holding out my hand to June and the Old Biddies.

A few minutes later, weighed down by five leather bags in various shades of beige, mauve, and lavender, I made my way back to the foyer. It seemed like several people had had the same idea and I groaned inwardly as I saw the queue of women outside the ante-hall, all brandishing their bags to be deposited. Still, it was moving quickly and I was just stepping up behind the next person at the counter, getting ready for my turn, when a woman jostled me, trying to push in front of me.

I turned to her in annoyance. "Excuse me! I think I was here first—"

She ignored me, giving me another shove and elbowing me out of the way. I stumbled backwards and dropped the bags.

"Hey!"

The woman didn't even glance at me. Shoving her bag at the attendant, she grabbed the numbered ticket and disappeared back into the crowd. The attendant leaned over her counter and looked at me sympathetically.

"That was well out of order," she said. "She should've at least apologised or offered to help you pick 'em up. D'you want a hand?"

"No, it's all right—I can manage," I said with a sigh as I bent down to retrieve the handbags. Luckily, most of them were securely zipped or clamped shut, but one must have had a loose clasp because it had opened as it turned upside down, spilling the bag's contents everywhere.

Cursing, I knelt down to gather the items, scooping them up and dumping them unceremoniously back into the bag. *Honestly, it's ridiculous how much rubbish old ladies keep in their bags!* I thought irritably as I gathered packets of tissue, lipsticks, loose change, safety pins, dental floss, faded receipts neatly tied with a rubber band, an old-fashioned chequebook... Then my hand froze as it hovered over a tube of hand cream. Lying next to it was a small tin. At first, I thought it was the kind used to hold breath mints, but then my eye caught sight of the words on the tin cover:

ITCHING POWDER
Ingredients: *Mucuna pruriens*
Warning: Do not use on sensitive skin.
Not suitable for children under 9 years of age.

Slowly, I picked up the tin, my mind racing. *Is this what was used to tamper with the powder used on Gaz? Whose handbag is this?*

I rummaged in the bag and pulled out a ladies' wallet. Flipping it open, I stared at the photograph tucked next to the credit cards. It showed a kind-faced man with bushy eyebrows, and standing next to him, clutching his arm and smiling widely, was June Driscoll.

CHAPTER TWENTY-FOUR

The evidence was there in my hands: the Old Biddies' sweet geriatric friend was the culprit behind the malicious prank on Gaz. It was simply too much of a coincidence that she would be carrying itching powder in her bag for another reason. In fact, as I recalled the conversation I'd had with Sharon, it all clicked into place. June had been the last person that Sharon had used the powder on, before she used it on Gaz, and Sharon had even left her make-up bag with the widow while she had gone to the toilet. There would have been more than ample time for June to tamper with the powder. *And it certainly seemed to have worked*, I thought grimly. With Gaz out of the contest, the odds had increased in the granny band's favour and they had nabbed one of the two coveted Finalists' positions.

But did it go much further than that? If June had been willing to use sabotage, would she have been willing to resort to murder too? The rhinestone that had been found at the crime scene—that could easily have come from June's Elvis costume. But what about her alibi? I thought back to the day I had found Lara's body. When I had scanned the Waiting Area while looking for Cheryl, I'd seen the Old Biddies next to Mr Ziegler, adjusting their costumes… but had I seen June with them? As I racked my brains, trying to remember, Devlin's words came back to me: "*A few members of the cast say that they saw the granny band, but they weren't able to identify each one individually.*"

The only ones who would be able to tell me for certain were the Old Biddies themselves. They would know if June had been with them the whole time. I stuffed everything back into the bag, shoved it—together with the others—at the attendant, then hurried back to the dining room.

But when I got there, I stopped short in confusion. The Old Biddies were nowhere to be seen. Neither was June, I noted with a flicker of panic. *Where have they gone?* I scanned the room again, craning my neck to look above the crowd of people milling around, and noticed that a few of the other contestants were missing too, such as Gaz, Tim, and Albert, as well as Monty Gibbs himself, my mother, and Stuart Hollande. Trish and her collie weren't there either. I relaxed slightly. Perhaps the diminutive businessman had taken a small group—including June and the Old Biddies—to another part of the manor to show them something?

Telling myself not to let my imagination run away with me, I went over to the buffet and began to fill a plate. I would simply wait for the Old Biddies to come back and then find a good moment to talk to them about June, I decided. And in the meantime, I might as well eat. But as the minutes ticked past, I found the uneasy feeling returning. Finally, I set the plate of half-eaten food down and stood up. I couldn't just sit here—I had to go and search for them.

At that moment, Monty Gibbs marched in through a doorway on the other side of the room, followed by a small group of people, including my mother and Stuart Hollande, several contestants, and the roving camera crew.

"...and I'm plannin' ter upgrade ter an IMAX system later this year. S'not normally installed in private residences, right, but as yer just seen, mine is bigger than most 'ome theatres and I'm 'aving a system custom-made," Monty was saying.

There were murmurs of appreciation from those clustered around him. I scanned the faces quickly and felt the surge of alarm again as I saw that neither the Old Biddies nor June were in the group. Where were they? Was it really just a coincidence that June and the Old Biddies should have disappeared at the same time? My four elderly friends were the only ones who could confirm where June was at the time of Lara's murder. Her alibi rested on the assumption that she had been with them the whole time on that day, and if they were gone, nobody would be able to prove or disprove that...

I walked up to my mother, who was chatting with Stuart Hollande, and waited for a lull in their conversation before saying casually:

"Mum, you haven't seen Mabel and the others, have you?"

"Mabel? Oh, yes, I think I did see them, darling—just as we were going with Monty to see his home theatre. They were going outside."

"Going outside?" I said, surprised. "In the dark? What on earth for?"

"I don't know, darling. They didn't say, although they seemed to be in quite a hurry."

"Was their friend June Driscoll with them?"

"I'm not sure—I'm afraid I wasn't really paying attention. She may have been with them."

Stuart looked at me curiously. "Is something wrong?"

"Er..." I hesitated. What could I say? That I suspected a little old lady of being the murderer and I was worried she might harm her little old lady friends to protect her alibi? It sounded crazy even in my mind.

Besides, I didn't know that the Old Biddies were

in danger. For all I knew, they might have just gone off on one of their mad schemes again and I would look very silly if I sounded the alarm and sent out a search party, only to find that they were just snooping somewhere they shouldn't.

I plastered a smile to my face. "No, no, everything's fine... Um... excuse me—I might just pop out and have a look for them."

"Don't forget your coat, darling—it's very chilly outside," my mother called after me.

I ignored her warning and hurried out, but I hadn't gone far when I wished that I had listened to my mother after all. The house had been heated like a furnace and I'd been feeling hot, but as I walked across the courtyard I could feel my skin cooling rapidly in the cold night air. I wrapped my arms around myself and shivered as I paused at the edge of the terrace and peered out across the lawns sloping away from the house. It was hard to make out anything beyond the faint swell of the grassy lawns and the dark blur of trees in the distance. A faint glimmer at the bottom of the slope in the distance reminded me that there was a lake down there; in fact, I could see that the path leading from the terrace curved across the lawn and wound its way down towards the water.

There were a few other people out in the courtyard, most of them braving the chill to have a smoke, and I could also see a couple, wrapped warmly in their coats and walking hand-in-hand, coming up the path from the lake—presumably having just taken a romantic stroll down to the waterfront. I was just about to approach them and ask if they'd seen any little old ladies wandering about when I heard a loud whistle, and the next moment, a furry shape came bounding out of the darkness. It was followed by a woman crossing the lawn on my right. It was Trish and Skip. The dog walker had sensibly put her coat on before going out and even had a thick woolly scarf around her neck, and she looked warm and flushed with exercise.

She saw me but made no effort at a greeting, ignoring me completely as she walked past. Skip had different ideas, however. The collie rushed over and jumped up in delight, putting muddy paws all over me.

"Down, Skip!" Trish admonished.

The collie wagged his tail and looked so happy to see me that I couldn't help but smile.

"It's okay," I said, brushing the dirt off my dress. "It's going to get dry-cleaned anyway."

Trish looked surprised. "Oh... most people get stroppy when dogs jump up on them."

I crouched down to make a fuss of the collie, laughing as he tried to lick my face. "Oh, he's just gorgeous! Have you had him from a puppy?"

For a moment, I thought she wasn't going to answer, then she said: "Yeah, from eight weeks. He was the runt of the litter."

"Really? Who would have guessed that he'd grow up into such a big, beautiful boy?"

Skip raised his left paw and held it out, as if asking to shake hands, and I laughed and took it.

"He's just adorable," I said warmly. "Some dogs are really well-trained but they're a bit robotic, you know? But Skip is fantastically obedient and still has masses of personality."

"*Woof!*" said Skip, as if agreeing with me.

I laughed and was shocked to hear Trish laughing too. It was a rusty sort of sound, more of a cough than a laugh, but it was there nevertheless. I glanced up and saw that her face had softened, and she even had a smile at the corners of her mouth. It was amazing the difference it made—she looked like a different person.

Blimey. So the way to her heart is through her dog, I thought. Slowly, I stood up again, wrapping my arms around myself as I wished again that I'd put my coat on before coming out.

Trish said suddenly: "You're shivering. Here..." She unwrapped her scarf and handed it to me.

I was so astonished by her unexpected kind gesture that I stood looking blankly at her for a moment, before hastily taking the scarf and wrapping it around my shoulders. It was wide, thick, and woolly—more like a shawl than a scarf— and it tucked snugly around me. I pulled it close and looked at her gratefully.

"Thanks," I said. I hesitated, then added, "By the

way... I was really surprised by the results of the voting. I thought you and Skip deserved to go through to the Finals."

She stared at me for a moment, then said gruffly, "Thank you."

"Um... you didn't happen to see the Old Bi—I mean, the group of old ladies from the granny band out here, did you?"

Trish shook her head and pointed around the side of the house. "No... but I took Skip down that way to do his business so I might have missed seeing them."

I turned to look again at the path winding down the sloping lawn. "Um... Do you mind if I borrow your scarf for a bit longer? I just want to go down the path a bit to have a quick look for them."

"Sure. Take it. I'm warm enough—I don't need it—and I'm going back in anyway." Trish turned towards the house and whistled to Skip, but for once the collie was disobedient, trotting instead down the sloping lawn towards the band of trees in the distance.

"Skip!" called Trish, sounding annoyed and also slightly embarrassed.

"He probably doesn't want to go back in," I said, laughing. "You can hardly blame him. Exploring out here is much more interesting for a dog."

"Yeah, he was getting pretty restless in there, which is why I brought him out." Trish made a sound of impatience, then—without another word to me—she marched off after the dog. It was an abrupt, almost rude end to our conversation, and previously I would have been offended. But I was beginning to realise that Trish's brusque manner didn't really mean anything—it was just the way she was. My feelings towards her mellowed. The woman might lack social graces but she wasn't a bad person, and what I had seen as an unfriendly attitude was probably just a cover for her lack of confidence in social situations.

Turning, I pulled the warm woolly scarf tighter around my shoulders and set off down the path towards the lake.

CHAPTER TWENTY-FIVE

The path was paved and well-maintained, but it was still tricky negotiating the incline in high heels. The lake also seemed to be farther away than I'd thought. I was just wondering whether to give up and go back to the house when I met someone coming up the path. It was Albert. He looked at me curiously but didn't say anything.

"Hi Albert—have you just come up from the lakefront?"

He nodded. "I wanted to look in the boathouse that Mr Gibbs was telling us about. I heard that he's got the new MasterCraft XStar with a 5500 GDI Ilmor Engine and a ZFT4 Tower," he said in the wistful tone of someone who knew they could only dream of such luxuries.

"Did you happen to see the old ladies when you

were down there?"

"No, but I didn't actually look in the boathouse. I heard some voices and... um... I thought it might be a couple who were... you know..." In the dim light, I couldn't see him blush, but I could hear it in his voice.

"You heard a man and a woman?"

"No... just female voices. Actually, one was quite loud... sort of like booming, you know? It reminded me of my old primary school teacher, Mrs Adler. She was scary. Anyway, so I didn't go inside..."

I started down the path. "I'm going to pop down for a quick look."

He looked uncertainly at me. "Would... would you like me to come with you?" Without waiting for me to answer, he turned around and fell into step beside me. "I'll come... It's dark down there and... well, you're a woman."

I glanced sideways at his weedy frame and thought silently that he didn't look like he'd be much better than me in a fight. Still, I was grateful for his company and we walked in silence towards the lake. The lights and noise of the party faded away as we followed the meandering path. Albert's longer strides meant that I had to hurry to keep up and by the time we arrived at the boathouse, I was out of breath and much warmer.

The waterside structure looked empty and silent. I hovered uncertainly outside the door as Albert went up to one of the shuttered windows and peered in.

"I think I see a light," he muttered.

He tried the door. To my surprise, it opened easily. We stepped into a darkened hallway. There was a spiral staircase next to the door, presumably leading to the upstairs level, and then the hallway continued into the main part of the boathouse, opening into the huge vaulted space of the wet dock. Most of the area seemed to be filled with water: two large berths dominated the dock with finger piers stretching on either side between them. A gleaming speedboat was moored in one slip and a luxurious yacht in the other. The sound of water lapping, sucking, sloshing, and splashing echoed eerily everywhere.

"Hello? Mabel? Ethel? Florence? Glenda? Are you there?" I called, peering to see in the dim light.

The large double boathouse doors which faced the lake were firmly shut and the only light in the place came from a pair of round lamps fixed high on the wall. They were beautiful replicas of vintage brass ship lights, but they gave only a feeble orange light which seemed to create even more shadows.

"Can you find the light switch?" I called to Albert behind me.

"I'm trying..." he mumbled, groping along the walls.

I walked to the edge of one pier, looking around for any signs of life. Next to me, the yacht loomed, anchored by thick ropes to cleats at my feet and rocking gently in the water. Beneath me, the cold black water surged in the narrow space between the side of the pier and the hull of the yacht, sucking and swelling as if a sea monster lurked beneath.

"I don't think anyone's here..." I said in disappointment, turning around. "I think—Oh!"

Albert was standing very close behind me and something about his expression made the hairs prickle on the back of my neck.

"Did you find anything?" he asked.

"N-no..." I said, trying to put a bit of distance between us. I was right at the edge of the pier and if I stepped back, I would fall into the water. "Um... why don't we go back to the house now?"

"I don't think so," he said pleasantly. "You might talk to that police officer again and give him more ideas."

"What ideas? What are you talking about?"

"I don't need you suggesting that the police start comparing things—"

"The crumbs!" I said. My heart began to pound in my chest. "I was right—they're not from my scones. We don't use vanilla extract in our recipe... but I'll bet your mother uses it in hers, doesn't she?" I stared at him as the pieces all clicked together. "That day on stage, when my mother was asking you about home-cooking, you mentioned that you'd brought some of your mother's home-made scones with you. That's where the crumbs came from; they didn't fall off my clothes—they fell off *yours*, when you pushed Lara into the liquid nitrogen. *You murdered her!*"

"I had to," he said, still in that eerily pleasant voice. "She deserved to die, for what she did to my mother."

"To... to *your* mother?" I stared at him in bewilderment for a moment, then the remaining pieces of the jigsaw fell into place.

I thought back to the day I had walked in on Nicole and Lara fighting. The sexy singer had been boasting about her conquests and the memory of her jeering words rang in my head:

"I once had this chap leave his wife and son on Christmas Day—can you believe it? ...Didn't even say goodbye to his five-year-old son..."

And then I remembered my mother sitting with Grace Lamont, talking about the contestants:

"...That boy, Albert, for instance—he's from a single-parent family too... his father left them for his mistress and then died in a car crash, so they were left completely alone..."

I stared at the young man in front of me. The loving son. The diligent student. The budding magician. And the avenging killer of the woman who had destroyed his family.

"Did you know Lara was coming on the show? Was that why you auditioned?"

He laughed. It was a strangely happy sound, which sounded incredibly creepy in that echoing boathouse.

"No, I had no idea! I didn't even recognise Lara when I first saw her. And then one day, when I was passing the dressing room, I saw her undressing inside. She liked to do that, you know: leave the door open and wander around in her underclothes, so that any men who were walking past might see her. She called me in and asked me help unzip her dress. I knew she was just playing with me—it was like a game for her, to see how much she could tease you—well, anyway, when she took her dress off, I saw this tattoo on her inner thigh. It was of a naked woman with legs that, like, merged into a fish's tail. Sort of like a mermaid... but not like any of the usual mermaid tattoos..." Albert's eyes took on a faraway look. "And suddenly I remembered seeing that tattoo before. I was really little—about five years old, I think—and my Dad had taken me to the park for the afternoon while Mum was baking at home. And this pretty lady met us there... I remembered that Dad was kissing and cuddling her a lot and I felt very confused, because I thought he should be kissing and cuddling Mum... And the pretty lady was wearing really short shorts and I remembered seeing the tattoo on her inner thigh. When I asked her what it was, she laughed and told me it was a 'siren'—a beautiful woman with magic powers who could make all men love her."

Albert's eyes cleared and he refocused suddenly back on me. "That's when I realised who Lara was. It was the same tattoo, in exactly the same place...

and I thought: how strange that we should both end up on the same talent show, so many years later. It must be Fate—it was meant to be! That's how I knew I had to kill her. This was my chance, you see—my chance to make her pay." He looked at me with a blank smile and said, as if discussing the weather, "Do you know my dad left us on Christmas Day? Mum was serving lunch and he just got up and left. I don't remember much from my childhood but I remember that day like it was yesterday."

I stared at him, at those empty eyes and smiling face, as his calm, pleasant voice recounted that heart-breaking story, and thought: *Oh my God, he's completely mad.*

"And then I realised that I had the perfect weapon," Albert continued, his face lighting up. "The liquid nitrogen! I'd brought it for my act without realising how easy it would be to kill someone with it. You see? Fate again. So I planned it for the night of the Semi-Finals performances. I knew things would be chaotic backstage and nobody would notice anything much. And besides, I would be on stage so I'd have the perfect alibi..." He paused and frowned. "I didn't plan for her body to be discovered so soon. You were unexpected. But anyway, it didn't matter in the end. Although, of course, now you know too much so that's why I have to kill you too."

My heart gave a jolt at his calm words and matter-of-fact manner. It was actually scarier than if he had been snarling and violent. He was looking at me like a fishmonger eyeing a trout, trying to decide which section to fillet first.

"Uh... d-did you really hear voices here or did you make that up?" I babbled, just to keep him talking.

He laughed again. "Oh, I made that all up. I knew you probably wouldn't come down here otherwise and I needed to get you alone. See, I'd been wondering how to kill you ever since I heard you talking to the police officer on the coach. I knew I had to silence you before you started putting too many things together. Then you just walked right up to me and gave me the perfect opportunity! It's Fate again, see? It's meant to be."

Oh no, it bloody well isn't, I thought grimly. And I lunged to the side to try and get around him.

But he was ready for me. His hands snaked out and grabbed me, then shoved me hard. I screamed as I reeled backwards, my feet slipping on the edge of the pier.

And then I was falling...

I smacked into the black water and plunged into the icy depths.

CHAPTER TWENTY-SIX

It was cold... so cold...

And there was icy water in my mouth... in my nose... in my eyes...

I thrashed—kicking, clawing, flailing—as I struggled my way back to the surface...

I burst out of the water, coughing and gasping for a breath.

The icy water sloshed around me. I was so cold I was shaking violently, my teeth chattering like a rattle. I knew I had to get out of the water—at this temperature, hypothermia could set in in minutes, and then I would sink and drown.

I kicked weakly, treading water, as I looked around me: I had fallen into the narrow channel between the yacht and the pier. I reached out for something to pull myself out of the water. My hands met the smooth hull of the yacht on one side, my fingers slipping uselessly against the sleek metal. I turned and groped desperately on the other side, hoping to find a handhold on the side of the pier. But before I could reach it, something came down on me, shoving me back underwater.

It was a hand. Two hands. It was Albert bending over the side of the pier, his face determined as he held me cruelly down. In spite of his weedy physique, there was frightening strength in his arms. I choked and spluttered as water surged once more over my head. Panic gave me strength and I fought, wriggling and flailing wildly. I managed to pull free for a moment to burst once more out of the water.

"N-n-no-o-o....!" I screamed. "Sto...stop! H-help! H-h-hel... h-help... m-me!"

But my voice was drowned out by gurgling and choking as Albert grabbed me once more and pushed me underwater. Icy water rushed into my nose and mouth. I gulped and choked as it churned and foamed around me. I tried to fight back, but I was already beginning to weaken. My limbs felt like lead. It was a struggle even moving them in the heavy water.

Then I felt the pressure on my head ease slightly and I drew on the last of my strength to claw my way back up and burst out of the water once more. Above me, Albert had turned to look over his shoulder, distracted, and then my heart leapt as I heard the sound of barking, followed by Trish's voice.

"Hey! What's going on he—*Gemma!* Oh my God, what are you doing to her?"

There was more barking... the stampede of running feet on the wooden pier... an exclamation bitten off... and then the sounds of a tussle.

I looked up to see Trish struggling with Albert while the collie circled around them, barking frantically.

"Albert! What... what the hell is wrong with you?" demanded Trish as she grappled with him.

"It's no use fighting—you're not going to win," said Albert, still in that eerily calm voice even though he was panting with effort. "I've got Fate on my side... Everything will work out because it's meant to be... I can drown you too and nobody will know—"

"*What?*" Trish stared at him incredulously but had no chance to say more as Albert's hand suddenly went for her throat.

They reeled on the pier above me, grunting and cursing, then to my horror, Albert aimed a vicious kick at Trish's shins which caused her to double over in pain. He took advantage of that to give her a hard shove, sending her staggering over the edge of the pier and down into the water next to me.

SPLASH!

The impact caused water to surge over me once more and I fought feebly to stay afloat. The last of my strength was almost gone. I could feel myself sinking deeper into the cold water, but somehow I didn't care anymore. Everything was beginning to feel pleasantly numb... in fact, I could no longer feel the cold—instead, I felt weak and drowsy... *It would be so easy to just close my eyes for a second...* I thought, *I'm so tired...*

The sound of frantic barking roused me again and I opened my eyes with an effort. Skip was running up and down the pier, whining and barking and looking into the water. *Trish!* I thought suddenly. The black water beside me was empty. *Oh my God—where is she?*

Then I remembered that unlike me, Trish had been wearing her overcoat. It might have kept her warm on land but, once in the water, the heavy sodden fabric would have dragged her down like a lead weight.

"Tr-Trish?" I choked, peering desperately at the surface of the water, hoping for a sign of life.

Above me, Albert was leaning over the edge of the pier, peering as well. He smiled in satisfaction as the surface of the water remained unbroken. Then he turned towards me, his face determined once more.

"N-no... no..." I gasped, kicking weakly to try and move away from the edge of the pier.

He bent down farther and stretched for me. "It's no use," he said, almost kindly. "You can't get away."

Then something exploded out of the water next to us. It was Trish, looking like a creature from the Greek myths, her wet hair streaming from her head, her eyes wild, and her teeth bared as she surged upwards and grabbed Albert around the neck, yanking him down into the water with her.

He gave a cry of alarm and scrabbled frantically, trying to pull himself back. But he had been bending too far forwards as he stretched for me, and now his weight tipped him over. I heard a *thunk* and a sickening crunch as his head hit the side of the yacht, then he pitched forwards and fell into the water.

Another *splash*. Another swell which threatened to submerge me. I gasped and choked again, more out of reflex than anything else, since I no longer had the strength to even paddle weakly. I felt the water come up to my chin... then my mouth... my nose...

"GEMMA!"

Strong hands grabbed me and hauled me back up to the surface. I coughed and spluttered again. Trish was next to me, looking more like her old self now and less like some predatory nymph from the deep. She was holding me up with one hand and treading water with the other, kicking strongly to keep both of us afloat.

"Gemma—you've got to stay awake. Do you hear me?" She gave me a shake, splashing water in my face. "Come on, kick! Keep kicking!"

It was a commanding voice. A dog trainer's voice. And ridiculous as it seemed, I felt myself responding, reaching for the last ounce of strength to follow her instructions. As I began to kick feebly, Trish turned her attention to the pier where Skip stood, looking down at us.

"Skip—go fetch! Fetch the rope! Good boy—go fetch!" She pointed at a thick bundle of rope that lay coiled at the end of the pier.

The collie cocked his head and looked at her quizzically for a moment, then he wagged his tail and trotted over to the rope. It was thick and heavy, but he got it between his teeth and dragged the end towards us.

"Good boy! Bring it here..." Trish held a hand out.

A minute later, she had the end of the rope in her hands. She turned to me and said urgently:

"Listen, Gemma, I'll have to let go of you because I need both hands to pull myself up. It'll just be for a minute and as soon as I'm up, I'll pull you out. But you need to keep yourself afloat, d'you hear me? You have to keep swimming!"

I nodded weakly and moved my arms and legs through the water. It was less a dog paddle and more a drowning rat crawl now, but at least it was keeping me at the surface. Trish coiled the rope around her wrists a few times, before gripping it strongly with both hands, then she turned to Skip, still waiting on the pier above us, and called:

"Tug, Skip! Good boy, tug!"

The collie grabbed the other end of the rope and began to pull, growling as he backed away from the edge of the pier. Trish braced her body against the side of the pier and hauled herself out of the water, shouting commands and encouragement to her dog the whole time. A minute later, she crawled, panting and dripping, over the edge of the pier and stood up shakily. Skip pranced joyously around her, jumping up and wagging his tail madly. She gave him a pat, then quickly turned and bent down, holding her hand out to me.

"Grab my hand, Gemma!"

I stretched up, but my fingers could barely touch the tips of hers, and I didn't have the strength to surge out of the water. Trish lay down on her stomach and tried again. This time, she caught hold of my hand and I clung on for dear life as she pulled me slowly out of the water. My arms felt as if they were being wrenched from their sockets but I gritted my teeth and held on.

Inch by inch, I was hauled, dripping, out of the icy water, until finally I lay gasping and shivering on the edge of the pier. The wooden planks of the walkway pressed into my cheek and I'd never been so glad to feel a hard surface against my skin. Then I felt Trish draping something soft and warm on me. It was an old rug that she had unearthed from a corner of the boathouse, rough and dusty, but at that moment, more glorious than any fur coat as I shivered and clutched it to me.

"Th-th-thank y-you," I said, my teeth still chattering.

Trish slumped down next to me, wrapped in a similar rug, and gave me a weary smile as she patted Skip, who was trying to climb into her lap.

"Al-Albert? Is... is he...?" I looked fearfully towards the water.

"He didn't come back up."

"D-do you th-think we should try t-to—"

"Well, I'm not going back in," said Trish shortly. "So unless you want to dive back in the freezing water—for God's sake, Gemma, the man was trying to kill you! Why do you even care?" She looked at me quizzically. "Anyway, why was he going for you?"

"H-h-he wanted to silence m-me because I knew t-too m-much. H-he was the one who m-murdered Lara."

Trish's eyes widened. "Really? But why?"

I sighed. "It's a long story. I suppose you c-could say it was revenge... or m-m-madness..." Then I looked at her in admiration. "Oh my God, Trish—I thought he was going to kill us both! I d-don't know how you did it... the way you fought him... and... and the way you ambushed him from the water... th-that was incredible!"

She shrugged. "I knew he was expecting me to come up so I just held my breath and stayed under for longer."

"But wasn't it cold? Weren't you p-panicking? I

283

couldn't even think straight when I fell in—it was such a sh-shock. I was just terrified and thrashing around."

She shrugged again. "I don't know. I wasn't thinking about all that—I was just thinking about beating him." She looked up at me, her expression guileless. "He said I wasn't going to win... I hate it when people say that."

CHAPTER TWENTY-SEVEN

"Are you the girl who found the body?"

Bloody hell. Not this again. I looked up wearily from the stack of menus I was holding and regarded the young couple standing in front of me. For a moment, I felt as if I had jumped back in time and the events of the past week had never happened. Then I reminded myself that Lara's murder had been solved, the talent show was over, and life was back to its normal routine.

Well, almost normal, I thought, looking at the couple again. The gossip and salacious curiosity hadn't died down yet, and I was still getting daily visitors to the tearoom who came more to gawp at me and ask nosy questions, than to sample the excellent baking.

Still, as long as they stay and order food and

drink, that's all that matters, I told myself. So I forced a smile to my face and said:

"Yes, I am. Now, would you like—"

"And the killer tried to drown you, didn't he?"

I gritted my teeth. "Yes, that's right... So, which table would you—"

"Were you naked?"

"I—*what?*"

"When he tried to drown you, were you naked?"

"No! No, of course I wasn't naked! Where on earth did you get that from?"

"See, I told you," the girl said to the boy. "Dave was lying."

"Look, are you going to have some tea or not?" I said, losing patience.

"Oh." They shifted uncomfortably. "Um... actually, we've got to catch the bus back to Oxford. Sorry, another time!"

The tearoom door slammed after them, leaving me at the counter taking deep breaths and counting to ten. Cassie returned from serving a table and grinned as she saw my expression.

"Still enjoying your fifteen minutes of fame, huh?"

"If someone else asks me if I was the girl who found the body, there are going to be a lot more dead bodies!" I growled.

Before Cassie could reply, the door opened again, but this time I was pleased to see a serious-looking young man with thick-rimmed glasses and a shy smile enter the tearoom.

"Seth!" I said, smiling. "This is a nice surprise."

He returned my smile. "I had a morning free so I thought I'd make a trip out to my favourite tearoom in the Cotswolds. Also, I've got extra tickets to the new production at the Oxford Playhouse. It's for next Saturday... I was wondering if you two would like to go?" he said, his gaze going hopefully to Cassie.

"Oh, shame—I'd have loved to, Seth, but I've already promised my mum that I'd go to Bath with her," said Cassie.

He deflated visibly but tried to keep the smile on his face as he turned to me. "Gemma?"

"I'm going to have to say no too, Seth," I said apologetically. "Devlin and I have got dinner plans. With this latest case wrapped up, I need to grab the chance before he gets sucked into a new one!"

"Oh." Seth looked crestfallen. "Well, I suppose I could ask the other tutors at the college..."

"I'll tell you what," said Cassie. "I'm sure Barb would like to see the play. Why don't you ask her?"

"Barb?" Seth looked confused.

"She's the receptionist at the dance studio where I teach part-time. Pretty blonde girl; very bubbly and easy to talk to. I'm sure you'd like her, Seth. You can't just hang out with boring old me and Gemma all the time, you know—you need to go out on real dates," said Cassie with a grin.

Seth looked pained and I knew he was chagrined

287

that Cassie obviously didn't consider herself a candidate for a "real date".

"Er... th-that's okay," he said hurriedly. "I've got a couple of research students at the lab who said they'd be interested, if nobody else wanted the tickets. Um... so—is everything wrapped up on the case, Gemma?" He turned to me, obviously keen to change the subject.

"Yes, pretty much. I mean, there will be a trial, of course, but since Albert is dead—"

"Oh, did they find his body?"

"Yeah, they dredged the bottom of the lake underneath the boathouse." I sighed. "The whole thing is so tragic, really. I mean, I know he was a murderer—and he was planning to kill me and Trish too—but still, I can't help feeling sorry for Albert."

"Yeah, you could almost say that it was Lara's fault," said Cassie. "If she hadn't seduced his father and messed up his family, and if Albert had grown up in a stable home instead—"

"You can't excuse his actions like that," protested Seth. "Lots of people grow up in abusive homes or come from very poor, disadvantaged backgrounds, but they don't resort to murder. It's just a line you shouldn't cross, no matter how provoked you are."

"You're beginning to sound like Devlin," I said with a laugh. "According to him, murder is *never* justified, whatever the reason."

"Oh, rubbish!" said Cassie. "Devlin has to think that 'cos he's a copper, but what if a mother saw someone attacking her child and killed him? That would be justified, wouldn't it?"

"Ah, but we're not talking about that kind of murder. This is pre-meditated murder," said Seth. "Albert planned it all in cold blood."

"Yeah, actually, I still don't get that part," said Cassie. "How did he do it? If he was on stage and in full view of the audience the whole time, how could he have murdered Lara as well?"

"But he wasn't," I said. "That was the key and we all missed it, because we all fell for the illusion."

"Yes, it was his disappearing trick," Seth explained. "When he sat on the chair and covered himself with the sheet, he wasn't sitting there the whole time. The chair had a false bottom and he simply slipped out from underneath the sheet and then crawled, stomach on the floor, to the other side of the stage where he stood up and magically 'reappeared'. That's why he needed the liquid nitrogen: because it provided such a thick fog across the floor of the stage, it shielded him from sight. The stage was lit at the front, so anything moving in the shadows at the back, under the cover of the fog, would be almost impossible to see—especially if he was wearing black all over.

"But... but I watched that trick myself that night," said Cassie. "He's still there, under the sheet. You can see the shape of his head the whole time."

"That wasn't his head," said Seth, chuckling. "It's a little dome which is attached to the back of the chair. Normally it's flipped back, out of sight, but when Albert covered himself with the sheet, he also flipped the dome up and forwards, so that it propped up the sheet with a rounded shape, in the position where his head would have been. Then later when he reappears and walks back to the chair, he just makes sure that he pulls back the sheet in such a way that it flips the dome backwards, out of sight, over the back of the chair again."

"So... you mean, he was actually out of sight for several minutes?"

"Yes, and on the night of Lara's murder, instead of crawling across the stage, he crawled into the wings instead, where Lara was waiting for him."

"He had lured her there by sending her a note, promising to tell her the secret to winning the contest," I chimed in. "And she wouldn't have been expecting anyone to come from the direction of the stage—she probably thought somebody would come from the Waiting Area or other parts of backstage—"

"So she was facing the wrong way," Cassie guessed.

"Yes, Albert took her by surprise," said Seth. "Then he intended to crawl back on stage under the cover of the fog, and finish his act. But before he had a chance to 'reappear', Gemma came on the scene and discovered Lara's body."

"I must have just missed him," I said with a slight shudder.

"Hang on—Albert would have barely had a few minutes in between sitting in the chair and reappearing. How did he think he could murder Lara in that time?" said Cassie.

I shrugged. "It *was* a bit crazy but I don't think he was thinking logically. In fact, I think he believed that he had some kind of divine protection—you know, like it was Fate or meant to be. Because it was such a crazy coincidence in the first place that he and Lara should have ended up on the same talent show." I gave her a wry look. "And maybe he was right, you know? I mean, it was amazing that he managed to pull it off in such a short time. It shouldn't have been possible but the fact that he did it..."

"Karma," said Cassie, nodding cynically.

The door to the kitchen swung open and Dora stuck her head out. "Gemma! Come quick—you're on TV!"

"Oh no..." I groaned as I hurried into the kitchen, with Cassie and Seth at my heels.

Dora beckoned us over to the little TV screen that had been set up for her in one corner of the kitchen. As I walked over, I noticed that Muesli was curled up asleep on one of the kitchen chairs—little minx, she had sneaked in again!—and I was about to pick her up and chuck her outside when I was distracted by what was on the TV screen. It was a breakfast show and the presenters were discussing *From Pleb to Celeb* and Lara's murder.

"...because this murder has really gripped the nation, hasn't it, Rick?" the woman was saying.

"Ooh, yes, Julie! I know I've been glued to the news—it's really been like watching a real-life murder mystery play out before your eyes."

"And with such an exciting ending too!" said Julie. *"For those of you who've missed it, here is Gemma Rose again, the woman who unmasked the killer—and who nearly lost her life in the process—talking about her experience."*

The show cut to a clip from the recent news, in which I was being interviewed by a reporter from one of the major networks. I cringed as my own face filled the screen. I couldn't understand why so many people wanted a career in showbiz—I couldn't think of anything more embarrassing than seeing yourself on screen and hearing the sound of your own voice. *Ugh.*

"...tell us how you felt—were you terrified?" the reporter was asking.

On the screen, I answered in a stilted voice: *"Er... yes, of course."*

"Did you think you were going to die?"

"Well, I... I wasn't really thinking... I was just

reacting... I mean, you don't really have time to think when you're in the water... you're just trying to stay afloat... and... and not drown..."

Cassie guffawed. "Oh, very eloquent, Gemma. The next time someone is fighting for their life in the water, I must tell them your Tips for Survival: just try to stay afloat and not drown."

"Shut up," I said, giving her a playful shove.

Thankfully, the screen had reverted to the breakfast show and the two presenters smiled brightly at the camera.

"That was Gemma Rose talking about her near-death experience," said Julie.

"But luckily for her, someone heard her screaming... and with us in the studio today, we have the lady who came to the rescue!" Rick turned and looked as a thin woman with pale blue eyes strode through the doorway on the side of the set, accompanied by a collie.

"Oh my God, it's Trish!" said Cassie.

The dog walker sat down on the sofa, with Skip lying down obediently by her feet, and looked expectantly at the two presenters.

"So, Trish, it seems like you—and your lovely dog—are the heroes of the hour! How did you feel when you heard Gemma screaming?"

"I didn't actually hear her screaming at first—I was too far away. It was Skip. He started acting strangely; he kept whining and trying to get me to follow him."

"Ah, they say that animals have a sixth sense, don't they?" said Rick with fake wisdom. "I suppose he must have sensed that your friend was in danger."

"She's not really my friend. We just met on the show."

"Oh... er... right." Rick looked a bit nonplussed. "So when you went in the boathouse and saw Albert Hodge attacking Gemma, what made you react the way you did? I mean, you rushed straight over to help without thinking of your own safety. Weren't you afraid?"

"No. Why? Wouldn't you have done the same?"

Rick flushed. "Er... well..."

"But he pushed you in the water too," Julie hurried to step in. "You could have drowned as well. It was very brave of you to risk your life like that."

Trish shrugged. "I suppose."

"And the way that you pretended to sink and then ambushed Hodge from the water—that was a very clever move," said Rick, smiling ingratiatingly. "Really, it's quite remarkable when you think about it. The water was freezing, you were trapped, there was a man trying to kill you—most people would have given up in that situation! But you had the presence of mind to come up with a ploy to outwit *him. How did you do it?"*

Trish looked at him unsmilingly. "I just wanted to win."

I laughed and shook my head. "You know, Cassie, I never thought I'd say this but I'm *really* glad that Trish is so bloody competitive!"

CHAPTER TWENTY-EIGHT

I spent the rest of the day fending off more ghoulish curiosity, and by mid-afternoon I was exhausted and more than ready to go home. But there was still the teatime rush to get through. Four o'clock was mayhem at the Little Stables, and Cassie and I whizzed around the dining room, showing customers to their tables, taking orders, and serving tea, cakes, and sandwiches as fast as we could.

The Old Biddies normally came in to help during busy times, but recently they had been noticeably absent and I wondered if they were upset with me for exposing their friend. It had been an awkward moment when I'd had to tell them about the itching powder I'd found in June Driscoll's handbag, and even worse when the police and show producers had been informed, and the "Herb Girls" officially disqualified from the competition. I hadn't seen June since and I'd seen very little of the Old Biddies.

As the afternoon rush hour ended and I was wondering whether I should give them a call, the tearoom door opened and four familiar old ladies trotted in.

"Mabel!" I said with far more warmth than usual. "Glenda! Ethel! Florence! How nice to see you. How have you been?"

"We're fine, dear—we've just been very busy," said Florence.

Ethel nodded. "The flowers for Sunday service went missing from the church, you see, and the vicar was in such a flap!"

"Of course, *I* knew exactly who had stolen them," said Mabel loftily. "That chap who came to fix the broken window in the side of the nave—I thought he looked very shifty... very shifty indeed!"

"I thought he looked rather handsome, actually," said Glenda with a dreamy sigh. "That oiled hair and thin moustache... rather like Clark Gable, didn't you think? Ohhh... if I was fifty years younger—"

"Nonsense! He had 'criminal' written all over him," said Mabel.

"Well, as it turned out, the flowers weren't actually stolen—the vicar had put them in the vestry to stay cool and he'd completely forgotten," said Florence.

"He's getting dreadfully forgetful, isn't he?" said Ethel. "Last month, he gave the same sermon three times."

"More fibre in the diet, that's what he needs," declared Mabel. "I'll have to have a word with his wife."

Glenda looked around the tearoom. "I'm sorry we haven't been in to lend a hand, Gemma, dear. What with helping the vicar find his missing flowers and then helping June get ready to meet her new sponsor for Bill's group—"

"She's got a sponsor?" My ears perked up.

"Oooh, yes, haven't we told you? A wealthy American widow, who was watching the show, was so moved when she heard June tell the judges why we entered the contest, that she decided to donate a large sum of money to help promote B.E.A.S.T.! Her late husband had bushy eyebrows too, you see. She's coming over to London next week on a shopping trip and June is going to meet her—isn't that exciting?"

"Oh! I'm really glad," I said with a smile of relief. "I'd been feeling bad that I'd ruined her chances—"

"Well, she ruined her own chances really," said Mabel severely. "It was reprehensible, what she did to that poor boy, and she's very ashamed of herself. She's been to see Gaz personally to apologise, you know."

"He told her that he forgave her completely and

not to worry about it anymore," said Florence.

"That was extremely nice of him," I said in surprise. "Considering that she spoiled *his* chances in the competition—"

"Oh, but she hasn't!" said Ethel excitedly. "I mean, it's true that he didn't win the competition—"

"Everyone knew that the twins were going to win," said Mabel, waving a hand.

"—but after the show finished, a production company contacted Gaz and said that they'd like to feature him as a regular on one of their comedy shows. If all goes well, he might even get his own show someday!"

"Oh, good for him. He really was very talented..." I broke off as a family got up from their table and came over to the counter to pay.

"That was delicious," said the mother. "Noah is usually such a fussy eater but he finished everything on his plate!"

I smiled as I glanced down at the little boy beside her. His face was covered in jam and cream, and he had crumbs all down his top.

"I'm glad he enjoyed it," I said, handing her the bill.

"Oh, sorry... I don't have anything smaller," said the woman as she held out several large notes.

"Hmm..." I looked at the cash in the till: most of the smaller notes had been used up already.

"We might have some change, Gemma," said Mabel, starting to open her handbag, and the other

Old Biddies followed suit.

"No, hang on—I have some smaller notes in my purse." Pulling my handbag out from beneath the counter, I rummaged inside, extracted my purse, and found the necessary change. "Here you go."

"Thank you. And we'll definitely be back," said the woman with a wide smile. "We'll be telling our friends all about your wonderful tearoom too! Oh, before we go—could Noah stroke your cat?" She indicated Muesli who, for once, was being good and not trying to sneak into the kitchen. She was sitting on a cushion we'd placed for her at one end of the counter, quietly surveying the room.

"Oh, of course." I picked Muesli up and placed her on the floor next to the toddler.

"*Meorrw?*" she said.

The boy giggled and put a pudgy hand out to Muesli, who sniffed it curiously. Noah squealed in delight.

"Her name's Muesli," I said.

"Moosly!" said the little boy. "Moosly! Moosly!"

The little tabby cat eyed him in bewilderment, then looked at me. "*Meorrw?*"

The mother laughed, then caught hold of her son's hand. "Come on, Noah—we'd better go. Say thank you to the lady and goodbye to Muesli."

"Bye-bye! Bye-bye Moosly!"

The door had barely closed behind the family when it swung open again and my mother sailed in, resplendent in a cashmere silk dress and camel coat with matching gloves.

"Darling! Guess what? I'm going to be a judge again!"

I frowned. "A judge for what?"

"For Monty Gibbs's new show, darling."

I groaned. "He's got a new show already?"

"Yes, it was Grace who thought of it, actually—Grace Lamont, you know, from *Society Madam* magazine. I introduced them at the *FPTC* Finale after-show party and Grace suggested a splendid concept for a new contest. Monty will be one of the judges, of course, and he has asked me and Grace to be the other two judges on the panel. The production will begin next month."

"Oh, how exciting!" said Glenda, clasping her hands.

"It will be nice to enjoy watching the show this time, instead of being on it," said Florence.

"Perhaps one of the new contestants would like to use my lace doily earrings with their costume? We never got to wear them, you know," said Ethel, looking peeved.

"Is it another talent show?" I asked warily.

"Well, the contestants *will* be displaying various talents—but not singing or dancing or anything like that. No, they will be showing 'real' talents that are useful in the home," my mother declared. "The contest will be searching for *Britain's Best Housewife.*"

"What? That's a ludicrous idea for a show!" I

spluttered. "What are we—in the 1950s? No-one's going to enter—"

"On the contrary: Monty only announced the auditions yesterday and he's already been inundated with applications! And there are several networks who are vying to host the programme. There's been so much interest from the press too, and Monty says early polls show that people are fascinated by the idea."

"Fascinated?" I looked at her sceptically. "People want to see talented stars, not humdrum housewives. There's nothing glamorous about household chores."

"Oh, but you're wrong, darling. It's a great novelty. Anyone can sing or dance nowadays but how many people can change the sheets and make the bed in under two minutes?"

"I think it's a marvellous idea," said Mabel approvingly. "What this country needs is fewer ventriloquists and more people who can cook a good roast chicken."

"Yes, but—"

"*Meorrw!*" Muesli leapt up suddenly from the floor and onto the counter. She had obviously been feeling ignored at our feet and decided to join the conversation at face level. She padded across the counter towards my mother, climbing over my handbag in the process. The next moment, a horrendously loud buzzing filled the room.

"ZZZZZZZZZZZzzzzzzzzzzZZZZZZZZZzzzzzzzzz…!"

Every customer in the tearoom looked up from their tables, wide-eyed with astonishment. I froze and stared at my handbag, which was vibrating across the counter. Suddenly, I remembered the last time I'd been using that bag—the day I'd visited a certain discreet shop on Cowley Road...

"What on earth is that, darling?" asked my mother.

"Oh, that must be the Randy Rabbit," said Ethel brightly.

"The Randy what?" said my mother, looking puzzled.

"That's what the salesgirl called it. Gemma bought it from the sex—"

"Uh—yes! Never mind!" I yelped. "It's... it's nothing really, Mother." I grabbed my handbag and groped inside, desperately trying to find the switch to turn the vibrator off, while still keeping it out of sight in the bag.

"Well, it must be *something*—it's making the most incredible noise," said my mother.

"Er..." I looked wildly around. Every eye in the tearoom was still on me. "It's... um... it's an electric toothbrush! Yes, it's the new electric toothbrush I bought."

"Oh, really?" My mother looked excited. "Helen Green was just telling me that she's invested in a new electric toothbrush. She purchased the latest Braun model and she says it's marvellous—but yours sounds so much more powerful. What brand is it? Can I see—" She reached for my handbag.

"NO!" I snatched the bag out of her reach. "Er… no, Mother… you won't like it. I promise. It's… er… it's very poor quality. In fact, I'm thinking of taking it back for a refund." My fingers finally found the switch and the buzzing ceased. I sagged with relief as silence descended in the tearoom once more.

"Did that shop sell toothbrushes as well?" said Ethel, looking puzzled. "I thought—"

"So! Would you like to have some tea? Mother? Mabel? Glenda? Florence? Ethel? There are still some scones left and Dora made a delicious carrot cake today—"

"I'd love to, darling, but I really must dash. I'm meeting Helen at Debenhams for late-night shopping. The mid-season sale is on at the moment and apparently they have a new range of bamboo placemats. Shall I get you a set?"

"No, thanks, Mother, but you have a great time with Aunt Helen!"

I hustled her to the front door and waved her off. As I was about to turn and go back into the tearoom, however, I saw a sleek black Jaguar pull up at the curb. My heart skipped a beat as a handsome, dark-haired man with piercing blue eyes stepped out of the car.

"Devlin!" I said, breaking into a smile. "What are you doing here?"

He came up the path to the tearoom door and bent to give me a kiss. "Well, I finished work early and had a brainwave. I looked online and found a last-minute deal for a romantic weekend in the Cotswolds: two nights in a historic inn in Burford, luxurious room with four-poster bed and claw-foot bath, cosy open fire and gourmet dining..." He leaned towards me, his blue eyes twinkling. "And now I just need to find someone to enjoy all of that with."

I looked at him in delight. "Really? We're going away? When?"

He swept a hand towards his car. "Right now, Miss Rose. Go and grab your things, and we'll be on our way."

"Now? But the tearoom—"

"We can take care of the tearoom, dear."

I turned to see that the Old Biddies had come out of the tearoom as well and were hovering behind me.

"You go with your young man and enjoy yourself," said Mabel. "We can look after the tearoom with Cassie—don't you worry."

"Yes, you deserve to have some time off after working so hard recently," said Glenda.

"Make sure you eat well! You're getting too thin," said Florence, clucking her tongue.

"And don't forget the Randy Rabbit!" piped up Ethel.

"The Randy what?" said Devlin, puzzled.

"Never mind!" I said, my face red. Turning back to the Old Biddies, I said: "Er... well, thank you, that would be amazing. Oh! Wait, what about Muesli—"

"I'm sure Cassie can look after her for two nights," said Mabel, waving a hand. "She's done it before and Muesli loves staying with her."

Glenda had disappeared into the tearoom and she reappeared now with my coat and handbag, which she thrust at me. "Off you go, dear."

A few minutes later, I found myself in Devlin's car, still in a slight daze as we drove away from the tearoom. As we crossed the little bridge which led out of Meadowford, however, I sat upright and said:

"Wait—Devlin, I need to go home and pack some things. I haven't got any clothes for the weekend!"

He gave me a wicked grin. "I wouldn't worry—you won't be wearing much for most of the time."

I blushed and laughed. "No, I'm serious... I need to pack a few things. I have to have clean underwear. And I need my creams and things. I promise I'll be really quick."

He sighed and swung the car in the direction of Oxford, muttering, "Women..."

When we got to my cottage, I left Devlin waiting in the car outside while I ran in to pack an overnight bag. Grabbing things at random from my chest of drawers, I stuffed them into a small holdall, together with some toiletries. However, as I was lugging the bag down the stairs, I happened to glance at the dining table, where a package that had come in the mail yesterday was still sitting, waiting for me to open it. I paused and picked it up, staring at the logo of the online pet store, then—making an impulsive decision—I took the package out with me to the car.

"Did you say we're going to Burford?" I asked Devlin when I got in the car again.

"Yes, why?"

"Do you mind if we stop somewhere in the village, before we go to the inn? I'll be really quick," I said hurriedly as he rolled his eyes. "There's just something I need to do and if I don't, it'll be on my mind all weekend."

Forty minutes later, Devlin sat waiting with long-suffering patience in the car again as I walked down a lane lined on either side with charming Cotswolds-stone cottages. I wasn't sure of the number, only of the proximity to the village church, but I hoped that there would be a local "Old Biddy" to help me. And sure enough, I soon met a white-haired old lady who knew everyone in the village (and what they'd had for breakfast, lunch, and tea as well), who happily directed me to the correct cottage.

As I approached the door, a grey tabby cat emerged from the shadows and strolled down the path to greet me, and I smiled as I bent to pat Muesli's lookalike.

"*Miaow!*"

"Hello, Misty... I hope your owner is home?"

As if in answer to my question, the front door to

the cottage opened and a woman stuck her head out, calling:

"Mis-ty! Mis—*oh!*" She stopped as she saw me.

I straightened and gave her a tentative smile.

"Hi Cheryl..." I took a deep breath, then said in a rush: "Um... I just wanted to apologise again... about the... I should have asked you directly, instead of going behind your back... It was wrong of me to accuse you like that..." I fumbled with the package in my hands and thrust it at her. "Um... anyway... I just wanted to say I'm sorry, again.... And also to give you this. I saw it online and... er... I thought you might find it useful for Misty."

She took the package from me and slowly unwrapped it, then stared at the picture on the box.

"It's a GPS cat-tracking collar," I explained. "It links to an app on your phone, so you'll be able to track where Misty is wherever she goes."

Cheryl looked up, her expression surprised and touched. "Thank you. It's... it's really thoughtful of you." She hesitated, then said: "I really appreciate you coming out to see me. And you don't need to apologise—I've been thinking about things and I can see why you might have suspected me. I shouldn't have lost my temper like that. I suppose I was hurt, more than anything else. I thought we were friends—"

"We are," I said quickly. "I mean, we can still be friends... if you like?"

She smiled. "I'd like that very much."

EPILOGUE

The following Monday morning, happy and relaxed after a lovely weekend with Devlin, I felt much more ready to face my appointment with Grace Lamont. I had actually thought, after my insolent comments at lunch the other day, that the magazine editor would no longer want to feature me in her publication, so I'd been surprised when I received a text from her secretary on Sunday evening reminding me of the appointment. I'd almost been tempted to cancel—that lunch with her had left a sour taste in my mouth—but I decided that it would be silly to let my personal feelings interfere with good promotion for my business. The *Society Madam* magazine was widely read and could generate the kind of PR that would help make my tearoom a household name. *Well, at least in certain upper-middle-class households,* I thought with a wry smile.

The magazine headquarters were housed in the upper levels of a beautiful Neo-Jacobean building overlooking the High Street in central Oxford. I parked my bike, chained it to a nearby railing, and climbed the stairs to the second storey. Stepping into the editorial office was like stepping back in time, with chintz-covered sofas and lace curtains dominating the reception room. A girl was at the computer behind the desk, sitting so straight and erect that I wondered if a steel rod had been surgically grafted to her spine. She glanced up as I entered and said, in a well-modulated voice:

"May I help you?"

"Yes, I've got an appointment with Ms Lamont at ten o'clock."

"Ah yes... you must be Miss Rose. Please have a seat and I'll let Ms Lamont know that you're here." She rose gracefully and sashayed down the corridor, returning a few minutes later with the formidable editor of *Society Madam* herself.

Grace Lamont was dressed in pearls and twinset today, with her steely-grey hair pulled back in an elegant chignon and a pair of silver-wired spectacles perched on her nose. "Ah, Gemma... good to find someone of the younger generation who takes punctuality seriously. Now, tea or coffee?"

"Tea would be great, thanks."

A few minutes later, I found myself perched

nervously on the edge of a chair in her office, trying to emulate the receptionist's rigid posture while also balancing a porcelain cup and saucer on my knee. I was also desperately trying to remember the etiquette with regards to holding a teacup. Should you curl your little finger as you sipped your tea? Or was that very bad form? I never even thought about such things normally but being in Grace Lamont's presence was enough to make you paranoid about every move and gesture.

I lifted the cup, twitched my little finger out experimentally, then hastily tucked it back in as I caught Grace frowning at me. To cover up for my *faux pas*, I said at random:

"Um... this is lovely tea."

"Lapsang Souchong," said Grace. "I'm surprised you don't recognise the unique smoky flavour."

"Oh... er... yes, I did. I just meant that this is a particularly nice blend."

"Hmm..." Grace lowered her cup and eyed me speculatively. I tried not to squirm under her gaze. She picked up her handbag and placed it on her desk, then fished a fountain pen out of its depths and held it poised over an open notebook.

"Now, your mother tells me that you were originally working in a corporate job in the Antipodes?"

"Yes, in Sydney. I'd been out there for eight years—straight after graduating from Oxford, actually."

"And what made you decide to return to England?"

"Well, I suppose I was feeling homesick... and I'd always had a dream of opening a quaint little tearoom."

"And how long have you been in business now?"

"Just over a year. But we've grown heaps in that time," I added proudly. "We've even recently been mentioned in some guidebooks as a 'must-visit' attraction for the Oxford area."

Grace Lamont didn't look impressed. "What makes your tearoom different from the many others in the Cotswolds?"

"Oh... er... well, I suppose we try very hard to provide a genuinely traditional English tea experience. All our tea is served in fine bone china, our cakes and buns are made by hand, according to authentic local recipes, and we only serve British baking. Even our finger sandwiches only contain traditional fillings, such as cucumber and butter, and egg and cress—and our smoked salmon finger sandwiches are always served open-faced, with dill and crème fraîche on pumpernickel bread, just like in the old-fashioned recipe."

"Hmm..." said Grace again, carefully writing in her notebook in what looked like copperplate calligraphy. Finally, she looked up and said: "I am pleased that someone of your generation is taking an interest in our classic British traditions and, in the face of culinary invasions from Europe and even the Far East, attempting to foster continued appreciation of our national cuisine. I had hoped to write an article to that effect, featuring your tearoom as a leader in this important campaign. However, simply providing food and drink is not enough—the correct methods of serving and presentation are also of vital importance. It is the essence of what it means to be British." She leaned forwards and regarded me sternly. "I am concerned that you might not be completely *au fait* with the correct etiquette for afternoon tea, Miss Rose. For instance, I noticed that you stirred your tea clockwise just now."

I looked guiltily down at my teacup. "Oh... um... was I supposed to stir it anti-clockwise?"

"Certainly not!" snapped Grace. "Correct etiquette dictates that tea should only be stirred in a back-and-forth motion, from the twelve-o'clock to the six o'clock position. Similarly, I hope you never pour milk into the cup before the tea. It is tea first. Always." She rose and came around to the front of her desk, leaning on it and crossing her arms as she looked down at me. "I presume you are aware of the correct manner of serving tea in a group?"

"Er..." *Bloody hell. This is worse than being back at college, bring grilled for an exam!* I hazarded a wild guess. "Um... you serve the person next to you first?"

"Only if they are the most senior person in the room. Tea should always be served in order of seniority and status. And I hope you *never* lay the empty teacups out in rows and pour into them in bulk?" she added, glowering at me.

"Oh... um... never," I said, having no idea what she was talking about.

She nodded. "Good. Tea should always be served individually, with each cup filled and handed out one at a time. It might save time to fill them all at once but that is the lazy way... not the British way."

"Er... right... Of course."

"Now, scones..." Grace gestured to the platter heaped high with golden-brown scones, which had been placed at the front of her desk, within easy reach of both of us. I had taken one, as directed, but hadn't dared eat it yet, and now I was glad that I'd waited as I watched Grace expertly twist her scone so that it broke into two halves and then apply a precise dab of jam and clotted cream to each surface. I watched in awe as she lifted the plate and brought one of the halves to her mouth, delicately taking a bite without spilling a single crumb.

Taking a deep breath, I tried to follow suit, but my scone refused to cooperate. It crumbled into several pieces at the first touch and sagged under the weight of the huge dollop of jam I'd hastily heaped on top. Grace frowned as she eyed the mountain of cream and jam wobbling on my scone and made a clucking sound as I leaned down to cram the piece into my mouth.

"Ladies do not lean down to eat their food. You bring the portion to your mouth, not the other way around," she said, compressing her lips into a thin line.

Hastily, I straightened up again, losing hold of the scone in the process so that it fell with a *splat* onto my plate, sending bright-red jam in every direction.

Bugger! Bugger! Bugger!

I looked furtively at Grace and was relieved to see that she had been too busy walking back around her desk to see my mishap. As she pulled her handbag towards her and began rummaging inside, I dabbed my napkin on the spilled jam as surreptitiously as I could. Thankfully, I was wearing a patterned sweater in a mix of autumnal colours and the red smears on my clothes blended easily out of sight.

Grace extracted her leather-bound diary from the bag and looked at me. "Now... I wonder if you have any professional photographs of your tearoom that we might use with the article? If not, I can send my photographer over to you. In fact, that might be the best plan as I will need a portrait shot of you as well."

She eyed me critically over the tops of her spectacles. "I must insist, however, that you wear a dress on the day of the shoot, as well as stockings and high heels, please. No bare legs. And *definitely* no jeans." She shuddered. "The readers of *Society*

Madam are accustomed to certain standards and we cannot have our featured personalities letting the side down." She flipped through the pages of her diary. "The article will be in next month's issue and we will need the photographs ideally by next week. Which day would suit?"

I was really beginning to regret agreeing to this interview. This photo-shoot she was proposing sounded tortuous. I wondered if there was any way I could back out now. To stall for time, I lifted my teacup and pretended to take a long sip.

"Miss Rose?"

I started to swallow and reply, then froze and stared as a tiny furry face with beady black eyes popped out suddenly from the top of Grace Lamont's handbag.

It was the mouse!

I gasped and choked, spilling tea out of my cup and dribbling it down my chin.

"Miss Rose!" Grace looked at me in horror.

"Sorry, sorry..." I gulped, grabbing the linen napkin from my lap to wipe my chin. "It was... um... hot," I said lamely.

"One never slurps, no matter how hot the contents of the cup, and one certainly never spills tea in such an uncouth manner!" said Grace, bristling with outrage. She came back round to the front of the desk and leaned on it, crossing her arms like a schoolmistress while she regarded me with a disdainful gaze. "Mishaps do happen, of course, but even when they do, it is important to react with grace and poise. A simple apology or request to excuse yourself is..."

I nodded, barely listening as her voice went over my head. My eyes were glued to the mouse, which had climbed out of Grace's handbag, on the desk behind her back. It was now perched precariously on one of the gold buckles around the handles. So this is where it had disappeared to! No wonder Cassie and I couldn't find it in our potted palm at the tearoom—I remembered the way Grace had bumped into the palm and how her handbag had become entangled in its long fronds. The mouse must have grabbed the chance to dive into her bag and hide there, hitching a ride out of my tearoom (and away from Muesli's claws!).

I smiled to myself, reluctantly admiring the little creature's resourcefulness. But how on earth had it survived all this time in her handbag? It had been over a week since Grace had come to the tearoom, and it looked remarkably plump and healthy. As I watched, I got a hint of an answer: the mouse sat poised on its hind legs, its tiny nose wriggling as it sniffed the air, then—almost faster than the eye could follow—it scurried down the side of the bag, jumped onto the desk, and darted to where Grace had set her empty plate down next to her bag. Its little paws came out and snatched a morsel of scone from the plate, then it dashed back to the safety of the bag, disappearing once more into its depths.

A moment later, the mouse popped up again with a self-satisfied expression on its little face and crumbs on its whiskers. I wanted to burst out laughing. So that's what the clever rodent had been doing—living a life of luxury in Grace Lamont's Chanel handbag and getting fat on cake and scones!

It sat up once more next to the bag handle and rubbed its paws over its face, then scurried down onto the desk again.

"Miss Rose?"

I realised that I had been watching the mouse, open-mouthed, for the last few minutes and hadn't heard a word of what Grace Lamont had been saying.

"I'm sorry... er, pardon? Do you mind repeating that?" I said distractedly as I sneaked a glance at the desk again. The mouse had darted once more towards Grace's plate but halfway there, it had paused, its nose twitching. Then it turned and scampered towards the bigger platter of scones sitting at the centre of the desk. As I watched in horrified fascination, it ran over the large old-fashioned blotter, past the expensive Venetian-glass paperweight, and through the folds of a linen napkin before finally arriving at the platter holding the scones. Reaching up with its tiny paws, it yanked a raisin off a scone and held it to its mouth, nibbling enthusiastically.

"MISS ROSE—IS THERE A PROBLEM?"

I jumped. "Uh... no! No, problem! Sorry... please go on."

Grace glowered. "As I was saying: a lady is judged not only by her looks but by her manners and composure too. No matter how great the provocation, a lady should never react with undue emotion. She must always keep her voice low, her behaviour restrained, and she must *never* indulge in hysterics." She reached idly for her cup of tea on the desk. "Most of all, a lady should meet any adversity with graceful aplomb and never a— *aaaaiiiieeeeeeeeeee!*"

She jerked back from the table, staring in horror at the furry little creature hunched next to her teacup.

"*AAAAAAAAAGGGHHHH! MOUSE! MOUSE!*" Grace Lamont screeched, demonstrating the exact way a lady reacted with graceful aplomb by clutching her skirt and hopping from foot to foot, screaming: "*EEEEEEK! EEEEEEEEEK!*"

The door to her office was flung open and the receptionist rushed in, a look of alarm on her face.

"Ms Lamont? Is something the matt— *AAAAAAAAIIIIIIGGGHHH!! MOUSE! MOUSE!*"

I watched in disbelief as the two women ran around the room like headless chickens, shrieking and flapping their arms. Finally, taking pity on them, I picked up an empty teacup and, turning it upside down, clamped it over the mouse, which was still unconcernedly eating its raisin. Then I grabbed a piece of thick embossed paper from Grace's desk and slid it under the overturned cup. Carefully, I lifted the whole thing from the desk and flipped it over, then I raised the edge of the paper and peeked in.

The mouse was there, its long tail curled around its plump brown body as it sat up and looked around. It had little rounded ears, bright black eyes, and a tiny pink nose surrounded by delicate whiskers. I smiled. I didn't care what Dora said—it was adorable.

I placed a heavy book over the top of the teacup, then looked up. Grace and the receptionist were clutching each other, huddled in the corner, watching me with scared eyes.

"I'll just take it outside, shall I?" I asked with a smile.

They nodded wordlessly. Wisps of hair had escaped their perfect buns, and they were flushed and dishevelled. I had to resist the urge to make a sarcastic comment about "ladylike composure in the face of adversity".

Still, I couldn't help feeling vindicated and superior (okay, I'm only human), as I slung my bag over my shoulder, picked up the mouse-trapped teacup (with poise) and strolled (gracefully) out of the room.

FINIS

Don't miss Gemma's (and Muesli's) next
adventure in:

OXFORD TEAROOM MYSTERIES
~ BOOK 10

COMING SOON

Join my Readers' Club Newsletter to be
notified when it's released:
*(You will also get updates on exclusive giveaways
and other book news)*
http://www.hyhanna.com/newsletter

THE OXFORD TEAROOM MYSTERIES

A Scone To Die For (Book 1)

Tea with Milk and Murder (Book 2)

Two Down, Bun To Go (Book 3)

Till Death Do Us Tart (Book 4)

Muffins and Mourning Tea (Book 5)

Four Puddings and a Funeral (Book 6)

Another One Bites the Crust (Book 7)

Apple Strudel Alibi (Book 8)

The Dough Must Go On (Book 9)

All-Butter ShortDead (Prequel)

~ more coming soon!

**For other books by H.Y. Hanna,
please visit her website:
www.hyhanna.com**

GLOSSARY OF BRITISH TERMS

Bloody – very common adjective used as an intensifier for both positive and negative qualities (e.g. "bloody awful" and "bloody wonderful"), often used to express shock or disbelief ("Bloody Hell!")

Boffin – a person with specialist knowledge or skill, usually in science and technology, but often used in the sense of "a nerd"

Bollocks! – rubbish, nonsense, an exclamation expressing contempt

Bugger! – an exclamation of annoyance or dismay (also used to describe a person who is silly or annoying, or a person you feel sympathy for, depending on context)

Bum – the behind *(American: butt)*

Carpark – a place to park vehicles *(American: parking lot)*

Council estate housing – cheap housing provided by the government for those on low income

Clotted cream - a thick cream made by heating full-cream milk using steam or a water bath and then leaving it in shallow pans to cool slowly.

Typically eaten with scones and jam for "afternoon tea"

(to) Give a stuff – to care, usually used in the negative sense (eg. "I really couldn't give a stuff!" = I really don't care.)

Guv'nor - an informal term for one's boss or someone in a position of authority (particularly used in the police force to refer to a higher ranking officer); occasionally still used as a respectful term of address

(to) Have (someone) on – to deceive or fool someone, often in a teasing context (eg. "Are you having me on?" = "Are you kidding me?")

Hammered – very drunk

Hotchpotch – a confused mixture (*American: hodgepodge*)

Ice-lolly – sweet frozen treat (American: popsicle)

Knackered – very tired, exhausted

Let the side down – to fail to do your bit as part of a team, to disappoint your colleagues or team members

Loo – toilet; "loo bowl" = toilet bowl

(To not have a) Look-in – to not have a chance to do something or to succeed

MI6 – the British Secret Intelligence Service

Mingin' (minging) – derogatory slang term to describe something very unattractive or unpleasant

Natter – to gossip, have a friendly chat

Plonker – an idiot

Posh – high class, fancy

Queue – an orderly line of people waiting for something (*American: line*)

(to) Ring – to call (someone on the phone)

Row – an argument (pronounced to rhyme with "cow")

RSPCA - The Royal Society for the Prevention of Cruelty to Animals; the largest animal welfare charity in the UK

(to have a) Run-in (with something or someone) – an unpleasant encounter, usually referring to an argument

Shag – (v) to have sexual intercourse with or (n) the act; *shagging*

Stroppy – grumpy and irritable (often used in conjunction with "cow" to describe a bad-tempered woman who is unpleasant and unlikable)

(to) Take the micky – to joke about something, similar to "pull my leg"

Telly – television

Torch – a portable battery-powered electric lamp. *(American: flashlight. NOTE – different from the American usage of "torch" which is a blowlamp)*

Totty – a slang term for an attractive, sexually desirable woman

Vicar – a member of the clergy in the Church of England (similar to American pastor, minister)

Whinge – to moan and complain (usually in an annoying way)

SPECIAL TERMS USED IN OXFORD UNIVERSITY:

College - one of thirty or so institutions that make up the University; all students and academic staff have to be affiliated with a college and most of your life revolves around your own college: studying, dining, socialising. You are, in effect, a member of a College much more than a member of the University. College loyalties can be fierce and there is often friendly rivalry between nearby colleges. The colleges also compete with each other in various University sporting events.

Don / Fellow – a member of the academic staff / governing body of a college *(equivalent to "faculty member" in the U.S.)* – basically refers to a college's tutors. "Don" comes from the Latin, *dominus*— meaning lord, master.

Quad – short for quadrangle: a square or rectangular courtyard inside a college; walking on the grass is usually not allowed.

DARK CHOCOLATE & ORANGE SCONES RECIPE

(created and kindly donated by Kim McMahan Davis - *Cinnamon and Sugar... and a Little Bit of Murder* Blog)

It's often said that Great Britain and the United States are two nations divided by a common language—and this is true of their scones too!

The quintessential "afternoon tea" snack, English scones are round and compact, light and fluffy on the inside, and crusty on the outside; they are not very sweet and are usually plain with no toppings (although they sometimes have sultanas embedded) as they are meant to be eaten with jam and clotted cream.

American scones, in contrast, are usually larger and denser, with more butter and sugar, and are normally made with variety of ingredients added to the dough, such as spices, fruits, nuts, and even chocolate. They come in an amazing range of flavours—limited only by your imagination!

You can find the recipe for traditional English scones at the end of *A SCONE TO DIE FOR (Oxford Tearoom Mystery ~ Book 1)* but since this story featured scones too, I thought it would be fun to provide an American scone recipe for comparison. This delicious recipe has been specially created by the talented Kim McMahan Davis of the *Cinnamon and Sugar... and a Little Bit of Murder* Blog and features an eternally popular combo: tangy orange and dark chocolate!

<u>INGREDIENTS:</u>

Scones

- 2 cups (272 grams) all-purpose flour
- 2 teaspoons baking powder
- 1/4 teaspoon baking soda
- 1/2 teaspoon sea salt
- 1/3 cup (72 grams) granulated sugar
- Zest from 1 large orange
- 1/2 cup (112 grams) unsalted butter, cut into small pieces and frozen
- 1/2 cup (108 grams) sour cream
- 2 tablespoons orange juice
- 1 egg
- 1-1/2 ounces (42 grams) dark chocolate, chopped

Chocolate Orange Drizzle

- 2 ounces (56 grams) dark chocolate, chopped
- 1/2 teaspoon vegetable shortening
- 1/4 teaspoon orange extract

<u>INSTRUCTIONS:</u>

Scones

1. Preheat oven to 425 degrees (F) or 218 degrees

(C). Line a baking sheet with parchment paper.

2. Whisk together until smooth the sour cream, egg, and orange juice. Set aside.

3. In the bowl of a food processor, pulse together until combined (about 10 pulses) flour, baking powder, baking soda, salt, sugar, and orange zest.

4. Sprinkle the frozen butter pieces over the top of the flour mixture, then pulse until the mixture resembles coarse meal.

5. Add the sour cream mixture to the flour mixture and pulse just until the dough comes together. Be careful to not over process the dough.

6. Turn out onto a lightly floured surface. Sprinkle the chopped chocolate over the dough then gently knead into the mix. Again, be careful to not overwork the dough or it will toughen.

7. Place the dough onto the parchment-lined baking sheet and pat into an 8-inch circle. Cut into 8 wedges and move them slightly apart.

8. Bake 12 - 15 minutes. The scones should be golden and the center should look set. Cool scones on a wire cooling rack while preparing the glaze.

Chocolate Orange Glaze

1. Place the chocolate and vegetable shortening into a microwave-safe bowl. Heat on 70% power for 45 seconds. Stir. Heat in additional 20

second increments as needed, stirring after each heat cycle until chocolate is melted and smooth.

2. Mix in the orange extract and stir until smooth.
3. Drizzle the chocolate over the scones. Allow to set for 15 minutes then serve.

Enjoy!

ABOUT THE AUTHOR

H.Y. Hanna is an award-winning mystery and suspense writer and the author of the bestselling *Oxford Tearoom Mysteries*. She has also written romantic suspense and sweet romance, as well as a children's middle-grade mystery series. After graduating from Oxford University with a BA in Biological Sciences and a MSt in Social Anthropology, Hsin-Yi tried her hand at a variety of jobs, before returning to her first love: writing.

She worked as a freelance journalist for several years, with articles and short stories published in the UK, Australia and NZ, and has won awards for her novels, poetry, short stories and journalism.

A globe-trotter all her life, Hsin-Yi has lived in a variety of cultures, from Dubai to Auckland, London to New Jersey, but is now happily settled in Perth, Western Australia, with her husband and a rescue kitty named Muesli. You can learn more about her (and the real-life Muesli who inspired the cat character in the story) and her other books at: **www.hyhanna.com**.

Sign up to her newsletter to be notified of new releases, exclusive giveaways and other book news! Go to: **www.hyhanna.com/newsletter**

ACKNOWLEDGMENTS

A big thank you to Kim McMahan Davis of *Cinnamon and Sugar... and a Little Bit of Murder* blog, for creating a special scone recipe especially for this book and allowing me to share it with my readers!

Thank you also to Cat and Jon for their brilliant help in brainstorming title puns and for coming up with the title for this book.

I am very grateful, as always, to my beta readers: Connie Leap and Basma Alwesh, for their invaluable feedback that helps so much in polishing the first draft of the book. My thanks as always to my editor, Chandler Groover and proofreader, Heather Belleguelle—I feel very lucky to have the support of such a fantastic team.

And of course, to my wonderful husband, for his help in brainstorming titles, tackling plot holes and for always finding time to encourage and support me.

25971759R00203

Made in the USA
Middletown, DE
19 December 2018